BEYOND TIME'S EMBRACE

By

Tina Susedik

Beyond Time's Embrace

By

Tina Susedik

Cover design by: Wicked Smart Designs

Cover Photography by: JW Photography and Covers

Cover Models: Ginger Ring and Kevin R. Davis

Acknowledgments

There are always so many people to thank when a book is released. People who remind me I can do it. Even though this book was started and stopped many times since 1996, I finally finished it. Why so long you ask? Well, just a few things happened in between. Hubs and I bought a business and moved, I wrote and published four history books, three military books, three children's books and thirty-three romantic mysteries, which includes several stories for anthologies.

Hubs and I became grandparents to five grands, (absolutely the best part). Became a part-time sitter for those wonderful grands. Sold our business, got it back, sold it again. Moved two more times. Took many wonderful trips. And so many other things. But...I finished the darn book.

I would like to thank Tess Russ at Poised Pen Productions for the title of this book and all the work she does for me. Linda Robinson, Jane Yunker, Michelle Murray, and Jackie Ingram for reading, editing, and commenting on this book. Jean Woodfin for the amazing picture for the cover. If any of you know Ginger Ring, you may recognize the woman on the cover.

I can't forget hubs for his unending support. We have reached fifty-one years of marriage. Not sure how the time went so fast.

Chapter One

Present Day

A kick jolted Libby Daniels awake. She placed her hands on her bulging belly to rub away the pain.

"Baby kicking again?" Her husband, Ben, smiled. "He sure is a wild thing, isn't he?"

Libby looked out the car window. The sky was overcast. Swirls of gray mist rolled across the fields. She pressed her head back against the headrest and sighed. Why Ben had decided to do a Civil War Reenactment in West Virginia when she was only six weeks away from her due date was beyond her. She enjoyed the events, but the trip from Wisconsin and now back home had been long and tiring. Her doctor had given her the go-ahead to take the trip, but she wanted to be home.

Every summer they went to as many reenactments as they could. They both enjoyed history, but Ben's obsession with the Civil War was simply that—an obsession. When he'd heard about one in West Virginia, he'd nearly had a heart attack in his excitement. With the history of West Virginia breaking away from Virginia in the middle of the Civil War and finding out through an ancestry search how one of his relatives fought in West Virginia, Ben nearly did cartwheels as he rushed to his laptop and filled out the registration form in record time.

Libby glanced at Ben. She wasn't the only one tired. Ben had this obsession with driving being a man's job. Especially since she was pregnant again. Libby rubbed her stomach as the baby did flips. Ben was as excited as he had been when Charlie was born. Libby was excited, too, and was hoping for a girl. But she was tired of being tired. She was looking forward to being back to normal.

"Hey, hon, get me a pop, will you?" Ben asked. "How are you holding up?"

Libby struggled over her bulging stomach to reach the cooler in the back seat where three-year-old Charlie slept peacefully in his car seat. "I'm okay," Libby answered. "Hey, slow down, will you? I have to unbuckle my seatbelt to reach the cooler."

"Oh, hell, you'll be okay without your seatbelt for a few seconds," Ben replied in a gruff voice. "I don't know why you make such a big deal about those stupid things anyway. They make me feel trapped. I hate it when you tie up Charlie in his car seat. It looks like he's going to take off into space at any second."

Libby handed Ben his can and re-hooked her seatbelt. "And *I* hate it when you *don't* wear yours. I can see you flying through the windshield and bashing in your face."

Ben patted her on the hand like a child. "Ah, hon, you know nothing will ever happen to me. I'll be here to love you forever."

They were quiet for a few minutes as the sounds of country music flowed from the radio. In the silence Libby closed her eyes and thought about Ben's last statement. His profession of love always threw her. Libby had learned at an early age she was unlovable. Her parents had seen to it. In her twenty-eight years, she never got over the idea it was her fault they had to get married. The "sins" of her parents landed squarely on her small shoulders. When Ben first told her he loved her, Libby cried. It was the first time someone had ever said those words to her. They quickly married and Libby was removed from her parents' guilt. As much as she loved Ben, she still couldn't understand why he loved her.

Libby popped opened her eyes when the radio signal rose to a high squeal then instantly cut out. Static replaced the noise before it rose again to a high pitch.

"See if you can find another station, will ya? We must be out of range, but I don't know why we would be. We're heading toward the station, not away."

Libby pressed the buttons across the radio but found more static and whining. "That's odd." She pressed the buttons back to the beginning.

"What the hell?" Ben slowed the car down and pulled onto the shoulder.

Libby looked up from the radio and peered through the windshield. In the distance a wall of white rushed toward them. "Are we driving into a snowstorm?"

"Must be."

"It's impossible. It's too warm."

"With El Nino, anything's possible with the weather." Ben played with the radio. Even with satellite, he couldn't find anything.

"Let's wait 'til it passes." She stared out the window. "I don't like the looks of this. I feel strange, too. Like my head is floating."

"Must be the baby. I'm going on. It's not like I've never driven in snow before. Remember last year's snow in Wisconsin? I made it through it, didn't I?"

"Put your seatbelt on first," Libby begged. "This isn't natural."

"What—your woman's intuition working again?" Ben joked. "We'll be okay." He pulled back onto the empty highway and drove toward the white wall.

A tremor hit the car. "Ben, stop!" Libby screamed. "The car is shaking."

"What the hell is going on?" Ben yelled, attempting to move the steering wheel. "The steering wheel won't move. I can't control this thing! We're being pulled into the storm!"

A lightning bolt struck in front of the car. They were engulfed in a dark, swirling mass of clouds. Libby's ears roared like the sound of the ocean in a seashell. The temperature in the car dropped.

Ben tried to control the car as it began to skid and spin. "It must be a tornado!" Ben yanked at the steering wheel. In spite of the cold air, perspiration ran down Ben's forehead as he tried to get his foot on the brake.

"For God's sake, put on your seatbelt!" Libby screamed.

"I can't move my arms!" Ben shouted above the roar of the storm. "Can you see Charlie? Is he okay?"

Libby looked in the back seat. Charlie's eyes were wide with fright. Tears ran down his cheeks. His mouth was moving, but no sound was coming from him. "He's terrified. Pull off the road!" Libby shrieked. Like being on a Tilt-O-Whirl, she was pulled against her seat and could no longer move her head forward. Her shoulder-length blonde hair whipped around her face, and she was having trouble keeping her eyes open. Pressure increased on her stomach. She was going to explode. "The baby!" Libby screamed.

"I can't do anything. Hang on, we're going to crash!"

As Libby was drawn into unconsciousness, Ben's voice came from what seemed a long, dark tunnel, "Libby, I love you!"

Everything faded to black.

Chapter Two

West Virginia

March 1870

Bradley Kemble halted his chestnut stallion and slid off its back, nearly slipping as his boots hit the swampy muddy road. Brad had never seen a storm as bad as this, nor one coming up so fast. When he'd left his brother's farm it was a cool, spring evening with the sun high enough to give plenty of light for him to make the fifteen-minute ride to his farm. Brad enjoyed the West Virginia evening, with its hint of apple blossoms scenting the air, listening to the tree frogs sing and birds chirping.

Before he knew it, gusts of wind tossed branches from the trees lining either side of the road. Newly sprouted leaves whipped through the air and landed on the road around Brad's feet. A bolt of lightning struck behind him making both Captain and him jump. His horse reared and tried to bolt. A loud crack made the ground shake. Where was the nearest hidey-hole when you needed one? Ever since the War he jumped at any loud sound. Lightning and thunder topped the list. He looked behind him into the dark. A massive oak had fallen across the road.

Brad grabbed the reins. "Easy, boy." Brad pulled on the reins to lead Captain through the muck. "Looks as if there's no going back to Caleb's. C'mon. We can't stay out here. Let's get home to Whispering Pines."

Brad tried to hold on to his broad-brimmed hat when a gust of wind whipped it off his head. Through the slits in the hood he wore over his face, he watched it roll down the road into the dark. Instantly rain ran down the hood and into the high collar of his topcoat. He shivered as the icy water ran between his shirt and topcoat.

"Oh, hell." Brad reached into his redingote and pulled out a pocket watch from his vest. He sheltered the watch with his hand and tried to make out the time. "Been on this blasted road for twenty minutes and only halfway home." He gripped the reins and urged Captain forward. "We're not going back, ol' boy. This is going to take all night at this rate!"

Brad's rain-drenched clothes clung to him as he plodded on. "Damn this mask." He pulled off his gloves, and with cold fingers untied the strings around his neck holding the hood in place. He whipped it off his head and shoved it into his coat pocket. Immediately the cold, slicing rain cut into his face, as if someone were stabbing pins into his skin. He closed his eyes against the onslaught and wiped his hair from his face. Brad pulled the mask back over his face.

"At least I can open my eyes with this thing on," he muttered. Above the whining of the wind, the sucking sounds of his boots and Captain's hooves moving in and out of the mud were barely audible. Their progress was slow, but there was no shelter between his place and Caleb's. He would have to tough it out. He bent his head into the wind and dragged Captain on.

After what seemed like hours, Captain snorted and skittered sideways. Brad rubbed Captain's muzzle to calm him.

"Whoa, boy! What's wrong?" Brad looked in the direction of Captain's stare while holding a tight rein on his horse. A black shape lay across the road partially blocking it. "Damn, not another downed tree. That's all I need." He squinted through the rain. Not a tree, but a buggy. He ran forward yanking on Captain's reins as the horse yanked and pulled the other way. Brad finally tied him to a tree and left him whinnying and rearing.

Brad slogged through the mud toward the buggy and the screams of another horse. A black, covered buggy leaned on its side against a tree, its wheels spinning. A horse, attached to the buggy, lay on its side, its cries piercing through Brad's brain. Other than the horse's shaking legs, Brad couldn't detect any other movements. Giving the horse a wide berth so he wouldn't get kicked, he walked to the horse's head. Its pain was reflected in the whites of his eyes as he tried to get up. Brad knelt in the mud and rubbed the horse's head, trying to calm it. The horse screamed and brought its head up. Brad ran his hands down the horse's front legs. Its left foreleg was broken. He would have to destroy it. Before doing the awful deed, he needed to see if anyone else was hurt.

Brad climbed onto the running board of the buggy. By using his weight and rocking back and forth, he righted it. A moan came from the inside. He yanked open the door. A young woman, lying on the floor, peered up at him. Her arms were wrapped around a small boy. Was he sleeping, or injured? Rain seeped in through a loose canvas window flapping in the wind. The woman's hair was plastered to her face. Scared, green eyes stared at him.

"Please, help my husband," she whispered before passing out.

Brad looked around the interior of the buggy. Where was her husband? There was no one inside but the boy and the woman. He slammed the door shut. He had to find the man. Brad covered his ears at the horse's screams. He would have to destroy it before he could do anything else. He trudged over to Captain and pulled a pistol from one of his saddlebags.

He stood over the injured chestnut horse. "Damn, I hate this. I'm sorry, boy." Pointing the pistol at the horse's head, he closed his eyes and squeezed the trigger. The screams stopped but echoes of the shot rang through Brad's brain as he resumed his search for the missing husband.

He walked around the still horse, tripped on an object protruding from beneath it, and landed face down in the mud. Cursing, Brad rolled over and sat up, ready to toss the offending object into the trees. He wiped mud and leaves from his hood and crawled back to the horse. Brad's hand came in contact with a man's head. He jerked back and sat with his legs bent beneath him, his hands resting on his knees.

His eyes stared sightlessly at the sky, while rain ran in rivulets down the man's turned-up face. The horse covered the man's lower body, his left arm twisted under his back. Brad closed the man's eyes and mouth. Brad leaned forward into the mud and hung his head between his shoulders.

"Shit, now what do I do? The man's cold as a wagon wheel." He stood and sloshed to the buggy hoping to find something to cover the body with. Finding only the woman and the boy inside, he shut the door, went back to his horse, and removed a blanket he kept in his saddlebags for emergencies. After covering up the body, Brad unhitched the dead horse from the buggy. As he tried to decide how he was going to move the horse, a moan came from inside the buggy.

Brad yanked the buggy door open. The woman was awake again and holding her belly.

"Oh, God, you're with child!" he shouted. He climbed into the buggy and knelt on the floor next to the woman. "You can't have your child here. There's no one to help you."

If she weren't so scared, she'd laugh at the man's obvious comment. The mask he wore completely hid his face. His voice reminded her of a horror movie. Was he going to kill them? She scooted as far into the corner of the vehicle as she could and wrapped Charlie in her arms.

"Don't hurt us," she whispered.

"I'm not here to hurt you."

Even though his voice sounded reassuring, everyone knew killers could be kind one moment, and murderous the next.

"Please don't be afraid. I only want to help." He leaned a bit more into the...whatever they were in. "Are you hurt anywhere? Is the boy hurt?"

Libby tried to sit. Her head pounded and spun enough to make her stomach queasy. Maybe if she threw up on the man, he'd leave them alone. She lay back down. Perspiration broke out on her brow. "Except for a bump on my head and the baby kicking like crazy, I'm okay." The woman looked down at her son. "Charlie seems to be okay, too." She stared at the man. "Did you find my husband? Is he all right?"

He touched her arm. "I'm sorry, Ma'am, he was crushed by your horse. He's dead."

Tears welled up in her eyes. "Oh, God, I told him to wear his seat belt." She rested her chin on her son's head and closed her eyes, tears running down her cheeks. *Wait. Did he say horse?* "We don't have a horse."

"Ma'am, I think you're confused from the accident. Your buggy tipped over. Your husband was thrown. It looks like your horse broke its left foreleg and fell on him."

Dead? Ben couldn't be dead. A tremor passed through her body. This was a dream. A nightmare. Maybe if she closed her eyes, she'd wake up back in Wisconsin.

The man shook her shoulder. "Ma'am, what is your name?"

"Libby," she murmured. The spinning in her head grew stronger. "Ben," she whispered before everything went black.

Before leaving the calm of the buggy, Brad took in the strange clothes the woman was wearing. It seemed she had on... pants? Pants on a woman? He stared at them. They were pants all right, made of a soft material. On her feet she wore a type of footwear Brad had never seen before. They were all white with strings wrapped up the front. The thick soles were like the material in his mackintosh—soft and rubbery. Her son had on the same type, but his went up past his ankles and were black.

"Must be foreigners." He backed out of the buggy. He needed to get the woman to his farm before the baby decided to enter the world in a buggy. He ran back to the dead horse and trapped man. Was he the Ben whose name she whispered before passing out? He couldn't leave him out here. By daybreak he would be unrecognizable by wild animals in the area looking for an easy meal.

Brad leaned down and pulled out the man's pinned arm, then grabbed him under his armpits. Grunting and swearing, he tugged and pulled to remove the body from under the horse. His cold, wet hands slipped sending him backward into the mud.

He shook his fists at the sky. "Will you please stop raining?" Libby's moan came for the carriage again. "Shit!"

Brad rose from the mud and, after getting his hunting knife from his saddlebags, cut the reins from the dead horse's halter and tied them to its front and back legs. Then he ran over to Captain and untied him from the tree. Captain refused to move any closer to the bodies. He reared and kicked while Brad pulled him toward the buggy.

"C'mon, Captain. I don't like this any better than you do." Brad finally pulled the hood from his head and slipped it over Captain's. The horse calmed down long enough for Brad to knot each of Captain's reins to those attached to the horse. Brad jumped over the horse's body and grabbed the man under the arms again.

"Back, Captain!" Brad shouted through the wind. "C'mon, boy, back up."

Captain pulled back on the reins as Brad tugged the man the other way. "Back! Back." Brad grunted. Captain pulled harder, fighting the straps, trying to break loose. Brad struggled, tugging, yanking, his boots slipping in the mud. At this rate, his arms were going to be yanked from their sockets. Finally, with one loud snort from Captain, the dead horse eased away, and Brad dragged Ben free.

Brad sank into the mud, resting his arms on his bent legs, trying to catch his breath. His hair hung in his eyes. Not one part of his once-white shirt was clean. His once-white breeches were covered with mud. The strap of his left pant leg had broken and was halfway up his shin, his high boots caked with muck. Mud oozed into his boot, down his stockings. Cora was going to have a fit.

Using his knife, Brad cut the reins from the dead horse. He picked up Captain's reins and led the reluctant horse toward the buggy, fighting him all the way until Brad finally gave up.

"All right, you old piece of buzzard's meat." He tied Captain to a tree. "Guess I'll have to move the damn buggy myself."

"Ma'am, Ma'am?" Brad called out as he approached the buggy. *Better let her know what I'm going to do. Don't want to scare her and have her go into labor.* Before he opened the door, he remembered his hood. He took the hood from Captain, yanked it over his face, and opened the door of the buggy. "Ma'am? Miss Libby?" If so much time hadn't passed, he would have felt more relieved she was still passed out, her son resting peacefully in her arms.

His heart skipped a beat. Wait. Maybe the youngster wasn't asleep. Maybe he was dead, too. Brad entered the buggy and leaned toward the boy. What was his name? Damn. He couldn't remember.

"Boy? Boy?" Brad whispered. He put his ear to the boy's nose. The steady, warm breath wisped across his ear. He briefly closed his eyes. The boy was alive.

"Ben, is that you? Are you okay?" Libby whispered as she struggled to sit. She flinched, grabbed her stomach, and stopped moving. A large purple bruise marred her forehead.

Brad ignored her questions. Obviously, she had forgotten about her husband. "Now listen, Ma'am." Brad needed to explain what he wanted to do. "I'm going to move the buggy so I can hook my horse up to it. Don't be alarmed when you feel movement. I need to get you to my home."

She bit her bottom lip and frowned. He'd be confused, too, if he'd been in an accident. At least this time she didn't shrink away from him. Most people thought he was a monster because of the hood he wore. If they only knew.

Brad went back into the downpour. Grabbing the tongues of the buggy, he pushed it backward. His muscles stretched, pulled, and burned as he strained to move it through the mud. How far would he have to move the buggy away from the dead horse to satisfy Captain? He figured the farther, the better.

After moving the buggy to what he thought was a good distance, he went back to her husband. Was he wearing a Union uniform? It was hard to tell with all the mud, but after the war, the one thing he recognized was a Union uniform. He had one of his own crammed into a trunk in the attic. But why would this man be wearing one now? After all, the war had been over for nearly five years.

A roll of thunder brought a roar of cannons through his system. He closed his eyes. His body seized like it had the first time he was in battle. Now was not the time to be reliving the horrible images of blood, maimed bodies, and death. He shook his head. Would these nightmares ever go away? A gust of wind brought him back to the present.

It didn't matter what Ben was wearing, he needed to be taken to his home. Brad wrapped him in the blanket he'd taken from his saddle bag and struggled to lift him.

For a seemingly slight man, the weight of sodden clothes, the blanket, and lifeless body must have added pounds. Either that, or he was exhausted from handling Captain and the buggy. He was too heavy to lift, so Brad put his hands beneath Ben's arms and dragged him. The body's boot heels left deep grooves in the mud which quickly filled up with rain. Like a log, he rolled Ben up the end of the buggy and into the boot. The body thudded to the floor and rocked the buggy. Hopefully, Libby hadn't heard.

Brad untied Captain and hooked him up to the buggy. The horse had never pulled anything before, but Brad was banking on Captain's wanting to get back to his warm, dry stable. Come hell or high water, and there was plenty of both, the horse would pull the buggy. He wasn't about to pull it himself! Much to his relief, Captain didn't rebel and, after climbing onto the driver's seat and flicking the reins against Captain's rump, they set off for home.

Chapter Three

Libby pulled herself out of the fog twisting and swirling through her brain. She rubbed the bump on her throbbing forehead and flinched. Afraid to open her eyes to the pain, she called to Charlie. She let out a breath when he wiggled in her arms. For a reason she couldn't fathom, they were lying on the floor of the car, which seemed to be swaying and bumping. It reminded her of riding the train from Milwaukee to Chicago, without the noise or smell.

As she lay still, hoping to ease the agony in her head, the patter of rain hitting the roof of the car sounded more like rain hitting their tent when they went camping. She was getting wet from an open window. In the distance, as if coming through a tunnel, a man's voice called out. "C'mon, Captain, only a little way, now."

None of this made any sense. The last thing Libby remembered before falling asleep was telling Ben to put on his seatbelt, a snowstorm, and their car...

"Oh, my God." She pressed shaking fingers to her lips. The snowstorm, Ben trying to control the car, the car spinning, and Ben yelling he loved her. Then fade to black. Libby cuddled Charlie closer. The rolling of the baby made her less scared, but she needed to know where Ben was. She eased her eyes open.

Rain dripped from her eyelashes onto her cheeks. For the life of her she couldn't figure out where she was. It certainly wasn't their car. The interior of the vehicle was entirely black. On one side a piece of fabric flapped in and out, letting in the rain. What Libby assumed was a door with a fancy, scroll-worked black handle was on the opposite side. A large piece of canvas ran across the front of the vehicle. A worn, padded seat ran beneath the canvas.

Libby slid Charlie from her arms and carefully laid him on the floor. Trying to ignore the throbbing in her head, she pushed herself up and leaned against the seat. Sweat beaded on her forehead. Bile rose to her throat. She swallowed the extra saliva pooling in her mouth. The last thing she needed was to throw up. She closed her eyes and rested against the seat. *I won't throw up. I won't throw up. I'd better not throw up.*

While waiting for her head and stomach to settle down, Libby tried to get her bearings. It reminded her of the time she and Ben had ridden in a carriage at one of the reenactments they'd participated in. But why in heaven's name would she be in a carriage?

Maybe Ben was playing a practical joke on her and had hired a carriage to take them the rest of the way home. Ben was always teasing her about the books she read, and how she romanticized the past. Libby like to pretend she was living in the 1800's. But then she'd remind him of his Civil War reenactments, pretending to be a Union officer and he'd shut up.

Wherever they went, they visited historical sites and she visualized herself in long, full dresses, living in a mansion in the south with servants to help her with the house. Ben reminded her the historical romance novels didn't show the bad things about the past. Once he had told her if they were living in the 1800's she would probably die from childbirth or Charlie from scarlet fever. He was right, but it didn't stop her from escaping back a hundred and fifty years or so. It wasn't any different from what he did. Was it?

A roll of thunder echoed across the sky bringing Libby back to her present situation. Her mind raced trying to find an answer to where she was. The voice telling this Captain person to keep going didn't sound like Ben, but they were definitely in a carriage. It smelled like canvas, or leather, or a wet dog. She wasn't sure which. Maybe all of them. She would love to reach over and pull back the canvas in the front of the carriage to see what was happening, but strength eluded her.

Could she get herself up on the seat behind her? It would certainly be more comfortable than bouncing on the floor. She looked down at her bulging stomach. There was no way she would be able to get up in the small confines of the buggy. A familiar pressure in her pelvis and an aching in her lower back worried her. She hoped they were heading in the direction of a hospital.

Libby snapped her fingers. Maybe this was an Amish buggy. Had an Amish person come across them and taken them to the nearest town? The Amish in Wisconsin were always willing to help people in trouble. But where was Ben? Libby giggled in relief. He probably stayed with the car to make sure nothing was ripped off by some unscrupulous person. He'd wait for the police and tow truck, then meet them at the hospital.

As Libby let out a sigh of relief at having figured out their strange situation, a foggy vision passed through her mind. A man leaned toward her. He wore a mask of some kind; his blue eyes peered through slits, setting her protective genes into overdrive. She'd held Charlie against her and shrunk back into the corner of the buggy.

In a deep, soothing voice, he'd asked her if they were all right. In a slight accent she couldn't place, he'd told her not to be afraid; he wasn't going to hurt them. Then he left. Rubbing her bulging stomach, she frowned. The man had come back and told her something about Ben and a horse. Did he say it was their horse?

With a blinding light Libby recalled what the man had said. Her memory might be playing tricks on her, but what the man had said was very clear. She leaned forward and grabbed her stomach. "Oh, God, no! It can't be true!" Sobs reached up from the pit of her soul, her eyes welled with tears. Rocking back and forth Libby realized it was true. Ben was dead. She tried to keep from wailing. Besides Charlie, Ben was the only one who really loved her. Even if he teased her at times, there was no denying he truly loved her.

Libby put her fist to her mouth and bit on her fingers to keep from screaming and waking Charlie. He would never understand. Charlie had adored Ben. They were buddies. Charlie followed Ben around to the point where he would get irritated with his son. What on God's green Earth was she going to do? She was going to be a single mother with two young children. Lord only knew she wouldn't get help from her parents.

"Stop it!" This has to be a bad dream. A nightmare she'd soon wake from. She was always having terrifying dreams where Ben would desert her; telling her he had never loved her after all and walking off with a gorgeous blonde with an hour-glass figure. Her family would be standing in the background, pointing their fingers at her, laughing, reminding her how no one could ever love her. Libby pinched herself on the arm. "Please, let this be a dream. C'mon, Libby, wake up!" The pinch hurt. This was real. Ben was truly dead.

But where was he? Did the Amish leave him in the car? Was the man calling out to Captain an Amish man? Was he the one wearing the hood? *Think. Think.* Was there only one person? He hadn't been wearing a hat, which would have told her if he was Amish. But it could have blown off in the storm. The man had also worn a cape or cloak of some kind. She had never seen the Amish wear them. Neither did his voice have the slight German accent of the Amish.

But, if he wasn't Amish, who was he? Libby's head pounded with greater intensity. She would have to pray her rescuer was honest and would get them to a hospital soon. It could be possible Ben wasn't dead after all. If they could get an ambulance back to him fast enough, maybe they could save him. Libby wanted to lean forward and yell to the driver to go faster, but a pain gripped her stomach when the buggy hit a hole in the road. As she was flung to her side next to Charlie, she hit her head on the floor. Darkness descended once more.

Chapter Four

Brad snapped the reins against Captain's haunches. "C'mon, boy. We've got to get these people home." Captain seemed to be moving so slow, Brad checked the reins to make sure he wasn't pulling back on them. He could probably walk faster than Captain.

He wiped at the rain running past his eyes and down his mask and blinked. Was there a light up ahead? No one else lived between his place and Caleb's. No one could be out with a lantern trying to find their way. But then these people had been. What they were doing on this road in a storm like this, he couldn't imagine. Of course, he had ridden into the storm, so they probably had, too.

Brad urged Captain toward the light. Like a curtain pulled across a window, the rain stopped. The sun hung low in the sky ready to set behind Appalachian Mountains. A slight breeze whisked branches back and forth. Birds chirped. It was like walking through a dense wall of fog into a pure, crystal setting. No rain dripped from leaves. There were Captain's hoofprints in the dry road going toward his brother's.

"What the blazes?"

The buggy bumped from the muddy, slippery path onto the dry, dirt road, nearly unseating Brad in the process. Another moan came from the back of the buggy, but he didn't want to take the time to stop and investigate. While Captain plodded along, Brad stood and looked behind him. The raging storm was fading away. The storm didn't seem to be moving in any other direction. It was simply disappearing like fog slowly lifting on a spring morning.

Brad took off his mask and shook his head. This had to be one of the strangest storms he had ever seen in his thirty-two years. He urged Captain into a gallop. A row of pine trees loomed ahead on his right. He was close to the road to Whispering Pines. He was almost home.

He snapped the reins. "C'mon, old boy, we're almost there. A warm blanket and food wait around the corner."

Once they reached the narrow road leading to Whispering Pines, Captain needed no more encouragement. He was close to getting rid of the attached buggy and was more than eager to end the ordeal. With no more urging, Captain made the right turn to the farm. Brad feared the buggy would tip over in Captain's exuberance.

Towering pines grew on both sides of the drive, the wide, lower branches left untrimmed, barely leaving room for the buggy to pass. Brad liked the privacy the trees gave his home. Because of the eerie feeling given off by the close-growing trees, few hawkers or drummers came to the house. Brad or one of his employees made the six-mile trek to Romney to purchase goods not grown on his farm. Because the road was not often used by wagons or buggies, it was full of rocks and ruts. Brad flinched at the treatment his passengers were probably experiencing.

His stomach rolled. The last thing he needed was to help a woman give birth again.

As he rounded the last turn to his farm, a burst of pride filled him. Even though it wasn't the place he was raised in, it was his. Caleb, being the older brother, inherited the family farm on the death of their father.

Several years ago, the owner of Whispering Pines, Jack Castlewood, had died and left it to his only child, Belinda. Being more interested in spending her fortune rather than in running the place, Castlewood Manor, as it had then been called, quickly deteriorated. Belinda gradually sold off her slaves and land, which Brad purchased.

He refused to own slaves and hired many of them back as his employees, which didn't endear him to some of his neighbors. The Kembles had never kept slaves. The Castlewood slaves were more than happy to be treated as human beings and earn a decent wage. Everyone had worked hard the past two years to get the house back to its former grandeur and on a profitable track. It had been hard work, but worth it. The long, strenuous days kept the memories at bay, too.

Brad stopped the buggy in front of the large, two-story structure. A covered porch downstairs and a balcony upstairs ran across the front of the house. Eight white pillars supported the porch roof. On the second-floor balcony, sections of railings like white picket fencing were attached to the pillars, a safety feature. Long, green, double-shuttered windows ran across the front, again on both floors. The entrance on the lower level was a large, double door, while directly above it on the second floor stood a single door leading from the master bedroom. At night, when memories of better times kept him from sleeping, he would go onto the front porch and listen to the katydids until he became sleepy enough to doze in his rocking chair.

Three dormers ran across the slopping roof on the third floor. When slaves had taken care of the place, the house slaves had lived in those tiny, hot rooms. Brad had added windows on the opposite sides of the house to allow for a cross breeze. He then converted the rooms into an apartment for Cora, his housekeeper, and her family. Several chimneys were interspersed with the dormers.

The first order of business was to get some of those fires going before it got dark. He jumped from the buggy and checked on Libby and the boy, who were asleep. It would be better if he got the fires going in the extra bedrooms before he brought them in. At least the rooms would be warm. As he ran up the walk he called out to Cora and her husband, Zack. No one answered.

"Damn, I gave them the day off." He ran across the front porch and threw open the door. As he waited for his eyes to adjust to the dark interior, he took in the scent of beeswax Cora used to keep his home shining. A day didn't go by when she didn't have one of her girls running a cleaning rag across the furniture and floor. Sometimes he was afraid to walk across the floor for fear of adding a speck of dust to it or landing on his backside on the glossy surface. He glanced down at his mud-crusted boots and grimaced. Cora was going to have a fit for sure. There was nothing he could do about it and headed for the curved staircase running along the right wall in the large foyer. A door beneath the curve of the stairway led to the backyard where the summer kitchen was located.

When Brad reached the top of the stairs, he paused. There were six bedrooms. Three on either side of the hallway. His room was in front on the left side. If he went straight down the hallway, he would come to two spare rooms. On the opposite side were three other rooms. Two of the rooms had a connecting door between them. One was to have been a nursery. He would put Libby in one room and the boy in the other so the woman could hear her son if he cried during the night. The last room was another spare room.

Brad threw open the door to the nursery. As he attempted to start a fire, he tried not to remember how Lucinda had decorated this room. As he struck the matches and lit the kindling, his cold fingers gave him trouble. After several fumbling tries, a small piece of wood caught. He gently blew on it until the flame caught the bark and wood around it. If only the fireplace on the other side of the wall were open to this one, it would save time. He rose and pulled open the heavy drapes covering windows on the two outer walls. Even though Cora kept the room neat, Brad hadn't been in the room in over a year. The late evening light sent rays filtering through dust motes from the drapes.

He closed his eyes and took a deep breath before facing the ghosts this room offered. Letting out a shaky sigh, Brad opened his eyes. In one corner stood the small bed to be used by a nanny. A cradle stood to one side near the bed, an unused patch quilt laying over its side. A wooden rocking horse, from his childhood, sat in the opposite corner to the bed, its reins hanging on either side of the wooden head, the ends touching the floor. A massive dresser had been placed against an outer wall between two windows. Brad didn't have to open the drawers to know they were still filled with baby items lovingly made by his late wife, Lucinda.

Captain's whinny brought him back to the present. He yanked open the connecting door to the next room and started another fire. His hands had warmed, so he was able to accomplish it in no time. Before going down to get his guests, he pulled open the chifforobe and grabbed one of Lucinda's nightgowns and a long robe. This room had been set up for her to stay in if their child became ill. She had worried about waking Brad if she had to attend to the child, so the room was made into a second bedroom for her. It had never been used.

Brad tossed the robe on the bed before running back down the stairs, across the foyer, and out the front door. Libby looked up when he threw open the buggy door.

"Are we at the hospital?" she whispered as she pulled her hair from her eyes.

"Hospital?" In his experiences during the war, the last place he'd take someone was a hospital. "No, we're at my farm, Whispering Pines." He reached for her hand. "We need to get you and your son into the house and warm beds. Can you walk?"

Walk? She didn't even think she could straighten her stiff legs, let alone walk. Before moving, she tried to clear her fuzzy brain and focus on the man standing in the doorway of the carriage. He seemed to be standing in shade because Libby couldn't see his face. When Libby didn't answer him, he leaned further into the buggy.

"Ma'am, can you walk, or move?" The man reached out and put a hand on her forearm.

Libby focused on the large hand resting on her arm. Long, tapered fingers with a dusting of dark hair. Dirty ruffles from his sleeve partially covered the back of his hand, also dusted with black hair. There was a reassuring strength in the gentle way he touched her. Libby pulled her glance from his hand and looked at his face. No wonder she couldn't make out his features—he had a hood over his face. Recalling his soothing voice from before, Libby wasn't afraid this time. For some reason, she trusted this man. The man's voice finally penetrated, and Libby focused on his words.

"Ma'am, please. Are you all right? Can you move?"

"I'm awfully stiff. And I'm not sure if I can turn around to get out the door. My stomach is in the way."

At the mention of her pregnancy, Brad glanced at her stomach. Beneath his mask, his face grew warm with embarrassment as she rubbed her hand across her rounded belly. Except for his wife and his brother's wife, Colleen, Brad had never been this close to an expectant woman before. Most woman stayed in the confines of their homes when their time was near. What on earth was he going to do if the baby was born before Cora came back? He'd never be able to handle it.

Rousing himself from his musings, Brad took in Libby's predicament. Her legs were curled underneath her, her knees and stomach facing away from the door. With her back leaning against the seat, she had to turn her head over her shoulder to talk to him. How on Earth would she turn and stand?

"Ma'am, can you push yourself up and onto the seat?"

Libby put the palms of her hands on the floor on either side of her backside and tried to push herself up. "I'm too big and tired." Tears ran down her cheeks.

"Now, Ma'am, crying isn't going to help right now. We need to get you and your son out of this buggy and into warm beds."

Libby hiccupped back a sob and glanced around the cramped space. "Okay. What are we going to do?"

Brad thought for a second. There was no way she would be able to swing her legs around and slide out the door on her backside. Getting onto all fours and backing out on her hands and knees was out of the question, too. She was so big; she would scrape her belly on the floor of the buggy. Another idea came to him. One which would cause embarrassment, but Brad could think of no other way.

"If I crawl in the buggy and lift you, you could get onto the seat and then climb out."

Libby chewed on her bottom lip and looked at the narrow space. "I suppose it's the only thing we can try but be careful not to step on Charlie."

Brad placed both hands on the interior of the buggy door, pulled himself inside, and sighed. At least with his mask on, his worry wouldn't show. "I'm going to try really hard not to hurt you, Ma'am. I'm going to lift you under your arms. You grab my arms and help me pull you up. All right?"

Libby looked at the mud-caked boots straddling her legs then moved further up his body. His white pants were wet and coated with mud. A pant strap hung over the top of the high boots. Stirrups? Was he actually wearing stirrup pants? A man? Three-year-old He was even wearing a cravat. The only reason she knew the name of it was from the books she read. She had never actually seen anyone wear one.

"Ma'am? Are you ready?"

"Quit calling me Ma'am. My name is Libby."

"Fine, Miss Libby, let's get you out of here." His sigh seemed louder, almost eerie through his mask.

Libby raised her arms to help him. His hands brushed against her breasts.

"Sorry," he mumbled.

"Sorry for what? Let's just get this over with." The pain in her lower back made her irritable. If she didn't get out of this carriage soon, she'd scream.

He put his hands under her arms. "Now grab my arms and pull."

Libby did as he said. He lifted her high enough where the back of her legs hit the seat. Her leg muscles protested when she stretched them out. Great. All she needed now was a cramp. She rubbed her hands down her legs when a wail, like two cats fighting, pierced the carriage.

"Mommy! Let go of my Mommy! You're hurting her!"

Charlie grabbed the man's leg with one arm and tried to grab his hand with the other. Tears were streaming down his face. She'd only seen him this angry once when another young boy called Ben a damn Yankee while at a reenactment. If he gripped Brad's leg any harder, he'd draw blood.

"Let go of her, you're hurting her!" His scream was enough to pierce an eardrum.

"Charlie, stop it right now. He's not hurting me. Let go of his leg!"

"No!" Charlie voice was like a growl as he sunk his teeth into Brad's leg.

"Ouch! Dammit, kid! Stop it! Release me at once." He swung his leg out in an attempt to detach the boy while trying not to drop Libby. The teeth dug in further. "Lady, get your son off me."

Libby let go of Brad's arms, yet he managed to keep her from falling. "Charles Bernhardt Daniels, you let go of him this instant!" She pulled on his arm. "He's not hurting me. Let go of him so he can let go of me. I'm trying to sit down."

While Charlie released his bite on Brad's leg, he kept holding his pants, tipped his head back, and looked up at Libby. She gave him one of her teacher frowns. But Charlie was tenacious in protecting her. If the situation hadn't been so serious she would have laughed.

"I'm sorry. I don't think he's going to let go of your leg."

Even though she couldn't see his face, she imagined the pain on his face by having teeth imbedded in his leg. "Uh, I think I can sit down now." Libby touched the seat behind her. "If you could just move me back, I could sit down, and maybe Charlie will let go of you."

"I certainly hope so." Luckily, he didn't have far to go to set her down, but when the backs of Libby's legs hit the seat, she fell backward. With Charlie holding onto his leg, Brad couldn't keep his balance. He didn't want to land on her stomach, so he rolled to his side and landed on his back. He heard Libby let out a groan when she landed on the seat. Charlie let go of his leg and pummeled his lower back with his small fists.

"You hurt her! You hurt my Mommy! I hate you!"

Libby rolled to her side and sat up. She grabbed Charlie by the back of his pants. "Charlie! Stop hitting him! I'm okay. Charlie! Look at me! I'm okay!" She pulled him off Brad, onto her lap, and rocked him, murmuring into his ear to calm him down.

"See, I'm okay. The baby's okay. This man was only trying to help me up. I'm glad you wanted to protect me like a big boy, but you owe him an apology for biting and hitting him."

Charlie finally calmed down enough to look at him. He waited for the boy to shrink back at Brad's mask. His heart warmed when Charlie looked him in the face and apologized.

"Sorry." He frowned. "Why do you wear that thing on your face?"

"Shush, Charlie. You shouldn't ask such rude questions."

Brad sat up, leaned toward Charlie, and chuckled. "It's all right, boy. No harm done. Every boy should protect his mother like you did. Your mother should be proud of you." Brad winced as he stood up. He could imagine blood mixing with the mud on his leg. "Now, let's get you and your mother out of here and into some dry clothes and warm beds. You're a big boy, I'm sure you can help me."

Libby gave him a little grin. "Okay, Charlie, you can help the man, but you make sure you do what he says."

Chapter Five

Charlie slid from Libby's lap while Brad climbed out of the buggy. "C'mon, you little whippersnapper." Brad called to Charlie as he reached out to help him down.

He scowled. "My name isn't whippersnuffer. It's Charlie."

Brad chuckled. "I called you a whippersnapper, not whippersnuffer. But if you wish, I'll call you Charlie. Now, Charlie, let's help your mother down."

Brad stuck his head into the buggy. Libby was still sitting on the seat, her head bowed down, her hands in her lap. She glanced up when Brad called to her. Tears were streaming down her face.

"Is Ben really dead?"

"Yes, Ma'am. I'm afraid so." When she didn't say anything or move, Brad thought she hadn't heard. "C'mon, Ma'am. Miss Libby. We'll discuss this later. Right now, we need to get you out of this damn buggy." He paused. "Uh. Sorry for cussing, Ma'am. Bad habit."

Libby wiped away her tears and levered herself up from the seat. Brad reached into the buggy and grabbed her hands as she swayed.

"You're doing good, Miss Libby. Now, come toward me. Charlie and I will get you down." When she got to the door, he stood to one side. "Put your hand on my shoulder and step down. I'll keep you from falling. Charlie, be ready to take your mother's hand."

Libby stood in the doorway and looked down. The ground seemed a mile away. The man with the hood was calmly telling her to step down. Charlie was stretching back his little neck, watching. Her eyes grew wide. She tugged on her bottom lip with her teeth.

"Ma'am? Miss Libby? Two steps, Ma'am. You only have to take two steps down. I won't let you fall. Charlie and I will help you."

His calm, soothing voice seemed to finally register with her. She placed her hand on his left shoulder. He reached out for her with his right hand. Libby closed her eyes and stepped down.

"Good. One more," Brad urged.

"You did it." Charlie squealed as he ran over to grab her hand from Brad.

Libby gave Charlie a weak smile. "You did a good job helping, Charlie. Now let's get to wherever we're going."

Good. She seems to be doing all right. They passed between the large white columns, under a balcony, and through a tall doorway. As they entered the foyer, she stopped and gasped.

"Ma'am?"

"Let me rest a minute. I'll be okay." She clenched her teeth.

Brad held Libby up with his arm around her back, holding her hand. The grip on his hand was strong enough to cut off the circulation. *No baby! Oh, God, don't let her have this baby now! Wait until Cora comes!* After what seemed like an eternity, Libby straightened up, gave him a nod and they continued toward the stairs.

"Charlie, let your mother use the railing. You can..." Hell, he didn't know what Charlie could do. He wanted the boy to help, but how was the pertinent question.

"Charlie," Libby said. "Walk one step higher than me and let me rest my arm on your shoulders. That would help a lot."

Charlie grinned, obviously pleased to be helping again. He jumped up one step and reached for his mother's arm. Libby grabbed the railing. Even standing one step above them, Libby's arm never touched Charlie's shoulders. But the pride on his face as he held onto her arm and calmly urged her up the stairs, made Brad realized what a good mother this woman was. Would Lucinda have been as good? He couldn't wonder for long, though. He was too concerned about getting Libby into bed. Halfway up the stairs another pain came. They stopped again until it passed.

Brad swallowed around the lump in his throat. "Aren't these pains coming awfully fast?"

"I'm sure it's simply false labor. As soon as I can lie down, I'll be fine."

Since she'd already had one child, he could only assume she knew what she was talking about. The last thing he wanted to do after this evening's events was deliver a baby. One chance had been enough. Brad breathed a sigh of relief when they finally reached the second floor without having to stop again.

"We'll go down this hallway and turn to the right." They entered Libby's room. "Can you get yourself undressed, Ma'am?" She'd better be able to. There was no way he'd help a strange woman change. "There is a nightgown and robe on the bed. I'll take Charlie into the next room and get him into some dry clothes. Is that all right?"

"Mommy, I want to stay with you." Charlie held onto her legs.

Libby looked at Brad then down at her son. "It's okay, Charlie. I'll be right here. As soon as you're done, you can come back here. Go with..." Huh. "What is your name?"

"Brad. Bradley Kemble. You're at Whispering Pines, my farm."

"Charlie, you go with Mr. Kemble. I need to change, too." For some reason, Brad leading Charlie through a door at the end of the room didn't bother her. The rooms must be connected. On the same wall as the door, a fire burned brightly in a large fireplace, giving off shadows in the nearly dark room. She leaned against a post of the four-poster bed as another contraction came and went. At least this one was shorter and farther apart than the other ones. Hopefully, with rest, they would stop completely.

Libby turned toward the bed and gasped. Attached to the posters was a ruffled canopy with curtains swagged back and tied to the posts. A white quilt covered the bed, with several large, white ruffled pillows tossed at the head. It looked like a bed from one of her books.

She picked up a frilly, pink nightgown. The long sleeves had lacy cuffs. Three layers of more frilly lace curved from the high neckline to the breast line. "There's enough material in this thing to cover three pregnant women. Why would a gay guy have something like this?" She pulled off her tennis shoes, socks, sweatpants, and top. She let out a sigh of relief when she dropped her bra onto the bed. Since she was small on top, she usually didn't wear one, but while pregnant her breasts were bigger and heavier. Since she would be nursing, it would be a long time before she could go without one again.

Libby slipped the nightgown over her head. It slid over her bulging stomach leaving the hem ending at the middle of her shins. Whomever this once belonged to must have been short. A yawn made her eyes water. Exhaustion overcame her. It was an effort to keep her eyes open. It was as if someone had tied anchors to her arms and legs.

"I'll crawl into bed and Charlie can join me when he's ready." She pulled back the blankets, crawled between the cool sheets, and fell instantly asleep.

In the next room Brad was losing a battle of a thousand questions—and with a three-year-old no less. Every time he turned around Charlie fired another question at him. After each answer he gave, Charlie added "Why?" To add to his frustration most of the boy's questions didn't make any sense.

"Hey, mister, why don't you turn on the lights? Where's your TV? Can you turn up the heat? I'm cold. Do you have any ice cream? I'm hungry."

Brad eluded his confusing questions by mumbling something incoherent as he moved about the room looking for something for Charlie to wear. All the clothes in the dresser were for an infant. His son never had a chance to get as big as Charlie. As their child would have grown, his wife, Lucinda, would have lovingly stitched new clothes, which didn't help him now.

"Hey, mister, why do you wear that thing on your face? I want to see what you look like. Are you a monster?"

Brad walked to the bed where Charlie sat on the edge and squatted on his heels before the boy. "I had an accident and got a large cut on my face. The scar scares people so I wear the mask. Any more questions?"

Charlie tilted his head and squinted his eyes. "Where're your kids? Where's the baby for the cradle? My mom has a baby in her tummy. It's going to pop out soon."

He had to ask, didn't he. Should he ignore the boy's question about the cradle? Instead, he chuckled at Charlie's rendition of the baby popping out. "I know your mom's going to have a baby." He paused, trying to figure out what to tell Charlie next. If he avoided the question about the cradle, the boy would only ask again and again. Best to get it over with. "I had a son, but he died when he was a baby. I don't have any other children."

Brad's answer actually seemed to stop Charlie's questions—for a few seconds at least.

"Where's your wife?"

"My wife died, too."

Charlie's bottom lip quivered. "Will my Mommy and her baby die?"

A lump formed in Brad's throat. He pulled Charlie into his arms. Like the boy's small arms around his neck, fear wrapped around him. What would happen to him if his mother died in childbirth? The idea nearly knocked him to the floor. Charlie laid his head on Brad's shoulder. He rubbed the boy's small back in circular motions.

"Your mama isn't going to die, Charlie. Neither is her baby. I promise."

After comforting Charlie for a few minutes, the boy was back to his questioning self, breaking the spell of protectiveness.

"Hey, mister, you have anything to eat? I'm hungry. Can I see my Mommy? Can I watch TV before I go to sleep? Is this bed mine?"

Brad finally let loose and laughed. "Well, young man, let's get your clothes changed, we'll go see your mama, then get something to eat. Then you can climb into the bed. How's that sound?"

Charlie leaned back in Brad's arms and giggled. "Goody! But where're my clothes?"

"They are still in the buggy, but I'll find you something else to put on. Come with me and we'll look together." Brad set Charlie on the floor and stood. As if he trusted him, Charlie took Brad's hand, and they walked across the hall to Brad's room.

"Wow, this bed is humungous! Why do you have curtains around your bed? How do you get up on it?"

Here we go again. Brad sighed and searched through his wardrobe for something to put on the boy. He finally pulled out one of his white shirts.

"Here you go, Charlie. You can put this on." Brad handed the shirt to Charlie.

"A dress?" Charlie squealed then put his hands over his mouth. "I'm not a girl!"

What? "This isn't a dress. It's my shirt!"

"Then how come there's girl things on the ends?"

"Girl things?" Brad frowned and fingered the crisply starched ruffles. "These aren't girl things. All men wear ruffles on their shirts."

Charlie giggled. "My daddy doesn't."

At the thought of Charlie's father, his enjoyment of the boy wavered. Who was going to raise this delightful child? Who was going to be there to put him on a horse for the first time, or teach him to hunt? Or read? Should he tell Charlie about his father? Maybe he was a coward, but it would be better coming from his mother.

"It doesn't matter. You can wear this tonight as your nightshirt. I'll roll up the ruffles so you can't see them."

Charlie's eyes got big. "It's gonna be my 'jamas?"

"'Jamas?" The boy used so many strange words, but it would be better to go along with his strange vocabulary than to set him off on another round of questions. "Yes, you're going to sleep in this. Now let's get your other clothes off and you into my shirt." Brad picked Charlie up and set him on the bed. He started to pull off those odd shoes, but Charlie had other ideas.

"I can do it myself!" Charlie puffed out his small chest. "I've been undressing myself since I was a little kid."

Brad tried not to laugh as Charlie grabbed one of his shoes and tugged, falling backward onto the bed. The shoe went flying over Charlie's head onto the floor on the other side of the bed. In rapid order, the other shoe followed the first. Sounds of grunts filled the air as Charlie tugged, pulled, and rolled around the bed to remove each article of clothing.

Ignoring each piece of strange clothing as it was tossed to the floor was difficult. Finally, Charlie stood up in the middle of the bed, naked except for an unusual garment he wore over his private parts and displayed his bony knees and skinny little legs. The garment was white with some men wearing blue tights, red shorts, blue shirts, and a red flowing cape attached to their shoulders.

With his hands on his narrow hips, he grinned. "I'm ready for the dress!"

Brad came out of his musings about the clothes. "So you are young man. You did a great job, too. Come here and let me get this *shirt* on you."

After a few minutes of struggling with Charlie's short arms and the long arms of his shirt, Brad finally had the squirming boy buttoned up. He grabbed Charlie under his arms and swung him onto the floor.

"It's too big," Charlie whined. "I can't walk!"

Brad laughed, something so unusual in the past years, it shocked him. But he couldn't help it, which made Charlie's lip quiver. The sleeves of the shirt lay on the floor, the ruffled cuffs dragging behind him like a bedraggled puppy. Every time he took a step, he tripped on the garment and propelled himself forward.

"Fix this."

Brad raised an eyebrow at Charlie's demanding tone.

"Please?"

"Come here. I'll help you." It took a few minutes for him to roll the sleeves high enough so Charlie's hands were sticking out. "Now what?"

"Can you stick the shirt into my underpants?" Charlie asked.

Underpants? What the heck were those? Charlie stretched out the material at the waistband. Oh. Underpants must be what he was wearing over his privates. "Sure, I can tuck them into your underpants." After a few tries, Brad came to the conclusion there was way too much shirt for the boy's pants.

"How about if I carry you so you won't trip?"

Charlie scowled and opened his mouth. "I'm a big boy. I don't need to be carried."

"So you are, but it would help me a lot if you would let me carry you. I never get to carry children, especially ones as big as you. Besides, I don't want you falling and knocking me over."

"Okay." Charlie sighed. "But I'm not a baby!"

Brad made a show of struggling to pick up the boy. "You are a big one, aren't you?" Charlie rewarded Brad's cleverness by flexing his muscles. "Strong, too."

"Can I see my mommy now?"

"All right. I'm sure she's anxious to see you, too." They left his room and entered Libby's.

The fire had died down making it difficult to see. Brad went to the side of the bed. Charlie flexed his knees as he were ready to leap from his arms onto the bed. Brad put a finger to Charlie's lips.

"Shh. She's asleep."

Charlie slumped in Brad's arms. "But I want my mommy."

"She's tired, Charlie. Let's go find something to eat, and when we come back, maybe she'll be awake. All right?"

After nodding, Charlie laid his head on Brad's shoulder. "How about my daddy? Can I see my daddy?"

Brad hated lying to the boy. "Not right now. He's busy." Before going down the stairs, Brad lit a candle sitting on a table in the hallway and carefully started down the stairs.

"How come you don't turn on the lights?"

"This is my light."

Charlie shook his head. "No, I mean real lights."

Since he had no idea what Charlie was talking about, Brad quickly changed the subject. "A big boy like you must be hungry enough to eat a bear. What would you like to eat?" Cora had left some cold meat and potatoes in the pantry for him.

"Pizza! Can I have pizza?" Charlie bounced in his arms.

"Pizza? I'm fresh out of pizza today." They entered the kitchen. There the boy went again. Talking in riddles. "How about some meat and potatoes? They make a man strong!" He set Charlie on a chair by the long wooden table standing in the middle of the room and flexed his muscles.

Wooden counters and cupboards surrounded two sides of the room while a cast-iron stove sat next to the pantry door. A large fireplace with bread ovens built into the side graced the last wall. The room was rather small but had plenty of windows to allow the summer breezes to cool it off. Brad lit the two lanterns hanging above the table.

"Do you gots any hot dogs?"

Brad shook his head.

"How 'bout pasgettios? They're my fav'rit after pizza. I have them every day at the babysitter's."

When would this child ever make sense? What kind of food did he eat anyway? "I don't have any of those things."

"Don't you gots any food in your house? Are you poor?"

Poor? Him? With all the meat hanging in the smokehouse, vegetables stored in the cellar, cows for milk, and chickens for eggs, he was a far cry from being poor.

Eggs. Milk. Why of course. "Eggs, I have eggs. Do you like eggs?"

Brad perked up and nodded until his sandy-colored hair fell into his face. "Scrambled eggs. I love those. Can you make toast, too?"

At this moment Brad was grateful his mother had made her sons learn more than the running of a farm. She insisted they learn to cook and so they would be more appreciative of their future wives if they knew how hard they worked. For once in his life Brad saw the usefulness of those tortuous cooking sessions. If only he could remember how to do it.

"Sure, I can make scrambled eggs. We can have bread instead of toast, though." Cora made toast every morning for him, but how she did it...

"Okay. Can I help? I help my mommy all the time."

Brad hesitated. What could a three-year-old know about cooking? If he were kept busy, maybe it would keep him from asking so many questions.

"All right, Charlie. You tell me how your mommy makes her scrambled eggs, and I'll make them the same."

As Charlie rattled off instructions about milk, eggs, salt, pepper, and butter, Brad threw wood in the still-warm stove. He added a few pieces of tinder and kindling and in no time had the stove hot for cooking. He searched for the ingredients Charlie said were necessary to make "prefect" scrambled eggs.

Making the eggs with a young boy was a lesson in mess, but still enjoyable. He didn't remember having fun cooking as a child. This time if an eggshell got into the bowl, no one yelled. He and Charlie simply dug it out and Brad wiped them on his already filthy clothes.

After they had their fill of the slightly underdone eggs, bread, and milk, Charlie's eyes began to droop. If he didn't get the child up to bed, he would fall asleep at the table, probably with his face on his dirty plate.

"Come on, young man, let's get you to bed."

Brad chuckled at Charlie's jaw-cracking yawn as he reached up his arms to be carried. No concerns about being a baby now. It was a struggle carrying both the boy, who seemed to get heavier by the minute, and the candle.

Before they were half-way up the stairs, Charlie was asleep. Since his wife had died, he'd trudged up the stairs many times in the dark, so he blew out the candle, set it on a step, and went the rest of the way up the unlit stairs and hallway.

A dim glow from the fireplace in Charlie's room helped guide Brad to the bed. Carefully, he laid him at the foot of the bed, pulled back the sheet and blanket, placed Charlie on the sheets, and covered him.

"'Night, Mommy and Daddy," Charlie murmured as he stuck his thumb in his mouth and snuggled down in the blankets.

"'Night, Charlie," Brad whispered back. He pulled the hair away from Charlie's eyes. The desire to give him a kiss on his forehead was overwhelming. Before he could do something so personal, he turned away. This was not his son. Even though Charlie was fatherless, he couldn't begin to think about taking over the job. They probably had other family somewhere to go home to. He wouldn't let himself get attached to the boy.

After building up the fire and banking it for the night, Brad took one last look at the boy, checked on Libby, who was still sleeping, and left to take care of her husband.

Chapter Six

Brad rested his head against the copper bathtub and let out a sigh. He was exhausted. He could barely lift his brandy snifter from the stool sitting next to the tub. A clock from the living room below him chimed 11:00. The last two hours since putting Charlie to bed had been grueling.

Brad shuddered. If getting the man into the buggy had been hard, it was nothing compared to getting him out. After leaving Charlie, Brad went outside to find Captain had pulled the buggy onto the front lawn and was nibbling at the new spring grass. He'd had quite a time getting the stallion turned around and back in front of the house. The only way it would work was to go down to the barn, fix a feed bag, and lure Captain back to the house. He hung the bag over the horse's neck to keep him from searching out more grass.

Then came the job of lifting Charlie's father from the boot. It had been several hours since Brad had placed him there, and in that time the man seemed to have gained fifty pounds. And fatigue was catching up with Brad which didn't help. While resting against the buggy after his second attempt, Brad realized once he got the man out, he had no place to put him. He wasn't about to put a dead person on any of his furniture. Laying him on the dining room table wasn't appealing, either.

In the barn, he came across an old door. He hauled it to the parlor, placed it across two dining room chairs, and covered it with a blanket. Before going back outside he hauled water to his room and hung it on the hook over his fireplace. Hopefully, by the time he was done hauling the body in, the water would be hot for a relaxing soak.

After several tries and more swear words than he'd heard during the war, he was finally able to pull the body from the boot. Too heavy to carry, he dragged him across the foyer, and into the parlor, leaving trails of mud from the man's boots. Another mess for Cora to clean up. He heaved the man onto the door and pulled another sheet over him, keeping his face uncovered. Throughout this process, Brad prayed for forgiveness for the rough way he treated this poor man.

Brad slid down in the tub trying to soak his back, instead making his knees protrude from the water. The hot water relieved his aches, the brandy his pains. He closed his eyes. What would his son have been like if he had lived? Would he have been so free and full of questions? Would Brad have been a good father? After his short time with Charlie, he probably would have. He had enough patience with the boy's crazy questions to fill the hayloft. He made Charlie laugh and feel important. Oh, and those little arms around his neck—well... Brad wiped away a tear running down his cheek. How could something so simple be so powerful?

He chuckled recalling Charlie's "shirt dance." It must have been a game he played with his mother. It took a few seconds for him to figure out when he held out the shirt for Charlie to put his arms in, Brad was supposed to move away from Charlie's arms, making the little guy spin in a circle as he tried to slip his arms into the sleeves. They both ended up light-headed and laughing on the floor.

Now the chances of having more children were non-existent. Brad had no intention of remarrying, unless he were able to find a woman who would love him for himself, scars and all, and not for his money. Before meeting and marrying Lucinda, he had been a typical bachelor, going out, drinking, playing cards, doing some womanizing. Celebrating the end of the awful war. Most of the women he met in his social circles, though, only wanted him for his money, and, he had been told by his sister-in-law, his extremely good looks didn't hurt, either. Even before he was scarred, his value was in what he owned and how he looked, not who he was inside.

He refilled his glass from the brandy bottle sitting on a chair by the tub. Belinda Carlisle was one of those. She was constantly trying to seduce him into her bed so he would have to marry her. She didn't want Brad's love, only his money and her old family farm. Since he bought it from her, Belinda believed she had a connection to him; one she not only wanted but deserved. He finally avoided social functions so he wouldn't run into her. The Carlisles had never been church goers, but since finding out Brad went every

Sunday, Belinda had become a "true believer." Brad became more and more disillusioned with women and their wily ways.

Then he'd met Lucinda at a party at his brother and his wife's celebrating the baptism of their fourth child. He was struck not only by her beauty, but by her sweetness. She seemed truly interested in him and his rebuilding of Whispering Pines. Lucinda and Caleb's wife, Colleen, had been childhood friends, and when Lucinda's family was passing through the area, they were invited to stay for an extended visit.

After two weeks Lucinda's parents left, but she stayed on. A month turned into two, then three, four, then wedding arrangements began. It had been love on both sides. Brad had never been happier or more content. His work on Whispering Pines had been worth it. He could bring his bride home and start a family.

When Lucinda had first seen the farm, she'd loved it. Her ideas for decorating fit with Brad's need for simplicity, mixed with her flair for elegance. The house took on life again. His employees adopted Brad and Lucinda's zest for life. When Lucinda became pregnant, Brad couldn't contain his joy.

Except for marrying her, the day Lucinda had given him the news was better than any other day in his life. He'd picked her up and twirled her around the room until they both fell to the couch from dizziness. Cora had given him a stern lecture about taking proper care of his wife since she was in "the family way." But beneath Cora's stern visage, he could see her happiness and joy at being able to raise "another Kemble."

Lucinda's pregnancy went well. She hadn't suffered from the morning sickness his sister-in-law had with each of hers. Lucinda thrived on Brad's attention and the growth of their child. With Cora's help, she took care of the house, and whenever she was resting, she was stitching clothes for the baby.

Then one Sunday evening when she was in her eighth month, her water broke. As always, Brad had given the employees the day off to spend with their families. After doing chores, he'd cherished their time alone. No one to interrupt their lovemaking and cuddling, no Cora to tell Lucinda how to take care of herself.

Lucinda had been lying on the sofa, eyes closed, her head resting on Brad's lap as he read to her from *The Last of the Mohicans*. She seemed more tired than usual, and as she listened to the story, she rubbed her hands over her large stomach. Occasionally she would comment on how tight it felt. When the hour grew late, Brad suggested they retire for the night. Lucinda would be more comfortable in their own bed. He helped her get up from the sofa and with their arms wrapped around each other's waists, they started up the stairs. Halfway up to their room, Lucinda stopped and let out a gasp.

"Brad, my water broke! It's too early!"

Brad heard the panic in her voice as he swept her up in his arms and took the rest of the stairs two at a time. He threw back the blankets on the bed and carefully laid her on the mattress.

"Get some extra sheets to put under me. Hurry, the pains are starting! Get some towels for the baby."

By the time he had come back with the sheets and towels, her pains were coming in rapid succession.

"I'm going to get Cora. You need help."

Lucinda took Brad's hand. Love and pain showed in her eyes. "I don't want you to leave me. We can do this together," she whispered as another pain gripped her.

His knees grew weak with helplessness. He'd helped birth plenty of animals, but this was different. But if Lucinda trusted him, he wasn't going to let her down. "I don't know what to do. Tell me."

"This is happening too fast. Cora said it would take a long time for the first one to be born." Another pain grabbed her. She pulled her legs up.

He slid the extra sheets beneath her and drew her dress over her stomach. His stomach flipped and head spun the sight between her legs. Lucinda was red and swollen, blood running onto the sheets. A small foot protruded from her.

Brad tried not to panic. "Honey, shouldn't the head be coming first?"

With tears running down her face, Lucinda looked at him between her legs. "Yes. That's what Cora and Colleen told me. What's wrong?"

"It seems the little fellow is going to enter the world landing on his feet. I'm sure everything will be fine." He wasn't so sure when she let out another cry. "Try not to push, Lucinda." *Oh, God I don't know what to do. Help me.*

Then he remembered what they did when a cow had trouble delivering. Heaven help him if this didn't work.

"Lucinda, honey, I'm going to try to help the baby turn around, so his head will come first. I know it's going to hurt." Her blonde hair was plastered against her blotchy, red face. Pain and trust showed clearly in her eyes. "I love you."

"I love you, too. Now do what you have to."

Brad took a deep breath and asked for God's help before pushing the little foot back into Lucinda's body. He tried to ignore her screams as he tried to turn the child. When he managed to get the child turned so his rear-end was facing out, Lucinda let out a piercing wail and the baby came out into Brad's hands followed by a gush of blood. The room went deathly silent.

The boy lay limp and blue in Brad's hands. He unwrapped the cord from around his neck, placed the infant face down across his hand, and patted him on the back with the other. Nothing happened. He picked his son up by his feet and spanked him. Nothing. Brad laid the limp form on the bed and put his ear against the small chest. Nothing.

A low moan from Lucinda brought Brad to her attention. The afterbirth expelled from her body along with more blood than was proper. He covered his son with a corner of the quilt before packing towels between her legs.

"How's the baby?" Her face was pale. With dark circles beneath them, her eyes were sunken.

Brad knelt on the bed by her and wiped the hair away from her eyes. "Our son is just fine."

"A son? We have a son?"

He kissed her forehead and swallowed around the lump in his throat. "Yes. You gave me a fine son."

"May I see him?"

"He's sleeping." There was no way he could tell her their son was dead. "I'll bring him to you when you're rested. Right now, I need to take care of you so you're strong enough to raise him."

Lucinda raised a shaking hand to Brad. "I'm going to die, aren't I?"

"Shh. No, honey, you're not going to die. I won't let you. I need you. Your son needs you." But even though he said the words, she was right. The bleeding hadn't stopped. Her skin grew paler and paler with each passing second.

"What should we name him?" Her voice was barely audible.

"I was thinking about naming him after our fathers: Caleb Barret Kemble. How does that sound?"

Lucinda closed her eyes. "It's a wonderful name. Brad, kiss me."

As he placed his lips against hers, she whispered, "I love you." A last puff of air passed from her mouth across his lips. Everything went silent.

"Lucinda? Lucinda? Oh, God, please don't let her die!" Even as he cried out the words, he knew it was too late. He had lost his beloved wife and son. Before he broke down in a puddle of grief, he picked up his son and placed him in a towel, laid him in Lucinda's arms, straightened out her legs, and covered them with the quilt. How long he stood beside the bed, watching their faces, hoping for a miracle to bring them back, he didn't know.

He didn't hear the buggies returning, nor Cora entering his room. He didn't remember his having to be pulled from the bed and the room by Cora and her husband, Joshua. or her calling in for more reinforcements. They finally dragged him into his study where Joshua plied him with brandy while Cora took care of Lucinda.

The funeral passed in a blur. He barely recalled throwing himself onto the grave. According to his brother, Caleb, he was like a man possessed. Later, after the funeral, he had locked himself in his study, where he proceeded to smash everything he could get his hands on. His brother and staff paced outside the door. Whenever they tried to break the door in, he would throw something at it and threaten to kill anyone who entered.

The final blow came when he hurled a brandy decanter against the fireplace and it flew back on his face. He welcomed the pain and blood running from his eye to his chin, but it would never equal the pain he had put Lucinda through. He passed through his pain and anger, not noticing his room had finally been breached.

"C'mon Mr. Bradley." Cora took hold of his arm. "Let me fix your face and get you to bed."

"Just leave me the hell alone!" He ran from the room, out the front door, and to the barn. Heedless of there being no saddle on Captain, he had jumped onto his back and flew from the house as if death itself was on his heels. They didn't see him for four days.

Brad touched the scar on his face as he pushed himself from the tub. The anguish was as strong as if it were yesterday. He wasn't sure if he could ever get rid of it. Something crashed on the main floor. Someone was in the house. The last thing he needed right now was a thief. Would this night never end? He put on his robe and slippers and tiptoed down the stairs making sure to avoid a few squeaking steps.

Chapter Seven

Libby rolled over, placing a pillow along her side to help ease the weight of her stomach. Something poked into her skin. She pulled at it. A feather? What was a feather doing in her bed? Wait. The storm. The car crash. A masked man.

She sat up and waited for her head to stop spinning. It was difficult to see her surroundings in the dim room. A tall piece of furniture resembling a wardrobe stood against the wall facing her. She didn't have anything like that. Across from the foot of the bed, a small fire burned in the fireplace. Fabric hung at the corners of the four-poster bed.

Libby lay back on the pillows and closed her eyes. Like a lightning flash, it all came back to her. If she were physically able, Libby would bolt out of bed. Ben was dead, she and Charlie had been rescued by a masked man driving a buggy. They were ensconced at his house at his farm. She recalled his deep, soothing voice, and something about taking care of Charlie. Libby looked toward the open door near the fireplace.

"Charlie! I need to check on Charlie," she whispered as she struggled from under the blankets. She swung her feet to the side of the bed. The baby kicked and her stomach growled. "Food wouldn't be a bad idea, either."

Libby shivered as her feet hit the cool floor. "Ooh, hardwood floor." She loved hardwood floors. A heavy purple velvet robe lay at the foot of the bed. She caressed it before slipping it on. It barely met at the middle, but she tied the cloth belt around her stomach, anyway. It was like being encompassed in something warm and wonderful. She waddled to the open door by the fireplace. The only other door, which Libby assumed led into a hallway, was closed.

The faint light from the fireplace to the connecting room guided Libby to the bed where Charlie lay sleeping, his chest rising and falling regularly.

She eased to the edge of the bed and pulled the blankets over his shoulders. What in heaven's name was he wearing?

The sleeves of a white shirt were rolled up to his thin wrists. Had the man who'd rescued them been true to his word and taken care of her son? Except for some hardened egg yolk at the corners of his mouth, he looked clean. She smiled to herself as she brushed a few strands of curly blond hair from his closed eyes. How had she and Ben created such a beautiful child; not only in looks, but in spirit, too? Ben had often told her Charlie had her spirit, but she never could see it.

Ben. Where was he? Besides a cradle, dresser, and rocking horse, there was only the bed Charlie was sleeping in. Where had Ben's body been put? What was she going to do without him? She had to find him—now! It was necessary to see for herself he was really dead. Even though he had probably been taken to a funeral home already, she would tear apart this house piece by piece until she was satisfied he wasn't here. Then she would demand to be taken to see him and make arrangements to bring him home.

As in her room, the closed door probably led to a hallway. A candlestick with a half-burned candle sat on a table next to the door. Several matches lay next to it. "Must be here for when the power goes out." It would be best to not turn on a light and wake Charlie. Using a trick she had learned from her brothers, she flicked her thumbnail across the tip of the match. It hissed and sparked. She quietly opened the door and with one last look at Charlie, stepped into the hallway.

The candle threw shadows against the walls and the two doors across the hallway. A dim light shone under one of the doorways. There was a splash of water as if someone were taking a bath. Hopefully, it was a bathroom. She could use one right now but it sounded as if she'd have to wait her turn. The other door across the hall and to her right was closed, with no sign of life behind it. She vaguely recalled coming up the steps on the grand staircase with Charlie and Brad. Not trusting herself to descend the stairs with a candle in her hand, Libby ran her hand over the wall, searching for a light switch. Where would one be hidden?

"Must be at the bottom." With her left hand on the railing and the candlestick held high in her right, she headed down the stairs. The higher she raised the illuminated candlestick, the more it lit her surroundings. After taking the curve in the stairs and coming to the bottom step, Libby paused. Which way should she go? There were five doors, all closed. One she thought probably went outdoors since it was in the middle of the large foyer. She quietly opened the door immediately to her left and stuck her head in. It was too dark to make out anything more than slivers of moonlight coming through drapes.

The other two doors directly across the foyer looked equally forbidding. No lights came from either one. Libby walked to the second door on her left and figured it must be below the room she was staying in. A glimmer of light shone under the door. She eased the door open and automatically felt the wall for a light switch.

"That's right, if this is an Amish home, there wouldn't be one." Several candles stood on several tables, flickering shadows on the walls. In the middle of the room, its back facing the door, was a couch. An old-fashioned pump organ stood in one corner.

She stepped into the room, taking in the tall windows and heavy drapes covering them. A fireplace was on the wall to her left. A long table, draped in something white stood in front of the couch, its bumps and contours resembling a— She gasped. Her heart pounded loud enough to wake Charlie upstairs. In her fear, she knocked over a vase sitting on a table next to the couch. The shatter of glass filled the silence.

"Oh, Ben!" Libby whispered, pressing her fingers to her lips to stop from screaming. She walked over to the table. "My poor, poor Ben." She laid her ear against his chest to listen for a heartbeat and to make sure he was not breathing. Tears streamed down her face onto the sheet. "Look, your face is caked with mud. Couldn't they have cleaned you up?" She picked up a corner of the top sheet, spit on it, and gently wiped his face. As if the baby felt Libby's anguish, it kicked against her ribcage. In an instant Libby went from misery to anger.

"You stupid, stupid man!" she screamed, pounding his chest. "You just couldn't put on your seat belt, could you? No, not Benjamin Charles Daniels. You were much too macho to do something as silly as strap yourself in!" When her anger threatened to engulf her, great sobs came from the pit of her soul. "I don't even know where we are, and you lay there just...just dead.

What are Charlie and I supposed to do? What about the new baby? It'll never know you and how much you would love it and Charlie."

After her initial outburst, Libby calmed. Tears dripping onto his mud-caked face, she ran her fingers gently over Ben's cheeks. "You were the only one who ever really loved me. Besides Charlie, who's going to now? Charlie and I loved you so much. This baby would have, too."

The urge to do something kept her from running screaming from the room, demanding someone take care of Ben. Where and to whom she had no idea. "I have to get this mud off you, I can't see your face, and Charlie can't see you like this." She took a corner of the sheet and again tried to wipe his face clean. She kissed his forehead. "What are we going to do without you?"

Brad crept down the stairs, a small pistol in his hand. So far, everything was dark and quiet. Wait. He had closed the parlor door, but now it was open, a woman's voice clearly raised in anger coming through the entrance to the room. No voice answered her. He was an idiot. What did he think, the dead man was going to carry on a conversation with a thief?

Stepping into the parlor, he slipped his pistol into his robe pocket and stopped. Libby was pounding the man on the chest, screaming at him. Did she hope to bring him back to life by beating him to death? Before Brad could approach and halt her ravings, she ceased her yelling, stroked the man's cheeks, and wiped them off with a corner of the sheet.

Her words were barely a murmur, but she was saying something about Ben's being the only one who'd ever loved her, and how she and Charlie had loved him. In life, Ben must have been one lucky man. Her comment about what she was going to do without him made Brad wonder what he was going to do with her. Where was she from? What were they doing in the storm? What was a seatbelt? What if she had the baby before Cora came back? He couldn't leave her and race to get his sister-in-law.

Brad must have made some sort of sound because Libby whirled around to face him. Luckily, he had put his mask on before coming downstairs. Her eyes, red and puffy from crying, filled with anger.

"Why didn't you clean him up before dumping him on this table?" Libby screamed at him. "Why isn't he in a casket? Don't you have any respect for the dead?"

If Brad hadn't been so shocked by her outburst, he would have laughed at the absurdness of her questions. "Ma'am, calm down. I didn't have time to clean him up. After taking care of your son, I barely had time to bring him in and clean myself up. I'm the only one here right now, and I had enough trouble getting your husband into the house, let alone cleaned up."

Libby bit her bottom lip and ran a hand over her husband's hair. "I'm so sorry for yelling at you. I just...just feel so awful. Besides Charlie, he's all I have—had." She dropped to her knees and sobbed into her hands.

What should he do now? He didn't know the woman, and crying women always made him uncomfortable. When Lucinda cried for some reason or other, he joked with her and helped her forget why she was sad or upset. There was no way he would joke at a time like this. Unthinkable. If it were his sister-in-law, Colleen, or his sister, Sybil, he would march right over and hold her until her fears were gone. His guess was most women were the same, so maybe it would help Libby.

"It's going to be all right, Libby." He joined her on the floor and put his arms around her. He placed his hand on the back of her head and pushed it against his chest. With each sob escaping from her, Brad was rewarded for his chivalry with a smack to his chin from the top of her head. He ignored the pain. "Shh, Libby. I'll make sure you and Charlie get back to your family. You'll be all right, and so will your baby." He rhythmically moved his hand up and down her back until her sobbing slowed. He had forgotten how good it felt to hold another human being. Even considering the reason he was holding her, his heart warmed from comforting Libby.

"My legs are cramping," Libby's hiccoughed comment broke into his thoughts. "I need to get up."

"Do you want to go back to your room?" His knees cracked as he stood and helped her from the floor.

Libby gave him a small grin. "Actually, I could use something to eat. I haven't had anything since lunch today and it was only a sandwich in the car. Do you think I could get something?"

"Uh, sure." *As long as it wasn't eggs. Maybe he'd be lucky and Libby would do the cooking herself.*

"Would you have any eggs? I have a strong craving for them."

Figures. He picked up a candlestick from a table and helped Libby from the room. "Do you like scrambled eggs?"

Libby shook her head. "Normally I don't, but for some reason I would like a plate of them, with some toast and grape jelly."

Here we go with the toast thing again! "I don't know if I can make toast,"—*or even know what the hell it is*— "but you can have bread with grape jam." *He hadn't yet cleaned up the mess from his and Charlie's meal.*

They were rounding the base of the stairs and heading for the doorway leading under them to the outside and then into the unattached kitchen when Libby stopped and grabbed the newel post.

"What's the matter?"

Libby grabbed her stomach. "My water broke."

Brad stared at her, trying not to let panic overtake him. When he saw the wet floor around Libby's feet, a familiar fear climbed into his throat. *Sweet Jesus, not again!* "I thought you said the baby wasn't due yet. You said it was too early."

She whooshed out a breath. "Don't worry. I wasn't really sure when the baby was due, so it may only be a few weeks early. Besides, I have plenty of time. I was in labor with Charlie for eighteen hours before he decided to enter the world. I sincerely hope it isn't as long this time."

Forgetting he had on his mask, he swept his hand over the top of his head. If he weren't wearing it, he'd pull his hair out. *And I hope it is. More time for Cora to get here. I'm not going through this alone again!* "Let's get you upstairs and into bed." He turned her toward the stairs.

"Why don't you get Charlie and take me to a hospital. Like I said, I have plenty of time." No sooner were the words said, than Libby grimaced and clutched the banister.

Beneath his mask, sweat beaded on his forehead. Thanks to his mask, Libby wouldn't be able to see how nervous he was. "There is no hospital." Even if there were, after seeing the field hospitals during the war, there was no way he'd trust a sawbones to deliver an ant let alone a baby. "You have to have the baby here. Unless you'd like to drop the babe on these stairs, we need to get you to your room."

Libby dug her teeth into her bottom lip as the pain held her in its clutches. "What do you mean there's no hospital? I can't deliver this baby alone!"

They headed up the stairs again. "Well, if you can wait until Cora comes back, she can help. Just keep the baby inside for—" *Oh, lord, how long before Cora does arrive? Too damn long.* "—as long as you can!"

"Oh, man, here comes another one. Stop." Her nails dug into his arm. "I need to stop!"

Brad held his breath as Libby did some type of panting, like a dog on a hot summer day.

"Whew! That was a powerful one. Maybe this baby won't take as long as Charlie did." A tear ran down her cheek. "I don't know if I can make it up the stairs."

Would it be bad if he cried along with her? *This is just like before. Please don't do this to me again!* "Can you carry the candle if I carry you?" Brad asked.

"Why don't you just turn on the lights?"

Brad grit his teeth. "Why do you and Charlie keep asking about lights? This damn candle is my light. Now, do you want me to carry you, or can you make it if I support you?"

Another tear rolled down her cheek. He was an ass for making a pregnant woman cry.

"I simply asked a question about the lights." She raised her chin. "If you can support me, I can make the stairs, but we'd better hurry."

It seemed she had to stop every ten steps to get through another contraction. Sticking a hand under his mask, he wiped the sweat from his face. He was getting light-headed as he matched her breath for breath. "Do you have to breathe like that?"

It probably wouldn't be prudent to kick at Brad's legs and send him down the stairs. She ignored him until the pain passed. "Yes, I have to breathe like that. It helps me focus on something other than the pain. It's called natural childbirth." *How could he be so dense?* An unsettling thought occurred. "You've never helped deliver a baby, have you?" Brad tensed against her arm. She was right.

"Yes. I have." His tone was clipped, almost angry. "Let's go."

Except for having to stop once more, the rest of the trip to Libby's room was uneventful. Brad was silent and withdrawn; Libby more concerned about being left with a man who she was sure hadn't a clue about what was going to happen. But then, most men didn't. Ben certainly hadn't. Even though he worried about her, his concerns were with the end result: a healthy son.

Libby climbed back into bed and pulled the covers up to her chin. Brad headed for the door. "Where are you going?"

"I'm getting some more sheets to put beneath you." He didn't look at her before practically racing from the room.

"Oh." Maybe he did know what he was doing, but he was a stranger. A stranger who was going to view her swollen body like no one but her doctor and Ben had. Then she remembered not even noticing her doctor when Charlie was born. Having a baby was the most natural thing in the world—nothing to get embarrassed about. If she kept telling herself that, she'd be okay.

Brad rushed out of the room as Libby started another contraction. How on earth was he ever going to be able to get through this? Maybe if he concentrated on what he needed for the birth and not what he'd have to do to help, he might be all right. Maybe. Possibly. Hopefully.

He ran across the hall to his room, threw on his pants and shirt, and grabbed more candles. As he was leaving the room, he noticed the pot of water still heating over the fire. Water! He remembered when he was with Caleb during the birth of Caleb's second child. Everyone was scurrying around with sheets, towels, and hot water. He wasn't sure what it was used for, but he'd sure as hell have some available this time.

He ignored Libby when he entered her room, stoked up the fire, put the pot over it, and lit candles around the room.

"Can I put these sheets beneath you?" So as to not distress her, he kept his voice low and calm, the total opposite of what was going on inside him. He wouldn't pay attention to seeing a woman's privates and concentrate on the baby. Having a baby was the most natural thing in the world. Except for Lucinda.

Libby flipped off the covers.

"What the hell are you doing?" Brad yelled.

"I'm going to pull back the blankets and spread out the sheets you brought."

"Get back in bed. I'll do it. You'll drop the babe on its head!" Women.

"I'm perfectly capable of helping. Now get on the other side of the bed and pull back the blankets."

Together they prepared the bed. Libby laid down several layers of sheets to make a thick, soft pad.

"Do you have any rope?"

He gulped around the lump in his throat. "Rope? What do you plan on having me do—pull the baby out?" At his comment, visions of him pulling out his son came to mind. "I'm not pulling your baby out. You hear me?" He'd had to help calves be born that way, but a human baby? Was she grinning? Did she think he was being funny?

She shook her head. "Don't worry, you won't have to pull the baby out. I thought you had delivered a baby already?"

He couldn't look at her. Now was not the time to explain how he hadn't been able to help his own child and wife.

"I want something to grab onto while I push. If you tie ropes to the posts at the head of the bed, I can use them to grasp onto. Also, do you have anything to put on the baby? I wasn't planning on it being born so soon and left everything in Wisconsin." She rubbed her stomach. "I need to lie down again. And don't forget to wash your hands before touching the baby."

I need to get out of here. His mind numb with her instructions, Brad rushed from the room to look for rope. Maybe he'd be lucky and the baby would come before he got back. He stopped at the bottom of the stairs. How could he be so callous? This poor woman needed him. Wasn't he a man? *Yes, but a chicken one when it came to what was going to have to be done. But it can't be any worse than what happened with Lucinda. At least my heart isn't involved with this one.* His heart in his throat, he ran to the barn for the rope she'd requested.

Libby seemed to be sleeping when he returned to the room. The hair around her face was damp, and dark circles had appeared under her eyes. She opened them as Brad started tying the rope to the bedposts.

"Are they long enough?" she whispered.

"I hope so." He handed one end to her and was satisfied to see she had plenty of rope to hold onto.

"Did you find something to put on the baby?"

"I found some diapers and a gown of some kind. There were some small blankets, so I brought them, too. There's a cradle for the baby to sleep in."

Another contraction gripped her. "Where did they come from?"

If he answered, he'd break down. His nerves were shot. Thank heavens this was happening at night and Charlie was asleep. What would he have done if he had to take care of the boy, too?

It seemed to Brad that as soon as the last contraction stopped, another started. After several more in rapid succession, her time must be near. He paced at the foot of the bed.

"Rub my back," she groaned.

He knelt at her side and rubbed her upper back.

"Not there. Lower. Harder. Rub harder!" Her voice rose to nearly a screeching level.

His arms grew tired from digging his palms into her back. Any harder and he would rub off her skin. With his other hand he wiped her face with a damp towel, wishing he could do the same to his face. It was getting incredibly hot under the hood.

Libby's groan reminded him of a charging bull.

"I need to push!" She moved onto her back and raised her legs. Her nightgown slipped to her waist, exposing her stomach.

Brad had forgotten how big a pregnant stomach could be, but he did remember being completely amazed how a life was stored in there.

Libby panted. "Can you see the head?"

Brad went to the end of the bed. He had to kneel on the bed to get closer. A dark bulge showed between her legs, her bottom swollen and distended. Brad had to swallow before he could answer, his mouth twice as full of saliva as usual.

"I can see the head." As soon as he had answered he poured warm water into a pan Libby let out a scream, pulling on the ropes.

"Damn you, Ben, for doing this to me!"

Brad would have been more shocked at her words if he hadn't been so engrossed in what was happening between her legs. It was nothing like his son's birth. Instead of a little foot sticking out, a head was emerging. Salty, stinging sweat ran into his eyes, burning them, making it difficult to see. He'd have to chance having her see his face. He pulled off his mask and tossed in onto the floor.

"C'mon, Libby. You're doing fine." This was the most amazing thing he'd ever seen. "The head is turning. Oh my. Its eyes are open!"

In the short time before Libby's body pushed the shoulders out, Brad wiped off the baby's mouth. Another push from Libby and Brad was holding a squirming, screaming, slippery human being.

"It's a girl. You have a daughter!" He wanted to laugh, to cry. He'd done it. No, Libby'd done it. No, by golly, they'd both done it!

As if she were a precious piece of antique china, Brad placed the baby on Libby's stomach. He recalled what Caleb had told him about having to deliver his third child himself. Since the brothers were so close, Caleb had told him everything. Tearing strips of cloth from Libby's nightgown, he tied two pieces to the cord still attaching the baby to Libby. With the knife Libby had ordered him to wash, he sliced between the strips, through the cord, freeing the infant from its mother.

Brad wrapped her in a blanket and placed her in Libby's arms.

"What are you going to name her?" Brad asked.

"Lucinda, after Ben's mother. Lucinda Marie," Libby murmured. "Lucy for short."

For a minute Brad couldn't breathe. His legs went weak. There was no way Libby could have known his late wife's name. "Pretty," he whispered. "Libby, I need to tend to you, first. Then I'll take care of the baby." He didn't need to worry about his mask being off and Libby seeing him. She only had eyes for the baby—Lucinda.

While Libby cooed, counted toes, fingers, ears, and any other part she could find, Brad carefully washed Libby using warm water and soap. He placed a small, clean towel between her legs, wrapped up the afterbirth to bury later, and removed the soiled sheets. He should probably help her change into a clean nightgown, but when he returned to her side, she was asleep, hair plastered to her face, a soft smile on her lips. One of her fingers was wrapped tightly in the infant's fist. It was beautiful. His heart leapt into his throat.

After changing the water in the washbasin, Brad carefully unwrapped Lucy's small fist from Libby's finger. The babe's strength surprised him. Cradling the infant in his arms he carried her to the washbasin sitting on a table near the fireplace. Her unfocused eyes gazed at him. They were blue. Would they change? Caleb had told him sometimes they did, but all his children's eyes had stayed blue.

Carefully Brad placed Lucy in the warm water. Instantly her legs recoiled and her arms flailed in the water like a blind boxer. Brad laughed.

"Hey, precious one, you keep wiggling and I'll drop you on your head like Mom dropped Caleb." It was a family joke, one Brad never let Caleb forget. "Then your big brother will blame everything you do on being dropped on your head."

Lucy calmed down while he talked to her. She seemed to take in every word he said, although he knew he could be talking about breeding his cattle and it would have the same effect on her. It was the tone of his voice, not what he was saying that was important. After cleaning her up and drying her off, Brad clumsily diapered her using the safety pins they'd bought in town and put her gown on. He fervently hoped the diapers would stay on, but then she wouldn't be dancing any jigs soon, so he figured it would be safe until Libby could take care of her. He wrapped her in a clean blanket and sat on the edge of the bed, simply staring at her.

"Hey, little one, it looks like you're going to have red hair like your mama's. Man alive, you're a beauty." Even with her crunched up nose and slightly pointed head, he thought so. Caleb had told Brad all his kids had been ugly when first born, but love tended to overlook their imperfections.

All his children turned out to be beautiful, according to Caleb, anyway, and Brad had to agree.

Brad ran his finger across the fluffy, red down on the top of Lucy's head and kissed her forehead. She stuck a fist in her mouth and closed her eyes. Her busy first day in this world had left her exhausted. Brad's emotions rose to the surface. He felt like he'd been kicked in the gut by one of his horses. Love. He couldn't and wouldn't love this child. It wasn't his nor could it ever be. Love. How could he love someone as quickly as he did this child?

He needed to put the infant down before she took over his soul. Brad laid the infant in the cradle, covered her with another blanket, checked on Libby, blew out all the candles but the one beside the bed, and left the room as fast as he could.

The smell of cold, dirty bath water greeted him as he entered his room. He longed to heat up more water and take another relaxing soak. The clock in his room chimed three times.

Shit was all he could come up with for the way he felt. He wanted a good, stiff drink, and a ride on Captain as far and as fast as possible. Instead, he dropped on the bed, curled up as if he were a child and instantly fell asleep.

Chapter Eight

Libby slowly woke from a dream about a little girl wearing a pinafore, ruffled pantalets, and her hair done up in ringlets. A tall, dark-haired man walked beside the little girl, holding her hand. They laughed at a puppy tumbling at their feet. In the dream a baby was whimpering. Gradually the whimpering became full-fledged screaming. She peeled her eyes open. This wasn't a dream.

She rolled over toward the crying and smiled. She'd had a little girl last night. Lucy. By the sounds of it, she's starving. About to sit up and swing her feet over the side of the bed, she paused. Someone was standing near the cradle. A woman, dressed in white, with dark hair cascading down her back, a hand resting on the end of the cradle, gazed at Lucy. Libby thought the woman was glowing, but decided it had to be her tired eyes playing tricks on her. Had to be the lighting shining on a nurse.

"Miss? Can you please bring my baby? I think she's hungry."

The woman glanced at Libby but didn't say anything before turning back to the screaming infant.

"Miss? Please, I want to hold Lucy." The woman continued to ignore her. What nurse does such a thing? What was going on? The woman finally leaned over the cradle and reached out as if to pick up the baby. She set watery eyes on Libby. Tears streamed down her cheeks. The pain on the woman's face pierced Libby's heart.

Wait. The woman wasn't going to steal Lucy, was she? She'd read about women who lost a child or couldn't conceive taking children right from the hospital. Libby swept back the blankets, ready to charge at the woman like a she-bear protecting her cubs.

A commotion from outside her door stopped her. Good. Someone was coming. Hopefully, they'd remove this woman from her room. A short, light-skinned black woman entered the room carrying a stack of sheets and towels. A long white apron was tied between her large stomach and overly endowed top. A white cap rested crookedly on her short, curly hair. A welcoming smile greeted Libby.

"My, my, my, but that baby sure do sound hungry. She's a'crowing with the rooster," the woman said jovially. "We best get the bottom changed and the top filled so's we can make her happy." The woman crossed the room, set her supplies on the dresser, and waddled toward the cradle.

Libby frowned. "What happened to the other lady?"

"What lady? You and I are the only ladies in this house. Besides me, Mr. Bradley lives here alone. I'm Cora—housekeeper, cook, nurse, and right now it looks like nanny."

Cora picked up the baby and carried her to Libby. "Sure is a pretty 'li'l thing. With those long lashes, must be a girl. What's her name? How did you come to be here? By the looks of her she must have just been born. Where's Mr. Bradley? How long you plannin' on stayin? Here honey, you take this sweet thing. If she keeps a squalin,' she'll wake the dead."

Libby cringed at the use of Cora's choice of words. Obviously, she hadn't seen Ben yet.

"Don't mind me, honey. I love to talk. Mr. Bradley says he could go a week without saying a word and there would still be plenty of talkin' being done in this house. I'll shut up now so's you can take care of the babe."

Libby gazed down at Lucy. Her heart swelled with love. "This is Lucinda Marie—Lucy. I'm Libby Daniels." A fierce protectiveness swept through her. Even stronger than when she'd had Charlie. Was she going crazy with her fierce thoughts? Maybe it was because Lucy was a girl and would need more protection than Charlie. Libby came out of her musings when she felt the mattress sag. She looked up and saw Cora sitting on the edge of the bed. Cora frowned at her.

"When I left yesterday mornin' to visit my family, I left Mr. Bradley to himself. How'd you come to be here? I didn't know he knew any women with child in the area. But then, I didn't know any, either."

Cora's silence led Libby to want to answer Cora's many questions. Libby closed her eyes to gather her thoughts. After letting out a long sigh, she began to tell what she remembered. Throughout the narrative Cora let out little sounds of distress or comforted Libby by patting her hand. When Libby mentioned Ben being downstairs, Cora's eyes opened wide, the whites showing around her dark brown irises, tears forming at the corners.

"Oh, you poor, poor thing. Here you are alone with no man to take care of you. What'll ya do now?"

As Libby switched Lucy to her other breast she wondered the same thing.

"I'll probably contact Ben's mother. She can send someone to get me."

"But you won't be able to travel for weeks," Cora told her firmly. "You'll need your bedrest to gain strength after birthin' this 'lil one."

Weeks? Where did this woman get the idea you had to stay in bed for weeks? When she'd had Charlie, she was in and out of the hospital in a day and a half. "I'll be up by this afternoon. Then I can call my mother-in-law."

Cora was shocked. "This after' noon? You'll do no such thing!" Before Libby could protest, Cora continued on. "Go on."

It took Libby a moment to realize Cora had changed gears and wanted her to continue the story. "Well, Brad got Charlie and me upstairs—"

"Charlie? Who's Charlie?"

"He's my little boy. He's three. He's sleeping in the next room. Anyway, I think it's the next room." Libby paused for a second. "Yes, I recall going there and checking on him before I went downstairs."

"Lord have mercy! Another child in this house!" Cora nearly fell off the bed in her excitement. "Praise the Lord. It's what this house needs, is lots of little ones."

"But I can't stay here, Cora. I need to get to Ben's family."

Cora patted Libby's hand in comfort. "Now, now, honey. Don't you fret none. We'll get you back to your family, but by the time Mr. Bradley sends out a messenger and returns, and after you're healed and rested, it could be a month before you're with your family."

Libby was getting too tired to argue, but she thought it was ridiculous to send someone out when they could just call. "Anyway," Libby continued her story, "I fell asleep and when I woke up, I went to find Ben. While I was downstairs, I went into labor, and Mr. Kemble helped me upstairs. He must have gone for the doctor, because the next thing I knew a man, not wearing a mask, was helping me deliver Lucy."

Cora frowned. "You say a doctor came out here and helped with the babe?"

"Yes. After Lucy was born, he took care of me. Then I guess I fell asleep. The doctor must have cleaned up Lucy, too, because she's spick-and-span and I didn't do it."

"Where was Mr. Bradley during all this?"

"I'm not sure. Maybe he stayed downstairs. Men don't care for those things," Libby answered as she released the slumbering baby from her breast.

"Here, let me take her, and you rest while I go down and fix you something to get your strength up."

A faint bit of sunlight came through the windows. *No wonder I'm still so tired. It must still be early in the morning. I must have slept only a few hours. I hope Charlie stays in bed for a while longer.* Cora slipped into the room next door. *Who was the woman with long hair?* was her last thought before slipping into a deep sleep.

Good. Miss Libby is falling asleep. After I check on her little boy, I'll check on Mr. Bradley. He must have had one heck of a night last night. After making sure Charlie was still asleep, she carefully opened Brad's bedroom door. She found him lying in a fetal position near the edge of his bed. Figuring he was cold, Cora covered him with a quilt she had folded on the end of the bed. *Yes, sirree, Mr. Bradley, you must have had quite a night. Doctor, indeed. If I don't miss my guess, I'm standing right here looking at him.* Shaking her head as she exited the room, she couldn't imagine the turmoil he must have gone through delivering another baby.

Brad was jerked awake by the sounds of someone being scolded. He couldn't imagine who Cora was nagging this time. At least it wasn't him. She was forever trying to get him to eat right, drink less, and find someone to marry and have a dozen children with. As Brad pulled off the quilt, he recalled the events of last night, or rather this morning. He'd laid out a man for burial, then had actually delivered a baby. Brad looked at the clock on the mantlepiece. Eight o'clock? He'd never slept this late in his life.

Brad sprung to the floor, his sore body protesting from yesterday's exertions. He twisted and stretched to release his stiff body. He was still wearing the pants and shirt from last night. They were wrinkled. Normally Brad would never have left his room looking like a vagabond, but Cora's yells were becoming persistent. He needed to rescue whomever she was attacking. With a sigh, he picked up his mask from the floor where he had tossed it before dropping into bed, yanked it over his face, and left his room.

The yelling was coming from the room across the hall, the one where he had put the woman, Libby. He wasn't sure he wanted to face her again after last night. Men don't usually get close to women they don't know. She would probably be embarrassed, too. Then he remembered she had thought he had been a doctor.

The door to the room was open. Hoping to avoid getting involved in the chaos going on, he leaned against the door frame, folded his arms across his chest, and viewed the scene before him. His faithful, yet forceful, housekeeper, Cora, was arguing with Libby, who was sitting on the edge of the bed. Libby's son, Charlie, was pulling his mother's arm one way and Cora was trying to push her with the other. Cora finally noticed Brad.

"Mr. Bradley, you have to help get this woman back into bed. She can't get up yet; it's too soon since the babe was born."

When Cora called out to him, both Libby and Charlie stopped their tug of war and looked up at him. Libby was blushing.

"Please, I have to use the bathroom. Would you please tell Cora it's all right for me to get up?"

Brad shrugged. "I wouldn't know if it's all right for you to get up or not, but I would imagine you know your body better than Cora does."

"Thank you, sir." She gave Cora one of her teacher looks. "When I had Charlie, I was up and about in a few hours. Women of today don't stay in bed or in the hospital for four days like they did before and if you don't let me up, I'm going to embarrass myself right here and now!"

"Four days?" Cora folded her arms over her chest. "Women stay in bed for at least a week, and if I have anything to say about it, so will you!"

This battle of wills was enjoyable. Lucinda had never argued with Cora, but believed everything Cora said and did to be the gospel truth. As he listened to their discussion, Brad felt a tug on his pantleg. Charlie was straining his neck to look up at him.

"Hey, mister, is that fat lady going to hurt my Mommy?"

Brad ruffled Charlie's hair. "No, Charlie, she's not. She doesn't want your mother to hurt herself. And you shouldn't call her the fat lady. Her name is Cora."

"I'm hungry and I don't think they're gonna feed me. Can you make me sumpin' to eat again?"

"Sure. Let me change my clothes first, and we'll see what we can find." Hopefully, Cora would already have something prepared, or they'd have scrambled eggs again.

"Can I come with you when you change?" Charlie asked as he watched his mother and Cora.

Brad couldn't blame the boy for wanting to leave the room. Even if Libby were to win this battle with Cora, he shouldn't be in the room when his mother took care of herself. "Sure, you can help me pick out my clothes for the day."

"You gonna wear one of those girl shirts again?"

Brad spirits lifted as he took Charlie's hand and headed toward his room. "No, I'll wear one of my work shirts."

"Good. I had to tell the fat lady I didn't like girl shirts. She laughed at me. Did you know I had to go potty in a pot and the fat lady didn't know how to tie my shoes? What are we having to eat?"

Brad chuckled. *Here we go again.*

It was early afternoon when Libby finally was able to be alone. Cora had left with her lunch tray after making Libby promise she would stay in bed and rest. Lucy was sleeping the sleep of the newborn after having had her fill, and Charlie was down for his nap. He had spent the better part of the morning with Brad, and when he came back to see her, he glanced quickly at his new sister, proclaimed her not as interesting as the new baby horse outside, and proceeded to talk non-stop about what he had seen and done. Every other sentence was filled with 'Brad said this' and 'Brad did that' and 'wait until Daddy sees this.'" She was getting rather tired of the man's name. When Charlie woke up from his nap, she was going to have to break the news about his father. Libby thought he was rather young to truly understand the impact of what happened, and even though he would miss his father, Charlie would bounce back and be his usual rambunctious self. Anyway, it's what Libby hoped. It was going to be hard enough to cope without Ben when Charlie threw fits.

Once she got things going here, she would go to her mother-in-law's home in Tennessee where she would have to help her deal with Ben's death. Then she could fly home and decide how she was going to handle the rest of her life without her husband. She definitely would want to continue teaching. She would need the income to support herself and the kids. Maybe she could get a job nearer Ben's mother and they could support each other. Both financially and emotionally. Her mother-in-law was always complaining she never saw enough of her grandchildren. Maybe she would be willing to babysit for them while Libby taught. There was plenty of room in her old farmhouse for the four of them. The antics of the kids could help her get over the loss of her son.

Libby mentally shook herself back to the present. No sense worrying about things before they happened. What she needed to do first was find out how she could leave here with Ben's body and get to his mother's. Libby closed her eyes and wiggled farther under the blankets. Maybe if she hid far enough under the blankets and then came out, she'd find none of this had happened.

After a few minutes she came up for air. A persistent need to relieve herself roared its ugly head. Libby tried to ignore the need when she thought about having to use the chamber pot residing under the bed. She couldn't believe it when Cora had brought it out for her to use. When Libby had insisted she would rather use the bathroom, Cora had looked at her in confusion.

Libby remembered thinking this was an Amish house, but since then, things didn't seem to point in that direction. Amish didn't wear bright-colored clothes like Cora's. They also didn't have non-family members take care of them. If this were an Amish home, Brad would have a wife or a mother to take care of him. His clothing didn't suggest Amish, either. If Libby didn't know better, she would have thought their clothes, speech, and way of living were more suited to the 1800s. She'd read enough historical novels and taught enough US history classes to know the time period.

Libby was struck with another thought. *Maybe this is one of those historical tour homes where the employees dressed and acted the part of the time period.* She had always thought it would be a fun job when she wasn't teaching in the summer. Ben thought she was crazy. Libby quickly dismissed the tour idea. If these people were employees of an historical home, they certainly were doing one bang-up job of acting like they really lived here. All she knew and felt right now was something strange was going on, and it wasn't postpartum blues or nerves or anything else making her feel this way.

A cool breeze washing across Libby's face drew her attention away from her thoughts. A scent of lilacs accompanied the breeze. All the windows were closed so she scanned the room to find the source of the breeze. A whisper of movement drew Libby's attention toward Lucy's cradle. She suppressed a gasp when she saw a woman standing over the cradle. It was the same one she had seen before. Her long white gown, which might be a nightgown, was blowing around her as if a strong wind were gusting against her. The woman's long, blonde hair was whipped off her face, exposing pale, stark features.

"Miss?" Libby called out in a voice she felt was far from calm. "Who are you? May I help you with something?"

As before, the woman reached out toward Lucy as if she were going to pick her up. Libby's stomach clenched, making her want to leap from the bed and grab Lucy away from the hands of this specter. Then the woman turned to Libby. Again, tears rolled down her cheeks. The sorrow coming from her kept Libby rooted in place. As much as she wanted to protect Lucy, she couldn't move.

As the two women stared at each other, Libby gradually became aware this woman posed no threat to either her or Lucy. There was something ethereal as well as maternal about her. Libby sensed shared events. Somehow, they were tied together. As Libby was about to speak, the woman glanced toward the door. Libby followed her gaze. Brad stood in the doorway, his stance tense.

Brad could seriously use a nap. He never realized how exhausting spending a morning with a three-year-old could be. He wondered if he would have eased into all this energy as his child had grown and not have been as tired as he was now. His lack of sleep last night hadn't helped, either. As much as he enjoyed his time with the lad, he was glad when Cora came and took him in for lunch and a nap. Brad thought of his own bed and wished he could fall into it, but he had other pressing matters to attend to. One being Libby's husband. Like it or not, he was going to have to face her and discuss the funeral as well as what her plans were.

As he approached her room, he tried to listen to Libby's soft voice. Was Cora taking care of her? Nothing shocked him as much as what greeted him as he entered the room. Libby was leaning toward her daughter's cradle. The scent of lilacs swept past his nose; one he hadn't enjoyed since Lucinda's death. It was one of her favorites. He closed his eyes as memories of her passed through his mind.

At his name being whispered, he glanced at the cradle. The sight of his wife standing at the end of the cradle, staring at him, made him want to run from the room. That, or run to her, grab her, and kiss her senseless. He knew neither was a possibility so he shut his eyes hoping he was dreaming. When he opened them, the vision was gone; only the essence of lilacs remained. It took him a moment to notice Libby was talking to him.

"Did you see her? Who was she?"

Brad shook himself back to reality, hoping Libby hadn't sensed his near panic. "See who? You're the only one in this room."

Libby knew she hadn't made up the vision but decided to drop it. "Are you okay? You seem nervous. It is okay to come into the room. The baby won't bite."

The urge to laugh was overwhelming. After last night, he of all people knew the baby wouldn't bite. Right now, he wished he could throw her comment back at her to break his tension, but she then might figure out he was the so-called doctor.

"I'm just tired. I spent the morning with your son. I didn't know how much energy is packed into such a small child."

Libby's eyebrows drew together. "I hope he wasn't too much trouble for you. He can be a bundle of questions and energy."

Much of which he didn't understand. "Don't worry, he was fine. We're both fine."

"Good," Libby answered in relief. "Sometimes he gets on people's nerves because of his incessant questions. Right now, he's recharging his batteries and will be going full force until bedtime."

Recharging batteries? What the hell did she mean? He chose to ignore yet another confusing comment by these strange people. He set the large book he'd carried in with him on a bureau, clasped his hands behind his back, and assumed what he hoped to be a stern pose. "I'm not here to complain about Charlie. There are several things I need to talk to you about. First, I want to congratulate you on your new daughter. Cora tells me she's a beauty."

"Do you want to see her or are you afraid of babies?"

He jerked his head up. "Afraid of babies? Of course not. Why do you ask?" Brad could have kicked himself for not having an immediate interest in the infant. He understood new mothers were extremely fond of showing them off. Libby couldn't know he already held a special spot in his heart for the little one.

"Most people at least act interested and want to see a new child. You seem rather...I don't know, ill at ease with me and Lucy."

Brad tried not to let out an audible sigh. "Ma'am, I was assured by Cora that both you and your new daughter were doing just fine. To me all babies look alike and aren't really interesting until they can walk and talk. But, if it'll make you happy so we can get down to other matters at hand, I will take a most heartfelt look at the newcomer."

"Well, don't put yourself out. I was only teasing. It isn't necessary to pretend an interest simply to please me."

Brad walked around the bed to the cradle. "It's all right. I guess since my brother has four, and I've seen, held, and played with every one of them, my interest in babies is not as high as if this had been the first I've ever seen." He glanced down at the cradle. "She is a pretty one just like Cora said," he complimented Libby.

Hi there, little precious. How're you doing this morning? We had quite a night last night, didn't we? I hope I did right by you. Will you remember me when you wake? Your face doesn't look so red anymore. I would give anything to hold you again, but your mommy thinks I don't like babies. Can't let her know how I feel about you, can I? She might figure out this isn't the first time I've set eyes on you."

Brad's heart swelled with pride as if he were the one responsible for creating this child, not just bringing it into the world. He was grateful for the mask covering his face so Libby couldn't see the moisture in his eyes. *Your daddy was one hell of a lucky guy. Oops, sorry Lucy, I shouldn't swear in front of children. I don't know when I'll see you again, precious. Take care, Peanut.*

"Yup, she's a beauty, Ma'am. You'll have to beat the boys off with sticks if I don't miss my guess." He walked back around the bed. "Now, can we get back to business?"

Libby bit her bottom lip and frowned. "I guess you mean Ben?"

Brad breathed a sigh of relief; happy she had brought up the subject first and hadn't gone into vapors or hysterics again. Last night had been bad enough. He stood next to the bed and looked down at Libby. Her face had gone pale and the recent look of adoration was replaced with anguish.

"I'm sorry, Ma'am, I mean Miss Libby, but we have to talk about your husband. I need to know where you are from so we can plan how to get you home."

"We're from Wisconsin," Libby answered. "We were heading home from a Civil War reenactment when we had the accident."

Civil War reenactment? Why would anyone want to recreate such an awful event? She had to be lying. "You traveled from Wisconsin to West Virginia in your condition?"

"It's no more than a twelve-hour drive. Of course that's going seventy miles an hour. Ben likes to drive fast."

Brad sat down in a rocking chair. "Wait a minute. Are you saying you came from Wisconsin to West Virginia in twelve hours? Must be some team of horses your husband has."

Libby drew in a breath then slowly released it. "What do you mean by horses? What are you talking about?" Her eyes widened. "Oh, you mean the horsepower under the hood. We have a plain old Taurus wagon, but like I said, Ben likes to drive fast. I mean he liked to drive fast."

Brad's head pounded. He must have slept less than he thought last night. This woman was making no sense at all. "Ma'am, I'm trying very hard to understand what you are saying. Having a baby must have addled your brain. No one can drive a wagon as fast as you're saying. Not in 1870 anyway. And this Civil War reenactment you're talking about? Why, the war has been over for more than five years."

Libby suppressed a giggle. She must be in one of those historic places where the employees pretend they live in a certain year. But this was getting ridiculous. If the man wanted to play games with her and pretend they were in 1870, then she would let him play on. She certainly didn't want to be the cause of him losing his job.

"So, you say it's 1870. How do I get Ben back home for his funeral? Actually, I thought we could get him back to his mother's place in Tennessee. Lord knows how upset she'll be."

"Where in Tennessee is he from? Maybe we'll be able to get him there before it's too late." He rubbed the back of his neck. "And I'm not *saying* it's 1870. It *is* 1870."

Whatever. If he wanted to keep pretending, let him. She had other problems. "What do you mean before it's too late?"

"Uh. Um." He got up from the chair and paced in front of the window. "Uh, when a person dies, and it gets hot like this, the body, uh, tends to, uh..." He paused at the window. "Ma'am, we have to get your husband buried right away. We're having a hot spell and we need to get him in the ground."

"Why can't you all a funeral home to take care of Ben's body, and then take it to his mother's?"

"Ma'am, there isn't an undertaker within twenty miles of here. By the time I sent someone into town, and waited for the undertaker to come here, it would be too late. For the sake of everyone who lives here, we have to bury your husband as soon as possible. Tomorrow morning at the latest."

This man was crazy. Crazy enough to harm her and her children? "Could you please ask Cora to come up here?" Her head spun.

Brad left the room, and a few minutes later Cora came panting into the room, wiping her hands on her apron. Brad followed her into the room.

Cora slapped her hands at her waist. "Mr. Bradley, what did you do to this po' woman? She looks ready to pass out. You should know better than to upset a mama who's nursing. You could ruin her milk."

"It's all right, Cora," Libby assured her, even though the thoughts going through her mind could really ruin her milk. "Cora, I need to know something. What year is it?" Libby held her breath as Cora stared at her as if she had two heads.

"Why, Miss Libby, you know it's the year of our Lord, eighteen hundred and seventy."

Can they both be playing the same game? They could be. There's no way I could have lost 154 years. I have to believe they're acting. If I don't and this really is 1870, I'm in big trouble. Big, big trouble. I'll play along until they slip up.

"Why don't you get me a telephone and I'll call my mother-in-law. She can make the arrangements to have a hearse brought here. You do have a phone, don't you?"

Cora gave a quick glance at Brad and frowned. "Ma'am, not only do we not have a phone, but I don't even know what a phone is."

All right. Cora sounded convincing, but she needed to press on. "Maybe we could have Ben's body flown back to Wisconsin. Where's the nearest airport?"

Brad brought his hands up to his face. Was he going to take his mask off? He released a breath, which, with the mask on, sounded a bit like Darth Vader.

Ha! I've got him now. Maybe he's frustrated enough to agree this is all a hoax and let me leave with Ben and the kids.

Instead, Brad pulled up the rocking chair next to her bed and sat down. He turned his head at Cora and through silent communication seemed to agree on something. Libby was even more surprised when he took her hand and slowly rubbed it. The motion was soothing to her rattled nerves.

"Libby, I haven't any idea what you are talking about. I don't know what this phone thing is, or what an airport is. I don't have any idea how you get from Wisconsin to West Virginia in twelve hours. And driving seventy miles an hour? That's ridiculous. The things you and your son talk about just don't make any sense." He paused a moment as if collecting his thoughts. "But one thing I do know is we *have* to bury your husband tomorrow. There is no time to take him anywhere but to the cemetery on my land. I wish we could wait until you're up and around to attend the service but seeing as Cora and I and a few of my employees are the only ones here, the service won't be large or long. Now are there any questions I *can* answer for you?"

Libby could think of at least a zillion questions, but Lucy chose the time to wake up to eat. Grrr. She didn't need the interruption, but answers.

Cora waddled to the cradle and relieved Lucy. "Sounds like this lil' one needs refilling. You just go now, Mr. Brad, while Miss Libby and I take care of this sweet thing."

Brad stood. Cora changed the baby's diapers. "I'll leave you alone now." With a curt bow in Libby's direction, he left the room.

Chapter Nine

An hour later Libby was finally left alone with Lucy, who was curled up next to her. Libby was growing fond of Cora but was glad when the bustling woman finally left the room to find something for Libby to eat.

Cora's closeness while Libby was nursing made her nervous. Cora seemed to take personal pride in what a good eater Lucy was and made sure both Libby's breasts got equal treatment from the baby. Cora had kept talking the entire time she was in the room, filling Libby with stories of being nanny to Brad, his brother, Caleb, and sister, Sybil. In Libby's mind it all came down to how much Cora loved babies and was happy to have them in the house again.

Any time Libby tried to ask Cora questions about what the year was or where she was, Cora either ignored her or changed the subject. Libby was getting the strong feeling Cora would just as soon have Libby stay here with Charlie and Lucy, whereas Libby only wanted to get back to familiar surroundings.

Libby laid her head on a pillow as she loosened the tightly wrapped blankets from Libby. Obviously, Cora believed children needed to be confined, while Libby thought babies should be able to wriggle and squirm freely. As she contemplated her new daughter, she let her mind wander to her conversation with Brad. While Cora was in the room, Libby had given the room a good once over, at least as much as she could while still in bed.

Something wasn't right here. There wasn't one light switch or outlet in sight, nor phone jacks or heat registers. There had to be some source of power. Even if this were an historical home, the employees would want electricity. Why hadn't Brad or Cora called for a doctor or an ambulance to take her and Lucy to a hospital to be checked out? It would certainly have been the first thing she would have done. Most places would be concerned about a lawsuit if they didn't take care of their customers properly.

Libby didn't want to think about the idea niggling in the back of her mind. But the idea kept coming closer to the forefront. What if it's really true? What if it really is 1870? Which was totally ridiculous. Things like that only happen in books. This is simply a big joke. If she concentrated really hard, reality would come back, it would be 2024, Ben would be alive, and they'd be on their way home.

Libby closed her eyes. Flashes from the past twenty-four hours flew across her mind. Ben and her in the car. The lightning. Snow. Their car spinning out of control. Ben yelling to her. Waking up in a buggy. Ben dead. A hooded man helping her into a house. His strange clothes and way of talking. His confusion at her questions.

1870... 1870... This was crazy. But what if it hadn't really been a storm? What if it was a time warp, or time window or something? There's enough of those things in movies and books, but could it happen in real life?

Libby punched a pillow as more images whipped through her mind. Cora's treatment of her. The pot under the bed she had to use. Those awful rags between her legs was carrying things a bit too far. There's no reason why pads couldn't be used. But what about all the oil lamps around, and the fireplace? And wouldn't a real historical house have air conditioning to keep the antiques from deteriorating?

Libby's head throbbed. She scooted herself to the edge of the bed, picked up Lucy, and placed her in the cradle. She slipped on a robe from the end of the bed. It was time to do a search of the room. Maybe some answers would get rid of her headache. Without Ben, it was time she took charge.

"Now, let's see if I can find something to put an end to this crazy 1870's idea."

Stiffly, she moved around the room, looking under the bed, peaking behind dressers, and lifting the rug for hidden outlets or registers. She moved pictures and checked behind the doors. She even checked the fireplace for removable bricks which might conceal anything modern.

Libby chewed on her fingernail in frustration. It was probably time to give up. The people here were too good at hiding modern conveniences. Then she spotted a leather-bound book Brad had brought into the room earlier.

A feather pen and bottle of ink rested next to it. It took a few moments for curiosity to overcome her natural ability to allow people their privacy. Tentatively, she ran her hand over the black book, picked it up and sat in the rocker.

'Whispering Pines, A Farm History,' was etched on the front. Nerves fluttered in her stomach while her heart raced. She opened the cover.

She continued to read quietly. "Castlewood Manor. The Chronological History of a Family Farm from its Beginning to Present Day Time." Beneath the title was written in bold script, "History of Whispering Pines from the year of our Lord, 1867 to Present Day Time. Owner: Bradley Christopher Kemble."

"1867?"

Libby was an avid history buff and was excited to learn about this historical place. Her hands shook as she read the first page. Now she was about to get some answers.

It didn't take long for Libby to became engrossed in the listings of marriages, births, and deaths of the Castlewood family for a several generations. She was vaguely aware of Charlie waking up and Cora talking to him about having something to eat and letting his mama get some sleep. She tried not to get upset as she skimmed through pages about the buying and selling of slaves as well as produce and animals. Her stomach did a flip when she reached the page titled, "Whispering Pines, Purchased June 14, 1867."

On the first page were entries stating the value of the land and buildings, amounts spent on refurbishing the farm, and what was paid to employees.

Libby sighed in relief. "They didn't own slaves. It looks like they came with the place and paid them as employees."

Scattered in between the listings were names of people who were born and had died. She recognized names from the old section of the book and followed family weddings and births. She noted the births of babies Libby surmised were grandchildren of Cora. With surprise she read the listing of Brad's marriage, but why it should have surprised her, she couldn't guess. He had said he was married. Or had he? She couldn't seem to remember.

"Marriage of Bradley Christopher Kemble to Lucinda Marie Chapman, August 25, 1866," she read slowly. "Lucinda Marie? Now that's a coincidence if I ever saw one." She didn't think of it again as she continued to browse through the next few pages. So absorbed in the details of refurbishing the house and trying to relate them to what it looked like now, Libby nearly missed several entries written in a shaky, masculine hand.

"March 15, 1868: Birth of Caleb Barrett Kemble, son of Bradley and Lucinda."

"March 15, 1868: Death of Caleb Barrett Kemble, son of Bradley and Lucinda."

"March 15, 1868: Death of Lucinda Marie Kemble, wife of Bradley."

Libby lowered the book to her lap, tears filling her eyes. Oh, the poor man. The pain he must have gone through.

"Wait a minute, Libby, they can't be the same man. The man in this book must have remarried and carried on the Bradley Kemble name. It can't be the same guy."

Mentally shaking off the idea, she continued through the book. There weren't as many entries after Lucinda's death. The handwriting was not as bold and sure as previously. It was as if life had gone out of its owner.

Libby came to the last entry surprised and disappointed when it ended in 1870. She had wanted to continue reading until at least another generation had elapsed. As she was about to close the book, the name Lucinda Marie caught her eye. Curious as to why Brad's wife would be in here again, she looked more closely.

"What on earth?" With shaking hands, she ran her finger under the entry. "Oh, my God!" In the same handwriting as the other entries was written:

"March 16, 1870: Death of Ben Daniels, husband of Libby."

"March 1870: Birth of Lucinda Marie Daniels, daughter of Ben and Libby."

The book slipped from her lap and fell to the floor.

"Mommy. Mommy!!" A voice came from a distance. Someone tugged on her robe.

"Miss Libby? You all right? Miss Libby?"

Libby opened her eyes and tried to focus on the two people in front of her. Both wore worried expressions.

"Mommy, talk to me. I need you!" The child said.

"Miss Libby, we need to get you into bed. You need your rest."

Libby felt herself being pulled up and guided toward the bed. Her robe was removed and the cool sheets gave relief to her hot body. She wanted to kick off the heavy quilt piled on her, but she didn't have the strength. Sleep. All she wanted to do was sleep and forget, but she couldn't remember what she wanted to forget. The murmur of voices grew more distant as she drifted off to a place where worries ceased to exist.

Libby was playing tug of war. She was at one end; light and voices at the other. The harder Libby tried to pull herself into darkness the more the light tugged her back.

"Don't fight. You'll be all right," a soothing voice whispered in her ear. "I'll take care of you. Go toward the light, Libby. Go toward the light..."

Peace filled her. As she reached toward the light she kept hearing the words: "Everything will be all right. Don't worry. Everything will be all right."

Chapter Ten

"I think she's waking up," Brad's sister-in-law, Colleen whispered. "What's she saying?"

Brad leaned over Libby to try and catch her words. "It sounds like she's saying everything will be all right." He pressed a hand to her forehead and turned to his sister-in-law. "She feels cooler, now. I'm not sure what Cora and I would have done if you and Caleb hadn't shown up when you did."

"Well, you know Caleb and his intuitions. If he says something is wrong with you, then we all fly over here to help. He hasn't been wrong, yet. Has he?"

Brad chuckled. "No, he hasn't." He walked over the window and looked out at his holdings while Colleen rocked and nursed Lucy. Even though he didn't know much about such things, he was glad Cora had come up with the idea of Colleen taking care of Lucy while Libby had been sleeping, or whatever she was doing, for the past two days. Evidently, Colleen had recently weaned her youngest but still had milk. Lucy had kept crying in hunger and the cloths dipped in sugar water Cora tried getting the baby to suck on didn't satisfy her. Luckily, she had taken to Colleen.

Colleen interrupted his thoughts. "Where's Caleb, now?"

Brad pulled aside the lace curtains. "He's outside with your brood and Charlie. They're playing some sort of game. Charlie has a rock he's trying to hit with a piece of wood."

"Where do you think they're from?"

Brad shrugged. "I don't know. The young one asks some mighty strange questions and uses words I never heard of."

"I know what you mean." Colleen chuckled. "Caleb says the same thing about the boy. He sure is cute, though. It's too bad about his father."

Brad left the window and sat on a chair next to Colleen. He thought he probably should be embarrassed having her nurse in front of him, but he'd seen it so many times, he was used to it. Besides, she was so discreet, he never could tell if she was feeding her babies or cuddling them. "I wish we could have waited to bury Libby's husband, but it was getting too hot. She's going to be mighty upset when she wakes."

"I wonder what happened."

Brad rolled his neck to release some of the tension of the past few days. "Cora says she came in here with Charlie to let him visit her. Libby was sitting in the rocker staring into space, mumbling something about it not being 1870. Earlier, when I had talked to her she questioned the year. She seemed to think it was some other year."

"I hope losing her husband and having the baby early didn't do something to her mind."

Brad rested his elbows on his knees, hung his head, and ran his fingers through his hair. "We'll have to see when she wakes."

The pair sat in companionable silence. Brad enjoyed being with Colleen. She didn't talk just to hear herself. When he needed someone to unburden himself and Caleb wasn't available, Colleen always filled in. She loved his brother to distraction making her a saint in his mind. Once he made the comment to her and she smacked him on the head with a wooden spoon. The idea only a saint could love Caleb sent her into a tizzy. Actually, it is what he thought, but now he kept it to himself.

Colleen broke the silence with a giggle. "Did you really deliver this baby?"

Brad grinned, making the scar on his face stretch and whiten. "Sure did, and I was scared to death."

A blush crept up Brad's neck and onto his face. He was such a handsome man. Even with the scar. Of course, in her mind, he was nearly as handsome as her Caleb. Both brothers were tall, well over six feet. Where Caleb had picked up their mother's red hair and finer features, Brad had taken after their father; thick, black hair, broad shoulders, and slim waist. Both had eyes the color of a clear summer sky. The best part about both men, though, was their generosity and kindness.

Why couldn't some woman see those qualities in Brad as Lucinda had? Looks weren't everything. Neither was money. Something both brothers had in abundance. As she switched Lucy to her other side, she thought of Belinda Castlewood.

The little hussy! Now, now, Colleen. Be a Christian. Belinda tries hard. Yeah, tries hard to capture Brad, even though she can't stand even touching him since he scarred himself. All she wants is his money and this farm back.

"Over my dead body!" she accidentally said out loud.

"What did you say?" Brad asked.

"Oh, nothing. I was thinking about Belinda. Have you heard from her lately?"

Brad let out a derisive laugh. "You know how word travels around this area. Somehow, she found out I have a woman staying here. I got a note from her asking if she could come out and visit. It said something to the effect that someone needed to protect the character of a woman alone staying in a bachelor's house. What a joke!"

"She's checking up on what she probably considers competition." Colleen let out an unladylike snort.

"And wants to make sure that, even though she flinches when she touches this scarred person, she is still able to get her clutches in me."

"Yes, well, some people think because you wear your awful mask, you're deranged, out to beat and maul people. I would love to see her reaction if you were ever to start taking it off." Colleen shook her head.

"It's something to consider the next time I need to get rid of her," Brad laughed back. "I'll let out a low growl and slowly start to peel this thing off."

Lucy's mouth popped off Colleen's breast when Colleen giggled. "I can just see her pulling out her hair as she runs screaming from the room."

Colleen carried Lucy around the bed and put her in the cradle. She stood next to the bed and watched Libby's slow breathing. "What are you going to do with her?"

Brad sighed. "I don't know. She won't be fit for traveling for a while, and with the strange things she talks about, I think she lives too far to contact her family. Hell, I don't even know where her family is from. She says Wisconsin, but people from Wisconsin don't talk like her and Charlie."

Colleen had a premonition, not unlike what her husband, Caleb, said he sometimes feels. Her eyes twinkled as she looked at Brad. "Maybe you should keep her."

Chapter Eleven

Libby drifted toward the whispering voices. Were Ben and Charlie planning something silly again? Ben liked to play practical jokes, harmless ones, but ones he was teaching Charlie. She drifted closer to the voices. It wasn't Ben's voice. There was an unrecognizable woman's voice and a more familiar man's. When her mind finally seemed to be resting quietly, she eased her eyes open.

A woman stood at the side of the bed. Her face seemed friendly enough, but her clothes, a long sleeved, high-necked blouse with lace running down the front, and a gathered skirt, looked out of date. She wasn't very tall, maybe five foot two or three. Her light brown hair was parted down the middle and pulled back to cover her ears. Libby couldn't tell what held it in place. At this point, as long as no one hurt her or her children, she really didn't care.

"How do you feel?" The woman's was soft and soothing.

Libby tried to answer, but her throat was dry enough to put a desert to shame.

"I think she needs some water." The masculine voice came from the other side of the bed.

Trying not to move her pounding head too fast, Libby turned toward the voice. Once she saw the man in the mask, she remembered everything. Knowing what she knew now, the couple's clothes and the furniture made more sense. It really was 1870, and Ben was dead. She closed her eyes to the emotional turmoil reeling through her body.

The woman came back with a glass of water. "Ma'am? Libby? Here, you drink this. It'll help you feel better." The woman put her arm around Libby's shoulders and helped her up.

"Nothing will make me feel better," Libby whispered as she lay back down and closed her eyes.

"We're all happy you've came out of your spell," The woman said. "Poor Brad has been worried sick for the past two days. Luckily, Caleb and I had come for a visit."

Libby's eyes flew open. "Two days? I've been out two days?" Her voice cracked. "Where's Charlie and Lucy?" Pounding head notwithstanding, she needed to see her children and tried to get out of bed.

A strong hand gripped her arm and kept her down. "Libby, you have to stay in bed. Colleen has been taking care of Lucy, and her husband, Caleb, and their children have been keeping Charlie occupied. Do you remember Cora?" At Libby's nod in the affirmative, Brad went on, "Well, she's been taking care of all of us."

"I have to feed Lucy. After two days she must be hungry." Several images of Lucy starving and emaciated passed through Libby's mind. She began to panic. "What's wrong with her? Why isn't she crying? I want my baby now!"

The woman Brad called Colleen tried to calm Libby down. "It's all right, Libby. She's fine. When she rejected the sugar-tit Cora tried giving her, I nursed Lucy. I had only quit nursing my youngest and still had milk left. I hope that doesn't offend you."

Libby shook her head. It was all too much to take in, but she was not one to let the kindness of others go unnoticed. "I appreciate what you've done. Thank you. Can I please hold her?"

Colleen leaned over the end of the cradle and picked up Lucy. A vague memory of another woman in the same position crossed Libby's mind. She looked closer at Colleen and Lucy. This was not the same woman she had seen before.

"There you go, sweetheart," Colleen cooed. "There's your mama."

Brad's heart swelled as Libby talked quietly to her daughter. Thankfully, Libby had finally woken and seemed to have all her faculties. Colleen's grin meant she felt the same. He was thinking about going to get Charlie when her next comment hit him like a brick.

"I want to see Ben and Charlie."

Brad cleared his voice, trying to stall for time while he found the right words. "Uh, Libby, I'll get Charlie for you in just a minute, but we had to bury your husband yesterday. You do remember he's dead?" Brad held his breath, waiting for her answer. Nothing so far had shown she would throw a fit, but he didn't want her passing out again, either. Nor did he want to find out she had forgotten everything.

Libby kept looking at Lucy. "I remember," she answered quietly. "You couldn't wait for me to get better before you buried him?"

Brad brought his hand toward his hair in frustration and stopped. Damn mask. "Ma'am, we just couldn't wait any longer. The weather is too warm, and..."

"I understand. You had to bury him."

Her quiet answers were getting on his nerves. He was glad she wasn't having fits or anything, but she was far too placid. He could understand how she might be feeling. Losing the one you love was the same as snapping the life out of yourself. Just because he had raised holy terror in his pain didn't mean everyone else had to react the same. They would all be wise to let her grieve in her own way.

What he thought he knew about her situation and what he figured she was remembering wouldn't help her grief any, either. Thank God she had her children to take care of and keep her mind off her husband.

"Could you please bring Charlie to me?" Libby interrupted his thoughts.

Colleen glanced at him and nodded.

Grateful for something to do, Brad left the room, ran down the stairs, and out the front door. Caleb and his children, along with Charlie, were still playing the game Charlie had called baseball. When Charlie mentioned the game, Caleb said he had read about a man who'd created the game. Of course, with Charlie's three-year-old way of speaking, they could be misunderstanding him.

"Hey, Uncle Brad, come and try this. It's fun," one of his nephews said, handing him the piece of wood Charlie called a "bat."

"Not now, Matthew, I have to take Charlie up to his mother."

Charlie ran up to Brad. "Is my mommy awake? Is she? Huh? Please, mister, can I see my mommy now?"

"Sure, whippersnapper, you can see your mommy now." Brad picked Charlie up and headed toward the house. "Your mommy is anxious to see you, but first I think we had better wash you up. Your face and hands are full of dirt."

Charlie laid his head on Brad's shoulder. "I just want to see my mommy," he whispered.

Brad patted Charlie on the back and thought about what the little boy had been through and how brave he had been. Chicken that he was, Brad still hadn't told him about his father. Brad kept telling himself the news should come from Libby, but deep down he knew he didn't have it in him to break the boy's heart.

"It'll be all right, Charlie. Let's go find Cora, get you cleaned up, and then take you to your mother." They entered the house calling for Cora's help.

Chapter Twelve

"I want to thank you for taking care of Lucy," Libby said to Colleen after Brad left the room. "I'm not sure I could nurse another person's child."

"Nonsense!" Colleen laughed. "We all do what we have to. I simply did what I had to so Lucy would survive. Besides, her crying was driving us all crazy."

"I'm sorry to have been such a bother to everyone." Tears burned behind her eyes. Her nose dripped as she tried to hold the tears back.

Colleen sat on the edge of the bed. "Now, don't you worry none, Libby. We're happy to help. If there's anything I, or Caleb, can do to help, just holler. Or at least let Brad know so he can send a messenger to our place. Oh, my goodness. You don't know who I am, do you?"

Libby shook her head.

"I'm Colleen Kemble. I'm married to Caleb, Brad's older brother. We own Winding Oaks a few miles up the road. We have four in our brood, the youngest is one."

"Nice to meet you, Colleen. I'm Libby Daniels. Ben was my husband and Charlie is my son." She glanced lovingly at Lucy. "You've already met Lucy."

"I've met Charlie, too. You have a wonderful son, Libby. You should be proud."

The two women sat in companionable silence. It was unusual for her to take an immediate liking to someone. But Colleen already felt like a sister. "Will Charlie be coming soon? I really need to see him."

Colleen rose from the bed, walked to the window, and glanced outside. "I don't see him or Brad. They must already be in the house. By the looks of my dirty bunch, I imagine Cora is cleaning him up before allowing him to see you."

"Would you mind if I had some time alone with him? Unless someone else told him about Ben, I will need to."

Colleen gave Libby a look of compassion and understanding. "I'm sure no one told Charlie about your husband. I'll leave you alone for now so you can collect your thoughts before seeing Charlie. If you need anything, pull the bell cord behind your bed. It rings in the kitchen where Cora or I will hear it. You rest a bit before they come up."

After Colleen left, Libby tried to 'collect her thoughts,' as Colleen had put it, but her thoughts kept rolling around and around, not settling on any one item. She played with Lucy's small, soft fingers, marveling at their perfection. From the length of them, Libby knew Lucy would have her own long, tapered fingers and probably her tall, thin body. One she'd been teased about her entire life.

By the time she met Ben, Libby was so self-conscious she could barely string three words together. Somehow Ben had seen through her shyness and outer shell. His teasing centered on what was good about her. Her kindness to children and others less fortunate. The way her smile lit up her eyes. He had told her once how a smile led the way to a person's soul and she had to have the most beautiful soul in the world. She believed him and blossomed into a pretty, somewhat more self-confident woman. As she grew, the situation with her parents worsened. Ben wouldn't let them harass her. He convinced Libby it wasn't her fault her parents had to get married and had a lousy marriage.

When they finally made love for the first time Libby felt as if she'd shed an old, battered coat and slipped on a mink one. At first, she had been embarrassed to expose her bony, flat-chested body to Ben, but he kept telling her how beautiful she was. When she tried to cover herself and make a joke about her small size, he told her 'what doesn't fit in the hand and mouth, is wasted.' Her laughter broke the wall she had made about her body.

Their marriage hadn't been perfect. She didn't know of anyone's that was. She loved Ben immensely and knew Ben loved her, but as her confidence in herself grew, Ben's need to take care of and protect her got on her nerves. Most times Ben had expected her to have the same opinions as his. When they didn't, he would stomp off by himself for a few hours. He would come back apologetic and life would get back to normal, but his need to be macho and have her be helpless caused a chasm in their relationship. To keep the peace, she learned to remain silent or agree with him in the presence of others. Sometimes Libby thought Ben liked her better when she was meek and mild. He was never mean, but she figured it probably gave him a feeling of power. But, why?

And now she never would. Instead, she was stuck in a generation where women had to keep to their place. Libby sighed at the irony. Just when she felt she was coming into herself and becoming more confident, she was somehow thrown into a situation where she would be suppressed. Anyway, it's what she had always read about women from the past. If only she had the strength to fight it. Right now, she barely had the strength to take care of herself and her children.

"Mommy! Mommy!"

Libby turned toward the door as Charlie raced across the room, ready to leap onto the bed.

"Whoa, there young man," Brad grabbed Charlie by the back of his shirt. "You have to be careful around your mother for a while. I think she would get upset if you were to leap on top of your little sister."

His face going from smiles and joy to a frown, Charlie stopped by the side of the bed.

"Come here, sweetheart." Libby patted the side of the bed. "You can climb up here but be careful not to push on my tummy. Maybe Brad could help you up."

"What do you think of your little sister?" she asked Charlie once he was settled on the bed. He was kneeling by her side, peering over her at Lucy.

"She cries way too much!"

Libby laughed and poked him in the stomach with her finger. "And you cried even more than she does, young man!" She laughed even more as his eyes grew round and determined.

"I did not!"

"Oh, yes you did. And you wouldn't quit until Daddy or I picked you up, changed you, and fed you until your tummy was ready to explode."

"Really?"

"Uh-huh." As Libby shook her head, she glanced at Brad who seemed to be engrossed in Lucy. Was she evil for putting a man who was afraid of babies on the spot? She couldn't help herself. "Brad, would you mind putting Lucy back into her cradle? I want to be able to spend some time alone with Charlie. She's sleeping, anyway."

Libby wished she could see Brad's face at her request. She could have sworn she'd heard him gulp but gave him credit when he came to the other side of the bed, carefully, and rather professionally, scooped Lucy up, and laid her in the cradle. After tucking a blanket around the baby, he gave Libby a short bow and left the room.

"Doesn't he like babies?" Charlie asked. "'Prob'ly thinks she cries too much, too."

"Come here, pumpkin, and lay down by me. I'm not sure if he likes babies or not. He probably hasn't had a chance to be around them much."

"He had a little boy once."

At Libby's questioning glance Charlie went on. "Uh-huh. He told me so. But he died."

"Did he tell you the name of his little boy?" Was it different from the one in the book?

"Nope. But he likes me. I can tell."

"And how can you tell?" Libby tickled Charlie's stomach making him giggle. "And tell me what you've been up to, squirt."

Charlie chewed on his bottom lip, then for the next five minutes filled Libby's ears with stories of Colleen's children, the creek they waded in, feeding the colts, playing in the haymow, feeding the chickens with Cora, and starting a game of baseball. "Do you know they never heard of baseball? That's silly. Everyone knows about baseball."

After reciting his actions for the past two days, he became quiet. "Where's my daddy? I miss him. When will he be back?"

Libby cradled Charlie in her arms and blinked back tears. How much would a three-year-old understand about death? Then she remembered Skipper. Hopefully, Charlie will, too.

"Charlie? Do you remember our dog, Skipper?" When he nodded, Libby went on. "Do you remember when he got sick?"

"Yup. He died."

"Do you remember what happened when he died?"

"You and Daddy buried him in the back yard, and I never got to play with him again."

"You're right. Well, something similar happened to your daddy. We had some kind of accident on the way home and Daddy got hurt. He died." Libby grew worried when after a minute Charlie hadn't said anything. "Do you understand what I'm telling you, Charlie?"

He solemnly shook his head. "It means I won't get to play with him anymore, doesn't it? I can't see him anymore, can I?"

Libby held him tighter as his small body shook. "That's right, honey."

Charlie's crying turned to sobbing. "I want my Daddy. I want my Daddy, now!"

"Shh, sweetheart." Libby rocked him back and forth in her arms, trying to reassure herself as much as her son. "It'll be okay. Everything will be okay." *Oh, God, please let everything be okay!*

In a flash, Charlie's face turned red. He punched the mattress. "I hate it here. I want to go home. Everything's stupid here."

Libby remained quiet giving Charlie time to vent his anger.

"There's no TV, no 'tricity, no phones, no cars. I wanted to call Grandma, but Cora didn't know what I was talking about. There's no toys, no movies, no bikes. They don't even have pizza or 'pasgettios! Where are we, Mommy? I wanna go home!"

Libby didn't know how to answer. Where were they? Somewhere in West Virginia? She wanted to go home, too, but it was better not to promise something she couldn't control to a three-year-old. He'd hold it to her forever. How on earth could she explain being shipped back over one hundred-fifty years to someone who had trouble understanding tomorrow, or next week? An hour from now?

"Charlie, I don't know where we are."

"Did Daddy take a wrong turn?" He snuggled against her.

Libby kissed the top of his head. *I guess he did if it's what you call taking a right on sixty-four and ending up in 1870.* "We're a long way from home right now, and I don't know how to get back. Maybe Brad can help us."

Would Brad believe they were from another time? Would he think she was crazy and try to get rid of her? Somehow, she would have to convince him she was of sound mind before explaining her situation. She had no idea what would happen then.

Gradually Charlie's body relaxed. Thank goodness he was falling asleep. As she kissed him on his forehead she heard him whisper, "Is Daddy buried in the back yard?"

Chapter Thirteen

Brad hated eavesdropping. In his mind it was the same as lying or cheating. Anyone caught should be punished. In this case, though, it was necessary. He needed to know more about this woman. Where they came from. How they happened to be on the road between his place and Caleb's.

After leaving Libby's room, Brad waited outside the door. He purposely left the door open to hear what was said between her and Charlie, hoping to gain some information to answer his questions. He suppressed a laugh when Charlie suggested Brad was afraid of babies and was pleased to hear Charlie knew he liked him. He shook his head in amusement when Charlie went into one of his rapid-fire descriptions of his day.

While Libby had been sleeping the past two days, Brad had taken the liberty of putting Charlie to bed at night and was the object of Charlie's daily reports. They never ceased to amaze him. His heart contracted when Charlie started yelling how he hated it here and what was wrong. Brad knew he would feel even worse if he understood what Charlie was going on about.

Libby's pain was obvious in her voice as she told her son about his father, and her frustration when she tried to explain she didn't know where they were, how they got here, and how they would get home. If his suspicions about them were true, Libby would think he was crazy. He hadn't even shared his thoughts with Caleb or Colleen. His brother and sister-in-law were open-minded about many things, but he was afraid they wouldn't go along with this idea. They would have him committed.

Finally, their voices were quiet. He peeked through the crack in the door. Libby held Charlie in her arms, and from their slow breathing they were asleep. He entered the room, walked quietly to the window and glanced out. Caleb and Colleen were walking down a path toward the creek, their children in tow. Caleb carried a blanket and Colleen had some towels tossed over her shoulder.

Must be going for a swim to wash the kids off. He glanced back at the bed. With Libby asleep, it was a good opportunity to go through her things. Brad went over to the trunks piled next to the fireplace by Charlie's room. Since having them brought up yesterday, he'd been anxious to go through them. To Brad, snooping through people's belongings was as distasteful as eavesdropping, but the clues to the mystery of who Libby was were locked inside those trunks. With Cora and Colleen's fussing and constantly in and out of the room, he hadn't had a chance to go through them until now. He wanted to have them put in his room, but he knew it would raise a few eyebrows.

Something Libby had said about it being 2024 kept running across his mind. At the time he dismissed it as the ramblings of a hysterical woman but combined with the strange comments made by her and Charlie, there was probably something to her comment after all. Yesterday he watched Charlie draw a picture in the dirt with a stick. When asked, Charlie said it was a car. A bigger version was called a truck. Of course, the drawings of a three-year-old couldn't be considered very accurate, but they were clear enough for Brad to know he'd never seen anything like them.

He kneeled in front of the largest of the three trunks. Since his back was to the bed, he pulled off his mask to be cooler. Beside them on the floor lay a fabric bag. He decided to check it first. Opening it proved easy enough since there were only two large hoops to pull apart. He dumped the contents on his lap. The first few items held no interest—just a comb and brush and some pieces of paper. He picked up what he thought looked like a small pocketbook. Shaking it produced a clinking noise, not unlike the coins he carried in his pocket. A metal clasp drew his interest. By pulling it one way, nothing happened, but when the pulled it the other, it opened. The dark interior reminded him of an open mouth lined with teeth.

Just as he thought—money. He picked up the largest coin. So small. Ridges along the edges. George Washington on one side, a building on the other. Brad studied the coin more closely. 2020. He looked again. Yep. 2020. Goosebumps rose along the back of his neck and up his arms. He placed the coin on the floor and picked up two more. One was copper and the other ridged like the larger one. He didn't recognize the faces on either one, but both had 2023 engraved on them. A quick check of the remaining coins showed dates from 1985 to 2023.

In a side pocket, he found a small card with Libby's picture on it, wrapped in something hard. The picture was in color and revealed how pretty she was when smiling. On one side of the card were the words Operator's License and on the other, Wisconsin.

So, she is from Wisconsin, but what did she operate? Is she a lady doctor or something? Not possible. Birth: 03/17/2000. Brad thought for a bit. Ah! March 17, 1800? Which would make her seventy years old. He looked again at the picture on the card. Not hardly. But if this were 2024 or even 1870, she is... Hell, how old would she be? His head throbbed thinking about it. Could this really be possible? Could she have somehow travelled back to 1870?

Brad thought about some of the stories he had read by people who, at the time, he believed had quite overactive imaginations. Someone traveling through time and visiting other places made him laugh. Later, in a more reflective mood, he wondered whether it was possible.

If one believed in God, and he did, one would believe God's hand was in everything. Was this an act of God? If so, why bring Libby to this place, at this time? He didn't remember the Bible giving any reference to acts of time-travel, but then it always amazed him how people could live so long in the Old Testament. The minister in his church always said God worked in mysterious ways.

Brad shook his head as he placed the card on the floor. He pulled out his pocket watch. It seemed like hours since he'd started snooping, but it had only been ten minutes. It wasn't time for dinner yet, and he should be able to go through a few more thing before Cora ambled up with Libby's dinner.

He flipped up the latch on the smallest trunk, carefully lifted the lid, and nearly fell in when a voice called out to him. Damn! Caught! He grabbed his mask and yanked it over his face.

A faint rustling sound woke Libby from her nap. She expected to see Cora bustling around the room on some errand or other. Usually something for

Lucy, so she was surprised to see a man kneeling on the floor. He had his back to her. His hair, waving to his collar with a slight flip at the ends, reminded Libby of the color of chestnuts. A perfect color for hair. Not only was it wavy, but seemed thick enough to lose your fingers in. She tried to get a better look at his face, but even though he was examining something, he kept his face forward. Then she understood what he was doing.

"Do you always snoop through other people's things?" Anger surged through her. "Are you looking for anything in particular or are you simply being nosy?" Shock went through her when the man grabbed a mask and yanked it over his head. "Brad. How dare you! Couldn't you have asked to go through my things?"

"I'm truly sorry, Miss Libby. I can assure you I don't usually do something like this, but I needed some answers about you."

"First of all, will you quit with the Miss Libby thing?" Her voice rose. She needed to calm down so she didn't wake the children. "Second, you could have asked me before digging through my things."

"I have wanted to ask you many questions since the day you wondered where you were, but you fell ill. Your comments made no sense, but when I combined them with some of the things Charlie has said, I began to realize you were from a different place and time. I needed to find out if my suspicions were true."

Heat rose to her face. "What do you mean? What are you trying to tell me?" Libby wasn't at all sure she could trust Brad with her secret.

"I found this in one of your bags." He handed her the card. "Are you really from 2024?"

Libby glanced down at her driver's license. It was hard to read through the tears welling in her eyes. "Yes," she whispered. "Is it really 1870?"

"Yes," he whispered back.

"Oh, God. How did this happen?" Libby looked at Brad searching for an answer. "What are you going to do with us?"

"I don't know how this happened," Brad answered. "I was hoping you could tell me. As for what I am going to do with you. Well..." He walked to the window and peered out, thinking of an answer.

Libby held her breath waiting for his reply. Brad seemed rather calm, but how would others react if they knew? Would they arrest her, or commit her to some kind of asylum for the insane? Would they be sold to a circus as freaks or sent off to fend for themselves? How would she earn a living? It seemed an eternity before Brad finally turned back to her.

"I think for now you should rest and get better. I also think we should keep this to ourselves. Others may react poorly and we may find ourselves with greater problems on our hands." He walked to the side of the bed and reached for her license. "I will take this for now and put it back with your things. I think it best I remove your trunks to the attic so no one else goes through them."

Libby was at a loss for words. "I... I don't know how to thank you. I was so afraid you would think I was crazy or something."

"No more so than my thinking I was crazy. I think I hear Cora coming upstairs. Let me put these things away before she gets here. If it would be all right with you, I would like to come back later and discuss this further, although finding another time when no one else is around will be a problem."

Libby smiled at him in relief. "That's fine with me. Whenever you can come back. As long as you don't ship me off to the circus!"

Without another word, he tipped his head at her and left the room.

Chapter Fourteen

Brad ran his hand through his hair in frustration as he sat at his desk desperately trying to go through his books. The past ten days had been torture. Actually, when Brad thought about it, the past two weeks had been hell. Ever since finding Libby and her husband and learning Libby was from 2024, things had gone to pieces.

Right after Brad had promised Libby he would come back and talk to her, Caleb and Colleen came back from their swim. It seemed there had been a disagreement about letting the girls swim in the creek along with the boys. Colleen said yes. Caleb, no. They ended up not speaking to each other and Caleb went back to his home alone. Colleen was still here with their children. They were the two most stubborn people on Earth.

The more he thought about it, though, the more he realized everyone he knew was stubborn. Every day Cora came to him complaining about how Libby didn't want to stay in bed. Cora was stubborn enough to keep her there; Libby stubborn enough to try to get up. So far Cora was winning, but Brad knew it was only because Cora was stronger—physically, anyway. As far as he was concerned, Libby knew more about it than Cora and could get up any time she wanted to.

Then there was Belinda Castlewood. In the past ten days she had been out to see him no less than five times. Each time she brought something for the poor woman stuck at an old bachelor's place. Luckily for him three times he had been out on his land. After a short visit, Cora and Colleen were able to convince Belinda to leave, telling her Brad wouldn't be back until dark. One of the times she came out of concern, he had come riding to the barns just as Belinda was leaving. He tried to swerve into the barn, but her eagle eyes caught him. He ended up having tea with her, trying to remain interested in her stories of visits to other neighbors. The only time his interest was piqued was when she brought up what their neighbors were saying about the mysterious woman staying at his residence. He wasn't sure if what they were saying were true or if Belinda was trying to get information out of him. That she was extremely curious about Libby was obvious to even the most dense.

The second time he got caught she came bearing gifts for the new mother and baby. Luckily for Libby, but not for himself, he had been coming out of his office as Belinda was about to go up the stairs. Her sneaking into his house was obvious, not only from the guilty look on her face and her stuttered attempts at explaining, but no one else had been in the house at the time. Cora and Colleen had taken the children for a swim and picnic.

Brad's strong hunch Belinda had been watching and waiting for everyone to leave became truth when she tried to seduce him, saying they were all alone and heading for the stairs again. He knew she was getting desperate when she tried the ploy. Belinda had trouble hiding the look of revulsion on her face when she touched his arm. Brad never knew whether to laugh at her or get angry when she tried her tricks. He wanted to laugh at her obvious duplicity and yell how he knew she was lowering herself to get his money and property.

It was too bad she couldn't see the disgust on his face. Maybe she would finally get the idea he wasn't interested. Nothing he said seemed to. She thought her coyness and sexuality were enough for any man. Brad believed if he'd ever marry her, she would succumb to his demands in bed on their wedding night and then cut him off for life. She would probably play the part of his loving wife in public, but his private life would be a living hell.

Brad was able to get Belinda out the door by saying he would come by to see her sometime. He took hold of her arm and physically escorted her from the house so fast, she was unable to pin him down to a specific day. Good thing since he didn't like to swear in front of women and telling her he'd come to see her when hell froze over would have probably put her in a swoon and he'd surely be stuck with her. After she was finally gone, he scanned the yard to make sure his sigh of relief hadn't blown down any trees.

To top off all the stubbornness surrounding him and the lack of peace he'd had, several of his mares were due to foal at the same time, which meant round-the-clock watches for him, his foreman, and his hired hands. They tried to take turns so everyone would get a chance to sleep, but they were all getting tired. The fourth night, after two mares foaled the night before, his favorite mare went into labor and was having difficulties.

In his haste to wake Brad up, Toby, Cora's son, tripped over a bucket, and fell into Joshua, his foreman and Cora's husband. Both men tumbled to the ground. Toby broke his arm and Joshua his leg. Not only did it leave Brad short-handed, but Cora was in a fit about her son and husband continuing their work in the barn. Every time she complained to him, he told her stubbornness seemed to run in her family. In his mind he wished he could hide out in the barn to get away from her harping, too.

Things out in the barn had finally slowed down and he needed to add the six new foals to his accounts. He was so tired the numbers swam before his eyes. The only thing giving him any peace lately was his growing relationship with Charlie. No matter how worn out he was, Brad made a point of putting him to bed every night. During the day he didn't see much of the boy because he was off with Colleen's children, but at night, when Charlie was all cleaned up and sweet-smelling, Brad would sit on the bed next to him and listen to the boy go on about his day.

Then came Brad's favorite words of the day.

"Tell me a story, Bwad."

Sometimes Brad told stories about his childhood with Caleb and his sister, Sybil. He could get Charlie giggling over the antics they pulled. Other times Brad made up stories like his mother used to. Truth be told, Brad thought the stories came easily to him and figured they were ones his own mother had made up. He couldn't remember the actual stories, but bits and pieces of them. He filled in details to help make a good story for the boy. He hoped.

One night when he was so tired he could hardly speak, Brad asked Charlie to tell him a story. During a tale about mice named Mickey and Minnie, Brad fell asleep, waking up hours later curled up next to Charlie. Before he could leave the bed, he had to pry Charlie's leg from around his throat. It was a good thing he woke up when he did, or Charlie would have choked him to death with his knee.

A few times when Brad went to put Charlie to bed, he found the boy with Libby. He wondered how she felt about the bedtime routine and asked her about it.

"I think it's a fine idea, Brad. It's not something his father did, but I always thought it would have been a good thing. Charlie's been telling me some of the stories you tell him. Did you and Caleb really empty a box of live crickets into your sister's bed while she was sleeping?"

"He sure did, Mommy. They gots a spankin,' too."

"You did?" Libby's grin matched the twinkle in her eyes.

"Yes, Ma'am. We sure did."

"And did you learn a lesson about not pulling pranks on your little sister?"

Brad knew Libby was trying to send a message to Charlie about his own little sister. He dropped his head down and let out a great sigh. "Yes, Ma'am. We surely did."

He was surprised when Libby giggled and answered in a sarcastic tone, "Oh, I'm sure you did."

Then she went on to ask about his day. Charlie was anxious to get to the storytelling so Brad wasn't able to tell her much, but it was enough to make him feel good about his day. He had forgotten how nice it was to share his day with someone. What had also surprised him was she genuinely seemed interested in what he was telling her. Afterward, he was let down whenever Charlie was already in his room and not with Libby.

A ruckus from the hallway outside his office brought Brad from his reflections. A pounding on his door brought him from his chair. "Now what the hell is wrong?" he muttered as he pulled on his mask and wearily opened the door.

Cora stood in front of him, her arms crossed beneath her hefty bosom, indignation written across her face. A pleased-looking Libby stood behind her, holding Lucy in her arms. "Mr. Bradley, I refuse to be responsible for Miss Libby if'n something happens to her."

"And *I* refuse to stay in bed and bedroom one second longer!" Libby jabbed her finger toward the stairs to make her point. "This is ridiculous. Women do not need to be pampered this long. I NEED TO GET OUTSIDE!" Her scream could have woken the dead.

"Sounds like a good idea to me." Cora grinned. "Not only does she want to go outside, but she wants to see her husband's grave. She can't walk that far."

Brad glanced back at Libby in question. What was Cora playing at?

"I most certainly can too walk that far!"

"Do you even know how far the cemetery is?" He held back a smirk when his question knocked the wind out of her sails.

"Well, no," she answered slowly. "But I'm sure Colleen or someone could take me there if it's too far to walk."

Brad leaned against the door jam and crossed his arms over his chest. He remembered how much he needed to see Lucinda's grave once he had come out of his drunken stupor. "It's really important to you, isn't it?"

"Yes," she whispered. "Please. Charlie needs to see it, too. He thinks his father is buried somewhere in your backyard like his dog was back home."

A look of understanding and sympathy crossed Cora's face. She patted Libby's arm. "I'm so sorry, honey 'chile. Now I know why the po' boy has been wandering around the back, looking like a lost soul. Of course you need to go see your po' husband's grave." Cora turned back to Brad. "Maybe Mr. Brad can hitch up the buggy and take you."

"I can walk," Libby insisted. "Brad must be too busy to drag me to a cemetery."

And way too tired. But she and Charlie needed this. "It really is too far to walk, Libby. Even if you didn't just have a baby. I'll have one of the boys hitch up the buggy, and I'll take you. We should have thought of it sooner."

Libby lifted her chin at Cora. "You never would have gotten past the warden."

"Humph. Just doin' my job," Cora grumbled as she headed down the hall toward the kitchen. "Try to do my job and all they do is complain. Nobody 'preciates nothin' 'round here."

After Cora had left the main house, Brad glanced at Libby. "I'll meet you in front in half an hour." He walked in the opposite direction from Cora.

Libby shifted Lucy to her other arm and contemplated what to do. Without her watch, she wouldn't know when the time was up. Waiting for Brad outside would be the safest thing to do. Shifting Lucy to her other arm, Libby headed for the door Brad had gone through. It was amazing how something as small as her daughter could become so heavy so fast. She must be getting weak. She was used to being active, exercising, and lifting weights. Two weeks in bed sapped all her strength. Since she'd finally won the battle against Cora she would be able to do more things. Inactivity was not a word in her vocabulary.

Libby smiled to herself as she settled onto a swing suspended by ropes from the porch ceiling. She set the porch swing moving with her feet and thought about how much she loved porches like this. Every time Ben and she would pass by a house with a large porch and a swing, Libby would sigh and say, "Someday, Ben, we'll have a porch like that." He would smile at her and say, "Yes, dear."

"Well, Ben. Here I am. On a porch swing like we always dreamed of. But where are you? Why aren't you here with me? Why did you have to die?"

Libby didn't want to start crying again. She'd done enough the past two weeks. Instead, she recalled the recent test of wills between Cora and herself. This morning when she woke, Libby decided enough was enough. She wasn't sore anymore, anyway not physically, and her bleeding was done. She couldn't stand the bed anymore, and if she didn't get out of it, she'd go stark raving mad.

She'd slipped her nightgown back on while deciding what to wear. Even though he hadn't been able to return to talk with Libby, Brad had been true to his word about removing her bags. They were nowhere in sight. She went to the tall wardrobe she had been dying to go through while confined to bed. The past two weeks were spent thinking about everything she wanted to explore before going back to 2024. Assuming she could get back to 2024.

The wardrobe was full of dresses, blouses, and skirts. Libby gave a prayer of thanks when one drawer contained her own underwear. "Wonder what Cora thought about these," she murmured pulling out her bra and panties. Libby searched through the clothes. Everything looked warm and heavy. Finally, in the back, she located a lightweight white blouse, and a long, dark blue, cotton skirt. Like in the historical novels she devoured, she should be wearing a corset of some kind and probably petticoats. But she wouldn't be able to put them on by herself and there were no petticoats to be found. The clothes smelled slightly musty from being hung in the back, but Libby was grateful to be out of her nightgown.

After donning the clothes, Libby realized the owner was someone much shorter than herself. Although the waist was fine, the bottom of the skirt was about two inches too short. There was nothing she could do about it, but if she rolled the sleeves up, no one would be able to tell they were too short. Normally the blouse probably would have fit across the front, but since she was nursing and her breasts were larger, it pulled across them. Then came the problem of what to put on her feet. The shoes, or rather boots, resting on the floor were way too small. As she spied her tennis shoes under the bed, Cora came into the room.

"What do you think you're doin', Miss Libby? You gets right back into bed."

Libby jumped. "Oh, Cora, you scared me. You shouldn't sneak up on people like that." How could a woman Cora's size, a walk so quietly?

"Good. I hope I done scared you right back into your bed."

"I am not going back to bed, Cora!" Libby stomped her foot like Charlie did when throwing a tantrum. But she was absolutely not throwing a tantrum. Was she? "There's no reason to. I feel fine. My bleeding's done, and I'm bored to death. I need to get out of here. Charlie and Lucy and I are going to see Ben's grave."

"You can't! For one thing you don't have anything black to wear."

"I can, and I will!" She yanked her shoes from under the bed and proceeded to pull them on, her jerky movements full of anger.

"What's them things you put on your feet?"

Oops. How was she going to explain tennis shoes to someone who had never seen plastic or rubber? "They're a type of shoe we have where I come from."

"The place you come from must be mighty strange." Cora shook a finger at her. "Even if you put them things on, you're not going anywhere."

Libby finished tying the laces and stood. "Who's going to stop me?"

Cora put her hands on her massive hips, her stance making Libby think of a drill sergeant. "I am."

Libby walked around the bed and picked up Lucy. "Do you think you can stop me when I'm holding Lucy?" Playing dirty felt good. She held back a cheer of success when Cora backed down. Libby hoped she didn't look too silly as she regally marched passed Cora, her red tennies squeaking across the polished floor, her white ankles showing beneath the blue skirt.

As she passed Cora and went out the door, Libby couldn't miss the nod of approval and smirk from the housekeeper.

Libby stopped the swing when Charlie called out to her as he raced across the front lawn with Colleen's children. Colleen followed at more sedate pace, calling out to the children to be careful.

"Mommy, Mommy," he called out in a breathless voice. "Brad says we're going for a buggy ride. Is it true?"

Libby wiped the perspiration from Charlie's face and brushed the hair from his eyes. "You need a haircut, young man. And yes. You and Lucy and I are going for a buggy ride with Brad."

Charlie leaned across her legs and reached out a dirty hand toward Lucy's fingers. Libby stopped him just in time. "How come you gots a dress on Mommy?"

"It's what women and girls wear here."

"Yeah, but you never wear a dress."

Libby sighed. "I know, Charlie, but sometimes we have to do things we've never done before. It makes these people feel better to have us dress like them. Do you understand?" When Charlie shook his head no, Libby went on. "It doesn't matter, honey. Why don't you go into the house and ask Cora to clean you up before we leave. You can't get into Brad's nice buggy all dirty, can you?"

Colleen came onto the porch as Charlie was trying to open the door. She ordered her oldest to help Charlie and then told the rest of them to go wash up, too.

"It's good to see you up and around, Libby," Colleen smiled as she sat down next to Libby.

Libby smiled back. She'd grown to like Brad's sister-in-law. She was down-to-earth and had a good sense of humor. "It's about time, don't you think?"

"Yes, well, I know what it's like to fight Cora. She was still living with us when I had my first two. Then she came to help Brad and stayed for Lucinda. She's in her glory now with all these children here."

Libby shook her head. "If you don't mind my asking, how much longer do you plan on staying?"

Colleen pulled off her bonnet and sighed. "I was hoping by now Caleb would be crawling back here, begging for me to come home. Maybe he doesn't need me as much as I thought."

"Well, you know how men and their pride can be," Libby said. "It seemed whenever Ben and I had a fight, Ben's fierce pride stopped him from apologizing first. As soon as I took the first step, he would hop right on the wagon with me and be as contrite as can be. I don't know Caleb well, but since he's a man, and they all seem to be alike, he's letting his pride get in the way of common sense. I enjoy visiting with you, but maybe it's time you took the first step and get things patched up."

Colleen grinned sheepishly at Libby. "I know you're right, Libby, but I'm cursed with the same pride and stubbornness."

"Think about what I said. As much as I hate to admit it, my mother-in-law was right when she says women are the peacemakers of the world."

"What are you wearing?" Colleen asked in an abrupt change of topic.

"I found these in a wardrobe in my room. I know the skirt's a little short, but it's all I could find."

"They must be Lucinda's, but I wasn't talking about the clothes, I was talking about what you have on your feet."

Libby swung her legs straight out and gazed fondly at her tennies. "They're my shoes. The ones in the closet were too small for me."

"I've never seen anything like them."

"It's what we wear in the north. They are warmer and more comfortable."

"Aah," Colleen responded as if being from "the north" cleared everything up. "What about the rest of your clothes?"

"None of them are right for here."

"Well, that settles it. I'll stay long enough to get your wardrobe situation fixed. I'll ask Brad if we can remake some of Lucinda's things. They're only hanging in the closet gathering dust."

How would she feel if someone wore Ben's clothes? "But won't he feel bad seeing her things being used?"

Colleen obviously didn't have the same concern. "He may, but it's about time he gets on with his life, anyway. A person can only mourn for so long."

"Do you think anyone will see us at the cemetery?"

"I doubt it. Why?" Colleen kept eyeing Libby's shoes.

"Cora thought I should be wearing black, but I don't have anything in the color."

Colleen huffed a breath. "Oh, those stupid mourning traditions. Men don't have to mourn for a year or sometimes two years. Only six months. They don't have to cover themselves from head to toe in black, even when it's hot and humid. I've heard of widows passing out in their black finery."

Libby agreed, but before she could ask questions burning in her mind, gravel crunched beneath horse's hooves.

"Here comes Brad now. I'll talk to him later. Leave everything up to me. Do you have a bonnet?"

"No." She did have a baseball cap in her bags, but like her maternity pants and tops, wearing it would certainly raise eyebrows.

"Here, use mine. You'll need one to keep the sun from burning your nose. With your fair skin you probably burn fast."

"You're right. Thanks." Libby couldn't help but admire the bonnet. She'd always thought it would be fun if hats had come back into style, and not baseball hats, either. This one was straw with a wide brim around the entire hat. It was held in place with wide ribbons coming down on either side to be tied under the chin.

"I know it's a little out of date, but the new ones don't keep your entire face out of the sun. I only wear it around our place or here. I'm outside so much with the children and taking care of my garden, and I do hate to freckle."

"This is fine," Libby assured her as she put on the bonnet. "Where is Charlie? I don't want to keep Brad waiting." With the bonnet in place, trying to see things from the side was like a horse wearing blinders. She couldn't see left or right without turning her head.

"I'll go hurry him along," Colleen offered with a wave in Brad's direction.

Brad jumped down from the wagon and came up to Libby. "I'm sorry I don't have the buggy, but the axle broke and Joshua hasn't been able to fix it since he broke his leg. I hope you don't mind."

"Of course not," Libby answered slowly. She wasn't concerned for herself, but for Charlie and Lucy. Brad seemed to read her mind.

"Charlie will be fine up there, but it might be a good idea to leave Lucy behind. It might be a bit jolting for her."

Libby mentally calculated how long it had been since she nursed Lucy. In another hour she would probably have to do so again. "I...um...how long will we be gone?"

"About two hours. Why?"

Libby's face heated. She didn't know this man well enough to explain her predicament. "Well, I, uh, can't leave her long."

"Why not? Cora certainly knows how to take care of her."

"Lucy um... I ..." Oh, the heck with it. "I will need to feed her again in an hour, so I can't leave her." Her face burned even more when Brad eyed her breasts.

As if he'd been caught with his hand in the cookie jar, he turned away from Libby and headed back to the wagon. "When the time comes, we'll find a place where you can feed her. Let's get going."

What was up with his abrupt change in attitude? It happened a lot with him. One moment he'd be friendly then suddenly he would become curt and walk away from her. She chalked it up to his missing his wife.

"Let's go, Mommy." Charlie tugged on her skirt. "Bwad's waiting."

Colleen stepped onto the porch and glanced at the wagon. "You're not taking Lucy in that thing, are you?"

Libby sighed. "I have no choice. I made such a stink about going to see Ben's grave and Brad's taking time out of his day, I can't back out now. I'll have to nurse her in about an hour, so I have to take her. What else can I do?"

"Wait a minute." Colleen slipped back into the house and returned a few minutes later carrying a pillow-lined basket with an umbrella attached to the front. Cora came out behind her with a large pillow and another basket. They took them to the wagon. Libby followed.

Brad frowned. "What's all this for?"

"Mr. Bradley, you can't expect Miss Libby to hold Lucy all the way to the cemetery. So's we'll put Miss Lucy in this here basket and set it behind the seat. The umbrella will keep the sun off her." Cora tossed the large pillow to Brad. "This pillow is for Miss Libby to sit on while she nurses the babe." She hung the basket over Brad's outstretched arm. "The basket has some goodies in it for lunch."

Libby flinched at Brad's clenched fists and red face.

"Lunch? But we're only going to the cemetery!" Brad yelled.

"Now, Mr.' Brad." Cora patted his arm. "You can't expect Miss Libby to bounce all the way to the cemetery and then turn right around and bounce right back. Not on her first day out of the birthin' bed. It ain't right."

Colleen nudged him toward the wagon. "Now, Brad. You need some time off. You've been working way too hard lately. You take Libby and Charlie to the cemetery then stop somewhere for a short picnic." She pointed at the large wagon. "Cora's right when she says Libby shouldn't be jounced all over the country in your contraption."

Brad whooshed out a breath. "Oh, all right. I know when I'm outnumbered. But I wasn't planning on jouncing her all over the country." His next words were spoken with painstaking slowness to emphasis his point. "We were only going to the cemetery."

Within a short time, Lucy was sleeping peacefully in the basket behind the seat, Charlie was squealing with delight at being so high from the ground, Libby was glancing around nervously for the same reason, and Brad was snapping the reins against the horses' rumps. As the wagon rumbled down the driveway, Cora and Colleen smiled at each other and shook hands. Their mission was accomplished.

By the time the novelty of riding in the wagon wore off and Charlie had settled down by laying his head on her lap, Libby thought it was safe enough to ride and talk at the same time. The pictures she had formed in her mind about riding in these wagons didn't do justice to the actual uncomfortable bouncing. Her one hope was the rocking and swaying would keep Lucy lulled enough to stay asleep a good while longer.

Libby fanned herself with her hand. "Is it always this hot?"

"Isn't it like this in Wisconsin?"

"Not in early June, it isn't," she answered.

Brad slapped the reins against the horses' rumps. "C'mon, boys. This'll take all day at this rate."

"I'm sorry about how this turned out. I only wanted to see Ben's grave. All this other stuff was Cora and Colleen's idea. I could have waited another day when I had planned things better with Lucy."

Brad glanced at Libby. Her bottom lip trembled. "You're a strong woman, Libby."

"Not hardly."

"I'm not sure how I would have handled things if I were in your shoes. Given the circumstances, you're doing great. I don't know anyone else who could have had those things happen to you and still be able to function. Most women would have taken to their beds on purpose. You only wanted to get out. I understand how it feels to lose someone you love. You've lost more than most."

Libby let out an unladylike grunt. "I'll say. One hundred and fifty-four years is a lot to lose."

He needed to change the subject and pointed at her shoes. "What are those things?"

"Oh, not you, too!" Libby sighed. "They're called tennis shoes. I didn't have anything else to put on my feet."

"Your ankles are showing. You shouldn't be showing your ankles."

"And I have a feeling you shouldn't be noticing, Mr. Kemble."

Brad laughed. "I'm sorry, but it's hard not to when they're attached to red, what did you call them? Tennis shoes?"

"Yes, tennis shoes. The boots in the wardrobe in my room were too small. But then, so are these clothes." When Brad didn't comment, she went on. "I hope you don't mind my going through the wardrobe in my room. I understand these clothes were your wife's?"

He shrugged. "Yes. I recognize them. Someone has to wear them."

"Your wife must have been a dainty woman."

Brad acknowledged the complement with a nod.

"Colleen is going to talk to you about fixing some of them for me. When she questioned me about my clothes, I told her we wore different ones in Wisconsin."

"By the looks of your clothes, I would say things change a lot in the next 150 years."

Libby frowned at him. "So, you finished going through my things? You could have left them alone once you knew for sure where I was from. You didn't need to keep snooping."

"I didn't go through your things once I put them in the attic. I made the comment from what I saw before you caught me. No matter what you think, snooping is not one of my favorite things to do."

The air was thick with displeasure. They rode in silence.

"Are we almost there, yet?" Charlie asked.

"I see there's one question surviving generations." Brad's laughter cleared the air. "I can remember asking the same thing when we would go into town with my folks. Seemed to take forever."

"Me, too. Are you going to answer his question?"

"Getting tired of riding?"

"I have to admit, my, um, backside is."

"It's only a few more minutes. We buried your husband in the family cemetery, which is almost to Caleb's place. Even though we call it the family cemetery, you'll find other people buried there, too. We share it with the Castlewoods."

"Aren't they the people who owned your place?"

"Yes. Belinda Castlewood still lives in the area, but everyone else in the family has passed on. You'll meet her eventually, I'm sure."

By the sarcastic tone in his voice, Libby wasn't so sure she wanted to. She was about to question him about the Castlewoods when he announced their arrival at the cemetery.

In her mind's eye, Libby pictured rows and rows of headstones in an open field, with a few trees scattered here and there. This cemetery was in the woods. If a person didn't know it was here, they would have passed it by. In a hundred years or so, unless there was family still around to care for it, it would probably be overgrown and neglected, the caretakers waiting for the newest stone to reach one hundred years so they could all be dug up and moved to a larger one, making room for development of houses or strip malls.

Right now, the fenced-in area was lovingly tended. Libby wasn't sure how they kept the grass mowed, but not a blade was out of place. Flowers grew in front of every headstone. Which one was Ben's and who took care of it? Again, Brad seemed to read her mind.

"Your husband's grave is set apart from the family." He helped her down from the wagon. "Colleen hasn't had a chance to plant flowers here yet, and only a wooden cross is marking the site." After assuring Libby of Lucy's safety at being left in the wagon, Brad picked up Charlie in his free arm and guided them around the perimeter of the graveyard. In a slight clearing a lone grave stood, a bare mound of dirt giving testimony to a recent burial. A bunch of dried daisies lay on the dirt.

"I want you to know we gave him a Christian burial. Even though a minister was not present, Caleb read from the Bible and Colleen sang some songs. The children picked flowers and we all said prayers. It was the best we could do. I don't know what religion you are, but God is God, and I believe your Ben is resting with Him now."

Libby rested her hand on Brad's forearm. Tears were backing up into her throat, making it difficult to talk. "Thank you so much for what you have done. I can tell you buried Ben with care, even though you didn't know him. It means a lot to me." Libby reached up on her toes and kissed the side of Brad's mask.

Before he could react, Libby sat on the ground beside the grave and put Charlie on her lap. Brad took the hint and left her alone. As he was walking away, he heard Charlie ask if that's where his daddy was buried, then the boy's tears when Libby told him it was.

For the first time since her death, Brad had no desire to visit Lucinda's grave. Instead, he wanted to keep an eye on Libby and Charlie. He also felt he needed to listen for Lucy. In Libby's state of mind right now, she probably wouldn't hear her. He leaned against a tree halfway between the wagon and Ben's grave. Libby rocked Charlie back and forth, occasionally wiping tears from her face. Eventually Charlie got tired of sitting and walked over to Brad.

"My daddy is over there. I guess he's not buried in your back yard."

Brad knelt down in front of Charlie. "No, he's not. We don't bury people in our yards."

"How come?"

"Well, you play in the yard, don't you?"

"Uh-huh."

"You wouldn't want to be stepping on your daddy now, would you?"

"No."

"Well, neither would I."

"Is your little boy in the ground here?" Charlie asked.

Brad was surprised the boy remembered being told his son had died. "Yes, he is."

"Can I see him?"

Brad raised an eyebrow. "You want to see where my son is buried?"

"Yup."

"All right. Let's check with your mother first." Libby was lying on her side on the ground next to Ben's grave, the bottoms of her red shoes pointing toward him. He would have been more shocked at her actions if they didn't resemble his when he first visited Lucinda's grave. By lying on the ground next to her, he felt part of Lucinda. Was Libby willing Ben to life as he'd tried to with Lucinda?

Brad decided not to disturb her. He led Charlie through the maze of headstones, being careful not to step on the graves themselves. When they finally stopped, Charlie flopped to his knees.

"Do you miss your little boy?"

"Yes."

"I miss my daddy an awful lot. Do you think he misses me?"

Brad crouched down behind Charlie and put his arms around him. "I *know* he misses you, Charlie."

Charlie leaned into Brad's chest. "Will you be my daddy now?"

Brad suppressed a laugh. It was a thought creeping into his mind too often lately. Although he didn't know Libby well enough to make her his wife, he would love to be a father to Charlie and Lucy. He reached up and touched his mask where Libby had kissed him. She did seem to be a nice person, though. Didn't care about his mask or what may be behind it. Brad brought his thoughts up short. What on earth could he be thinking? Libby's husband recently died. There was no way he would intrude upon her mourning. He didn't even know if her being here was permanent or not. Maybe all three of them would be whisked away as quickly as they came. It was a thought Brad didn't care for. He felt a tug on the bottom of his mask.

"Brad! Are you going to be my daddy or not?"

"Not right now, Charlie. I'll help take care of you and Lucy and your mother, but I can't be your father."

"Oh." Charlie hung his head. "How come my daddy doesn't have any nice flowers?"

"I guess no one had time. Would you like to pick some for him?"

"Sure. My daddy liked to pick flowers for Mommy. My Mommy loves flowers."

"Really?" It was a piece of information he filed away for future use.

When Brad and Charlie returned to Libby, she was sitting up, watching their approach.

"We picked flowers for Daddy."

"I see, honey. Daddy will like them." She took the bunch of dandelions and daisies from Charlie and placed them next to the dried-up ones.

"I think I heard Lucy crying. We'd best be going back," Brad said.

The wailing got louder as they approached the wagon.

"She sure sounds mad, Mommy. Why is she so mad?"

Libby laughed and moved faster to her daughter. "She's not mad, Charlie. She's hungry."

"Well, I'm hungry and *I'm* not screaming my head off!"

Libby ruffled her son's hair. "Since she can't talk, it's her way of telling me she's hungry,"

"Do you think she can hold off until we find a better place to eat?" Brad asked hopefully. They had reached the wagon where he helped Charlie and Libby up onto the seat.

"I don't know. Maybe if I hold her. How far do we have to go?"

Brad jumped onto the wagon bed. He scooped Lucy up in his arms and handed her to Libby. "How long can you keep her quiet? That's about how far we'll travel."

Libby was too concerned with getting Lucy quiet to think about the skillful way Brad had picked Lucy up and handed her off.

Libby was able to hold her daughter off until Brad found a spot along a creek. Brad brought out Lucy's basket and when he was handed her, carefully laid the baby in it. She immediately began to scream. Libby jumped down from the wagon before he had a chance to help her. He grabbed the pillow and a blanket Cora had tossed in at the last minute. At Libby's directions, he spread the blanket near a tree and propped the pillow against it. She picked Lucy up and undid her blouse, attached Lucy to her breast—all before she sat down.

"Cora must have thought we were going to gone for days." Brad pulled out fried chicken, hard boiled eggs, fresh bread, a chocolate cake, and a glass jar of lemonade. "She has enough food here for an army."

"I'm hungry enough to eat a bear!" Charlie reached for a chicken leg.

"Wait a minute, young man. You have to wash your hands first." Brad swung a squealing Charlie under his arm and headed for the creek.

While they were gone, Libby quickly switched Lucy to her other breast. By the time they came back, Lucy had slowed down her nursing and was nearly asleep. Libby turned her back to Brad and Charlie, buttoned herself up, and burped Lucy. A large gas bubble coming from her made Charlie giggle and brought a laugh to Brad.

"Did that sound really come from a little peanut like her?" Brad asked. "What do you think, Charlie, is your sister part bear?"

Charlie giggled and tried to burp louder than Lucy. Libby smiled at his antics as she placed Lucy in the basket. "Okay, Charlie, enough horsing around. Let's eat."

A short time later, with the remains of the picnic back in the basket, Brad lay prone on the blanket, his arms resting beneath his head.

Libby was in the same position, but with her head on the pillow and Charlie's head on her lap, sound asleep. Now was as good as time as any to talk with Brad.

"Brad?"

"Hmm?"

"I haven't had a chance to thank you for being so good to Charlie and me. Especially Charlie. Most men wouldn't take the time."

"I like the boy and his father is gone. I hope you don't mind, but a boy needs a man to help him grow up right."

Libby thought of all the boys in her class growing up without a father and how things were not working out. "I don't mind. I happen to agree with you. I don't want him to be a bother."

"He's not. Like I said— I like him."

"Do you really believe we're from the future?"

Brad shrugged and crossed his feet at the ankles. "I don't know why, but I do. I wish I knew how."

"Do you think we'll be able to go back?"

"I don't know. Do you want to go back?"

Libby was surprised by his question. "Of course I do. It's where my life is. Things are so different there."

"Better than here?"

Libby had to think about his question before answering. She didn't want to hurt his feelings. "Yes, in some ways. Medicine is better. People live longer. You can go from place to place faster."

"In these car things Charlie talks about?"

"Yes, in cars and planes, boats and trains."

"We have boats and trains."

"Yes, but they go faster in 2024."

"Does going faster make it better?" he asked.

His question took Libby aback. She thought about the fast-paced life she lived. Always racing around trying to get everything done. "I guess not."

Brad rolled to his side facing Libby. Tell me about your life."

"You already know I was married to Ben. We had a good marriage. I taught fifth grade."

Brad interrupted. "You taught? But you're married and have children."

Libby had to stop and recall why it should surprise him. Then she remembered the rules of the day. "In the future women can be married, have children, *and* teach, or be a secretary, a doctor, or even a lawyer. She can be and do anything she wants."

"What about the children? Who takes care of them?"

"We hire babysitters or put them in day care."

"You let strangers take care of your children? Doesn't sound right to me."

Even though she loved teaching, there were times when Libby believed it wasn't right, either. Guilt wrapped itself around her heart every time she dropped Charlie off at day care. She thought about all the children who were left on their own because both their parents worked or didn't care. But it was the way things were done.

"Anything else good about your time?" Brad asked.

"Indoor plumbing and showers. Showers are the best!" Libby responded emphatically.

"Explain."

"We have running water in our homes, coming from pipes. We turn a faucet and water comes out. You don't have to go outside to a little building to take care of business. We have toilets. Once you, uh, take care of business, you flush the toilet and the mess is swept away."

"Where does it go?"

"Into the sewers."

"What's a shower?"

Using her hands to help, she tried to describe the pipe coming out of the wall, allowing water to spray down on a person.

"Sounds like a waterfall," Brad said.

"Sort of, but with hot water and you're not sitting in your own dirty water."

"Tell me more of your time."

Libby closed her eyes and thought about 'her time.' Pollution? Wars? Pesticides in their food? Rape? Murder? Divorce? Noise? Right now, it was so incredibly quiet. No cars or planes. Even in the quietest moments of her day, there was some sound, no matter how faint. Even when she and Ben went camping in remote woods, there was still noise. Right now, it was peaceful.

Brad watched Libby close her eyes. She looked so serene. He wished he could see her thoughts; look into her world. But he liked the world he lived in. He couldn't imagine these car things all over the place or women leaving their children with strangers. Those shower things sounded nice, though. Libby's silence went on long enough for Brad to think she was asleep. He watched the slow rise and fall of her breasts. He felt the slow rise in a part of his body. Something he hadn't experienced in a long time. Why was he reacting to her this way?

"Brad?"

The sound of her voice nearly made him jump out of his pants. A quick look at her face reassured him her eyes were still closed. He rolled onto his stomach in case she should look his way. He certainly didn't want her to view his attraction to her.

"What?" he answered.

"Will you show me where you found us? Maybe we'll find some clues to help get us back."

Brad's stomach tightened at the thought of Libby and her children returning to their time. He made a quick decision. He wouldn't help.

"No."

Libby sat up quickly, toppling Charlie to the ground, waking him up. "What do you mean, no? We need to get home."

"I can't show you," Brad said. He jumped to his feet and stared down at Libby. "Let's get going."

"But why?"

There was no way he could tell her he wanted her to stay and why. Unfortunately, their peaceful afternoon was ruined.

Chapter Fifteen

Libby sat on a rocker on the front porch, fanning herself. Lucy lay on a blanket taking her afternoon nap. Brad was giving Charlie a riding lesson. Sweat ran between her breasts from the sweltering mid-August heat. She was bored. Bored and hot.

Summers in Wisconsin could get hot, but not for this long and not with this humidity. The only fan available to relieve it was the one she held in her hand and waved back and forth in front of her face. She and Ben never had air conditioning, but ceiling and floor fans went a long way to relieving the summer's heat. Libby glanced down at her daughter.

Lucky kid. She'd give anything to be able to wear a t-shirt and... Well, not diapers, but at least a pair of shorts, not a long skirt and blouse. At least she could wear a short-sleeved blouse. Thankfully, Cora had agreed Libby didn't have to wear black since she wasn't going into public.

She wiggled her toes against the plank porch floor. If she were lucky, no one would notice she wasn't wearing shoes. And if Cora knew she wasn't wearing one of those awful corsets, she'd have a fit! Bras were bad enough. Even her bra made her hot, but not wearing a corset was a small price to pay for freedom.

Freedom. Freedom to do anything she wanted. What she wanted was something to do. Back home, she would be rushing around trying to get the things done she didn't have time to do during the school year. By now she would be lamenting the lack of time before the next school year started. She'd be planning the year, making desk and locker tags, organizing her room, and probably feeling sorry for herself because she had to leave her children with a sitter.

Right now, she'd give anything to have something to do. Cora wouldn't let her help in the kitchen or with the housework. Libby was still considered a guest and guests didn't help out. It was also what Cora and her daughter were paid for. Once she suggested helping outside or in the barn. Cora nearly fainted. A suggestion was made to write letters to her friends. Only Brad knew she had no friends to write to. One night she decided to start a journal so when she returned to her time, she would have a record of her life here. Cora was happy thinking her writings were letters and no one seemed to notice the letters were never sent, and she never received any back.

The only thing ladylike she was allowed to do was take care of the flowers and garden. She was glad it was something she actually enjoyed. There were enough flowerbeds on the property for a gardener, but Libby and old Jacob got along. Sometimes while taking care of the beds, she could actually pretend she was back home.

If it weren't for her boredom and Ben's death, Libby would be content here. She missed Ben terribly. Several times she tried to get Brad to show her where the accident had occurred, but Brad was always too busy. Or so he said. He had finally shown her the buggy he found them in, but nothing more. Sometimes she believed Brad didn't want them to leave. Libby sensed the tensing of his body whenever she mentioned going home. She hoped by seeing where they landed the children and she would take off for 2024. Maybe it's what Brad thought, too.

Certainly, his relationship with Charlie was blossoming. Charlie rarely talked about his father. He took on Brad's way of walking and talking and spent his waking hours at the barn. Brad bought Charlie the pony he was having his lesson on. Libby was afraid once Charlie knew how to ride, he would follow Brad everywhere. But then, Brad didn't seem to mind. Libby chuckled. Was poor Brad even able to go to the bathroom by himself? Except for Charlie looking so much like his father, she could forget Brad wasn't his father.

Even Lucy was thriving. She was roly-poly, starting to coo and play with her hands and feet. When Brad talked to her, she smiled and laughed. If he ever took off his mask, would she think him a stranger? She should recognize his voice, though.

Libby sighed. Maybe one of the local schools needed a teacher. What would Brad's reaction be if she mentioned it? But why should she worry about what he thought? He wasn't her keeper. A little voice reminded Libby that, yes, he was her keeper. Without him, she and her children would be lost. Lord only knows what would have happened if Brad hadn't found them. She'd simply have to be brave and ask him about teaching.

Brad never talked about neighbors or their children, so she had no idea if there was a school nearby. She would have to ask Colleen the next time they were together. Someone must be teaching their children. Libby felt her resolve strengthening. She would demand she have a job around here. If not teaching, then something else.

Chapter Sixteen

Libby pulled back the heavy drapes in the front parlor and eyed the grey mist swirling around the front yard. Another dreary, rainy day. Even though it was only early afternoon, it felt like dusk. Cora told her this was the way winter was in Tennessee. Libby sighed. She'd been here seven months with, so far, no hope of returning home.

Libby had no better luck trying to get him to let her teach. He reminded her over and over married women did not teach. She reminded him she wasn't married. Brad said being married and being widowed were the same thing when it came to teaching young minds. She muttered something about the narrow-minded ideas of 19th century men. Brad laughed and asked her if women in her time had it so much easier. This started a discussion about women's rights, which, surprisingly, Brad agreed with. Yet she couldn't convince him to let her teach. She had to be satisfied with helping Charlie learn his letters and numbers. It barely fulfilled her need to teach. She resolved to talk to Colleen about it at Christmas.

Libby was looking forward to Christmas simply because there would be other people to talk to. Caleb and Colleen's children had been ill during Thanksgiving so they weren't able to get together. It turned out to be a terrible holiday for her. All she thought about was how her and Ben's families would get together. She glossed over the bad episodes when the families would start fighting, but dwelled on the good times, the warmth and laughter of the children. The teasing of Ben's siblings with each other. His mother's delicious food. Her remembrances depressed her, and she was glad when she and Brad finally put the children to bed and she could bury herself in her bed.

Christmas should be different. Libby wouldn't miss Ben any less, but the bustle of company would cover her pain. She and Colleen got along so well, too. It was like they were soul sisters.

Sometimes when she tried to remember people or places from home, Libby had trouble focusing on them. She was afraid her memories were fading and was worried about what it meant. Would she ever be going home? Brad tended to ignore her whenever she brought it up. She finally quit mentioning home except when he asked her questions about her life there.

Brad's love for Charlie and Lucy was certainly not in question. Their relationship was even stronger. A few times Libby heard Charlie calling Brad *Dad*. Libby's first impulse was to rush to Charlie and remind him Brad wasn't his father. Before she could do anything, she listened as Brad explained the same thing to Charlie. Several times after, when Charlie would slip up, Brad would remind him. Once Charlie's answer had been, "I know, Brad, but can't I pretend you're my daddy?" Libby's heart was being torn in two.

After Brad had taken care of Charlie while Libby was sick, he didn't want to give up his nighttime routine with Charlie, so they shared them. Since Ben had never helped Libby with bedtime chores, she found having someone help made it easier. It became a warm and comforting time.

One night, after the children were in bed, she and Brad sat on the front porch, Brad with a snifter of brandy and Libby with a lemonade. As always, when he had the chance, he asked her about her life. That particular night he wanted to know what she missed the most, besides her showers. With only the crickets as background noise, and no light pollution to dim the brightness of the stars, Libby realized what she didn't miss. Besides the noise, she didn't miss rushing around every day, although some rushing would have been welcomed to break the boredom. She did not miss television or radio, or even electricity. What she did miss was her friends and the ability to talk to them on the phone. Several times it would cross her mind to call Colleen and talk about everyday events. Then it would hit her how impossible it was to do. Instead, she started a list of things to ask her the next time they met.

The summer was spent recuperating and learning about her new life. Cora finally capitulated and let her help around the house. Even though she'd done the majority of the work in her own home, this was different. Most everything was done and made by hand. Something as simple as lighting an oil lamp took many tries to set the wick so it wouldn't burn black. What she couldn't get used to was the lack of toilet paper. She'd give her soul for some nice, soft toilet paper.

Then there was the first time she had used a handkerchief on Charlie's runny nose. Libby smiled as she remembered the shocked look on Cora's face when she tossed the piece of cloth away. At first she hadn't understood what she had done, but at Cora's gasp it dawned on her it would have to be washed. Tissues were so much easier.

One day after watching Cora take care of the laundry, Libby decided to be more careful getting her clothes dirty and wearing them more than once. At home she tossed her clothes into the laundry after a day's wear. But watching Cora scrubbing the clothes against the scrub board, and lugging pans of water back and forth from the kitchen for rinsing, gave Libby a new respect for laundry chores.

Libby mentally shook herself from her thoughts. She needed to concentrate on getting back to 2024. But more and more she was less and less inclined to ask Brad where the accident occurred. Was it because she knew he would say no or if she was becoming resigned to staying here? She didn't dislike it here; just needed something more to keep her occupied.

She couldn't shake off the feeling there was more to Brad's declining to help her. So many times she felt his eyes on her, yet when she would glance at him, he was turned another way. She enjoyed being in his company. More and more her thoughts would turn to him during the day, wondering what he was doing and what they would discuss at night after the kids were in bed.

Most nights they would meet in the parlor to read or discuss the day's events. Libby didn't have much to tell him, except when he'd ask about her other life. She began to look forward to these visits, and on the nights he was busy in his office or on the land, she missed his companionship. Guilt would bring tears to her eyes. Ben had only been gone seven months. She shouldn't be looking forward to seeing another man.

Noises from the preparations being made for Christmas seeped into the parlor. Tomorrow Caleb and Colleen would come with their crew. Brad and Caleb's younger sister, Sybil, her husband, David, and their two children were also coming. Then the action would pick up. If she were anything like her brothers, Libby would like her. It should prove to be a noisy holiday with eight children under the age of eight. Libby couldn't wait.

Libby set down her book. Who was making so much noise in the front hall? It reminded her of the time a team of little leaguers came into a restaurant she and Ben were at. The rambunctious group was filled with laughter and jokes. They weren't being naughty and their antics were bringing smiles to the other patrons. Ben had been hoping for a quiet evening together but finally got into the spirit of the children and accompanying adults. Libby loved it.

Curiosity finally got the better of her. She eased open the door and peered around the corner. Brad in the arms of a beautiful woman. Her hair was the color of a copper penny. Her tiny figure would have made any man drool. Brad was hugging her tightly as the woman gazed adoringly into his face.

"Bradley Kemble. When are you going to get rid of your stupid mask!" She smiled and tugged on his hood. "I hate it. I would think by now some woman would have fallen in love with you no matter what you look like."

A man appeared by the woman's side and put an arm around her waist, pulling her away from Brad. "Now, Sybil. Is this the way to greet your brother after all this time?"

"I suppose not, but my brother can be so stubborn," she added. "Now, where's this woman I hear you have staying with you?"

She must have made a sound because the three adults turned their heads her way. Before she could slip back into the parlor, Brad came to her, took her hand, and led her to his sister.

"Libby, I'd like you to meet my sister Sybil, her husband David, and their two children, Rosie and David, Jr. Sybil, David, this is Libby Daniels from Wisconsin."

Libby wasn't prepared for the arrival of their guests a day early and could only mumble, "I'm pleased to meet you." Sybil had the friendliest, bluest eyes she'd ever beheld. Their warmth and joy pulled her into their depths. She glanced up into Brad's mask. *Is this what his eyes are like?* Her pulse raced a little faster. His eyes probably held the same warmth as his sister's. Wow!!

"Are you two twins?" Libby asked Sybil as she turned back to her.

Sybil laughed. "Not hardly. This old man is one year older than me, but when he wasn't wearing his stupid mask people mistook us for twins." Sybil reached out a gloved hand and took one of Libby's in hers. "I'm so pleased to finally meet you. I've heard so much about you and your two little ones. We have sons the same age."

When Sybil let go of her hand, David greeted her the same way. She was out of her depth. Never had she met such warm, friendly people. It took her a moment, while Brad took their wraps, for her to come to her senses. Sybil was giving smiling looks between Brad and her like she had some kind of secret. David was helping Sybil and their two small children, with the same reddish dark hair as their parents, off with their wraps, mittens, and hats. Cora was bustling around grabbing outer garments and laughing with joy.

"Yes, sir. It is great having the family all together again." Cora clapped her hands. "This is going to be one fine Christmas." As she walked to the back of the house with the two children in tow, she mumbled "eight youngins bringing life back to this ol' house."

Sybil took Libby by the elbow and led her to the parlor. "You must find this difficult, meeting all of us at once."

Libby laughed. "I've already met Caleb and Colleen, so you're the only ones I don't know."

"Well, we'll remedy that!" Sybil assured her. "If you hear the boys calling me Billy, it's a nickname they gave me when we were growing up. I was such a tomboy, always chasing after them, trying everything they tried. I think my mother despaired of me ever turning into a lady."

David put an arm around her shoulders. "But a darn fine lady she turned out to be," he laughed as he wiggled his eyebrows suggestively.

Libby wasn't sure what to make of their banter until everyone laughed at his joke.

As they sat down, Libby and Sybil on the couch, and David in an armchair, Brad poured brandy for them.

"Billy, how did you hear about Libby and her children being here?" Brad handed a glass to her.

"Did you ever hear the term 'writing a letter,' dear brother?" Before he could answer she went on. "Obviously not since I haven't heard from you in a year. Luckily, Caleb didn't inherit the inability to put words on paper. I know everything that's happened in the past few months. Besides, we spent the night with Caleb and Colleen last night, and we had a nice long chat with those two." Sybil looked between Brad and Libby and grinned.

Brad raised an eyebrow. "You spent the night with them? I thought you were coming straight here."

"We were," David answered. "But we got an early start out of Boston and once we got within a few hours of their place yesterday, we decided to go on instead of staying in another miserable wayside inn."

"It was better for the children, too." Sybil turned to Libby. "Where are your children? I hear they're adorable."

Libby smiled at her. She couldn't help it; the woman's friendliness was infectious. "They're taking naps right now, but Charlie should be getting up soon. He's so excited about Christmas, I had a hard time getting him down. I thought I'd have to sit on him."

"Our two are just as bad," Sybil agreed. "Wait until Caleb and Colleen get here later with their four. It'll be total chaos."

Brad raised an eyebrow. "They're coming today, too? I thought you were all coming over tomorrow after church. Are you *all* staying overnight?"

"We sure are, dear brother. Their wagon is loaded down with food and presents, kids and servants. In fact, I think I hear them coming now."

Brad tried hard not to let his disappointment in the change of events show in his voice. He'd been looking forward to Christmas Eve with Libby and her children. For the past month he'd visualized a family Christmas Eve. He shouldn't think this way, but more and more Libby, Charlie, and Lucy were like his family. He wanted to see the joy on Charlie's face when they brought in the huge tree, decorated it, and lit the candles. He could hardly wait to give the boy the runner sled Brad made for him and the cradle for the doll Libby made. He knew Lucy was way too young to appreciate the cradle, but it made him proud and happy to do something for them.

Brad glanced at Libby. His heart skipped a beat. Not only was she nice to look at, but she was a wonderful person inside. Every morning since they'd arrived, Brad looked forward to getting up and seeing what the day, and her family, would bring. By mid-day he was thinking about their evening meals together. He came to enjoy her tradition of everyone sitting down to eat at the same time and not shoving the kids off to bed so they could eat alone.

Then they would sit with the kids. Charlie would ask Brad to help with his blocks and Libby would play with Lucy. Sometimes the four of them would lay on the floor and play with the toy soldiers from Brad's childhood. Lucy babbled and played with her hands and feet while the rest of them set up battle lines and knocked over each other's men.

Then after they put the children to bed, he and Libby would sit in the parlor and read or talk about his day or her life in the future. Brad understood how much she missed her husband. But it bothered him when she would ask to see where the accident had occurred. So far, he had managed to come up with excuses not to show her, but some day he would have to. The thing was, he was afraid. Afraid if he took her to the accident site, she would disappear. The thought of Libby and her children leaving made him break out in a cold sweat. He'd not only fallen in love with Charlie and Lucy, but he was falling in love with their mother, too.

"Bradley?" a soft voice broke into his thoughts. "Are you all right? Are you coming?"

He glanced up at the frown on Libby's face. Her hand was resting on his forearm, sending shockwaves throughout his body. For the umpteenth time in the past few months, he was glad she couldn't see his face and the desire written across it, which was disarming. She didn't seem to mind that he was disfigured and saw him as a human being and not a monster. He made a promise to himself to keep her with him as long as he could. Maybe she would even fall in love with him.

"What's wrong? You look ready to bolt to your room."

"Where are we going to put everyone?" she whispered.

Why did her saying 'we' make his heart skip a beat? "Don't worry. Cora and the staff will take care of it. With Caleb and Colleen's staff here, there are plenty of people to handle it."

"Will they open up the other rooms of the house?"

"Yes." He slipped her hand into the crook of his arm.

"But I have to help Cora decide where to put everyone."

Brad sighed. He was never going to be able to change her mind. In the past few months, he'd come to learn when she set her mind to something, there was no way to change it. "Go ahead and find Cora. Let her know everyone will be here tonight." Before the words were spoken, Libby lifted her skirts and raced down the hall.

Chapter Seventeen

Sybil took a place on a settee. "Where's Libby going?"

At Brad's nod, David poured brandy for him and Brad and a sherry for his wife. Brad took the drink and leaned against the edge of a bookcase. "She's checking with Cora about where to put everyone and whether we have enough food for supper tonight." He raised an eyebrow at his sister and took a sip of his drink. "After all, we weren't expecting you until tomorrow. Nor did we know Caleb and his crew were going to stay over, too."

Sybil looked over the rim of her glass. "Libby's taking over the household already?"

Brad chuckled. "Not really. She feels she needs to repay me for taking her and her children in after the accident."

"Has she seen you without your disgusting mask?"

"No. And I see no reason for her to do so."

David tipped his glass at his brother-in-law. "How can you marry someone who's never seen your face?"

Brad blew out a mouthful of brandy and coughed when part of it went down his throat the wrong way. "Marry? Who said anything about marriage?"

Sybil gave him a side-eye which always made him nervous. She was up to something. One that had given him grief while growing up. She was going to tease him relentlessly until she received the answer she wanted. Being the youngest child and a girl gave her the idea he and Caleb should bow to her every command—which they usually did.

He smiled behind his mask. He loved his sister dearly and, as much as he liked to think she was, there wasn't a spoiled bone in her body. She simply liked to give her big brothers a run for their money. And she did. He could very well imagine she was the same way with David. Lord knew the man was besotted with her.

Before she started in again, he'd better answer her. "I have no plans to marry Libby."

Sybil rose, closed the library door, then retook her seat. She flapped a hand at him. "Take off your awful mask and relax. I doubt she'll come barging in. I imagine she's too busy organizing the troops."

After removing the mask, he ran his fingers through his hair and sighed. The damn thing was hot, even in winter weather. It had been so much easier to live his life without it before Libby and Charlie arrived.

Now he needed to convince, if not himself, then his family he wasn't in the market for marriage. "Look. Libby lost her husband and is trying to adjust to life here. It hasn't been easy with all the changes."

Sybil frowned. "What changes? Things can't be so much different in the north. It isn't in Boston, anyway."

Damn. Leave it to his sister to jump on his words like an alligator on a fish. He refilled his glass to give himself time to think about what to say. Never in a million years would he be able to explain to them where Libby was really from. He still had a few moments himself when he didn't believe it. But he couldn't deny the proof in her handbag.

So, what to tell his family. His sister inadvertently helped.

"I can't imagine losing David in some strange place and being left alone with two small children." She held out her glass to her husband for a refill. "Have you made any inquiries to her family in Wisconsin?"

"We haven't heard anything from her or his family." While not an outright lie, guilt filled him at the subterfuge. How did one contact people who didn't exist for one-hundred and fifty-four years?

David filled Sybil's glass and took a seat beside her. "What else is she having trouble with?"

"The weather. It's much warmer here. She's from a city and isn't used to the quiet. She also didn't have any help at home and was a schoolmarm. She's used to being busy. Anyway, it's what she tells me."

"She's a schoolteacher?" Sybil widened her eyes. "But she was married."

"Well, if there's a shortage of teachers, it doesn't matter if a woman is married or not. Anyway, it's what she says. Besides, why can a married man work, but not a married woman?"

Sybil smirked. "Seems like you two talk a lot. Must keep you from being lonely."

"Leave it alone, Billy. I'm not marrying her."

David patted her hand as if to say to stop pushing her brother. "Who took care of Charlie when she was teaching?"

"She had a neighbor who took care of him."

Sybil scowled. "It's simply awful when a husband doesn't support her."

"I agree, but like I said, life is different up north." He sat down in a green, winged-back chair in front of the fireplace. Heavens, he hated lying. "Uh. Things aren't as settled there as they are here."

"Huh." Sybil stood and pushed the matching chair closer to Brad.

Brad rolled his eyes. Sybil was digging. He was doomed. No way was he going to tell them about where Libby was from without her permission.

"Colleen says she's very nice and seems to like her."

"She is and Colleen does."

"Do you?"

"Do I what?"

"Like her."

Brad held back a growl. Sybil was unrelenting. Why hadn't he kept his mask on? It would have been easier to hide his reaction to her questions. She was way too observant. "Of course, I like her." Had he kept his voice neutral enough? "But it doesn't mean I'm going to marry her."

Dave stood behind his wife's chair and placed his hands on her shoulders. "When did you find them?"

Sybil took one of her husband's hands and rubbed it against her cheek.

A pang stabbed Brad's heart. How he missed those loving touches, those signs of caring. Would he ever have that again? Libby's face flashed in his brain. "Sometime in March."

Sybil frowned. "She's been here eight months and hasn't tried to go home? Whyever not?"

Damn. This was something he and Libby should have discussed, but with his family's early arrival, there hadn't been time. His family was too damn smart, too. Frantically trying to come up with some reasonable answer, he was relieved when someone knocked. His relief was short lived.

"Brad? It's Libby. My I come in?

Sybil chuckled. "First name basis, huh?"

"Where the hell is my mask?" He grit his teeth when Sybil held it in the air. "Give it to me," he whispered. Without thinking, he stuck out his tongue at her as if he were five years old and she'd hidden his favorite slingshot.

"Very mature, Bradley. Very mature."

He held out his hand. "Please."

She waggled a finger at him. "Uh-uh, my dear brother. It's time to face the music. If she screams and runs away at your scar, you know she's not the one."

"Dammit, Sybil. How many times do I have to tell you I'm not marrying again."

"Huh. Keep telling yourself that." She rose and tossed the mask into the fireplace where it burned in a flash. "Come in, Libby."

Brad jumped up and turned his back to the door. His stomach clenched. Sweat beaded on his forehead. No matter what he'd told his sibling, having Libby see him without the mask scared him to death. What if she was revolted? What if she hated him for hiding his face from her?

"Cora and I have the sleeping arrangements all settled." Libby stopped. Who was the man with his back to her? His form seemed familiar. Why was Sybil grinning like the Cheshire Cat? The tension in the room was thick enough to cut. What was going on?

She took a few more steps into the room. "Where's Brad?"

Sybil held a hand to her lips, but her eyes were shining. "Why, he's right there." She pointed to the tall man with his back to her.

"Brad?" Where was his mask? Had he decided to let her see his face? She held her breath. Was he so disfigured, it would shock her?

"Leave the room, Libby."

Huh. Like heck she would. She'd spent the last eight months wondering what color his eyes were. If he were as handsome as his brother. Which was wrong. She was a widow. But then, what sane person wouldn't wonder why someone would hide their face?

"I will not. Not until you turn around and face me."

Brad's shoulders drooped and he hung his head. "I can't."

"Bradley Kemble. Turn around."

"Oh, oh, big brother. Sounds an awful lot like an order." Sybil tapped a finger against her lips. "Sounds like a teacher voice, too. Or like Mother when you did something naughty."

"Sybil. Shut up."

"Fine." Sybil stood and took her husband's hand. "C'mon, dear. I know when I'm not wanted."

Brad's chuckle was more like a growl. "So, you finally figured it out. Don't let the door hit you in the back when you leave."

Brad closed his eyes and let out his breath. They were gone, but what now? He only had the one hood. Maybe he could stay in the library until he was sure Libby was in the kitchen, or dining room, or Charlie's room, or her room.

Heavens, he was a coward. How would he explain not showing up for dinner or putting Charlie to bed? After all, it was his turn.

He headed to the decanter on a side table. He needed another brandy. Maybe an entire bottle. Yes, he was a coward of the worst kind. Something alerted him. He wasn't alone in the room. Libby? He took a deep breath and turned on his heel.

Libby didn't say a word. Simply stared at him then took a step closer. "Why, you are every bit as handsome as Caleb."

What? That was all she had to say? Belinda... Well, he wasn't going to think about what that woman did when she first saw his scar. Or anyone else. Why did people think a scar made a person evil, stupid, or deranged?

"What did you say?"

"I said you are as handsome as your brother."

His stomach went back into its proper position. "That's what I thought you said."

Libby frowned and stepped closer until she was a mere two feet away. "What? Did you think I would run screaming from the room as if you were a monster?"

"You wouldn't be the first one to do so."

She raised her hand as if to touch his scar. He took her wrist. "Don't."

Libby dropped her hand. "I'm sorry. I guess I understand why you hid your face, but on the other hand, I don't. Why would you care what people think? Do you hide from your nieces and nephews, your brother and sister?"

"No."

"They are the only ones who matter. Don't you think?"

Brad shrugged. She was right. It was time to face his demons, both inside him and those who turned their backs on him. "I guess. You don't mind my scar?"

"Having been able to know you these past months, I understand you are more than your outer shell. You are kind, considerate, smart. I could go on and on, but I can't think of any more adjectives."

If he'd thought earlier he was falling for her, he was positive now. But what should he do about it? Take her to where the accident occurred and hope she didn't disappear? Keep her here? Wait a few months and begin courting her? He ran a hand over his face, the ridges of his scar rubbing against his palm.

"Brad. Libby. Dinner is on the table. We're waiting for you. Caleb and Colleen are here, too." Sybil rapped on the door but didn't open it.

"We'll be right there, Sybil." He searched Libby's face to look for any lies she may be telling. By now she probably was aware he was successful and could support her and her children. Was she after his money? No. Not possible. If she were, she wouldn't be asking to see where the accident occurred. She wouldn't be wanting to go home. Plus, there was no guile in her eyes. They were as honest as the day was long.

He took her elbow. "Shall we? We can continue this discussion at another time."

The closer they came to the dining room, the louder the noise level became. Eight children under the age of eight, four adults, Cora, and the other servants, made for a rambunctious group. In accordance with tradition, one he hadn't followed since Lucinda had died, everyone on the farm partook in the festivities. To make things easier, the meal was buffet style. The table was set for sixteen with smaller tables set up for the children.

The side tables were laden with turkey, ham, various types of potatoes, yams, okra, gravy, and so many desserts someone with a sweet tooth would be in his glory. His mouth watered. Someone like himself.

He stopped Libby in the doorway of the room, taking in the laughter, teasing, and joking taking place. His heart swelled with joy. How he'd missed this. Going to Caleb's for the holidays wasn't the same. This was *his* house. His family, including his employees, filling the house with love.

Libby tapped his arm. "Look at Charlie. With all the children to play with, he's in his element." Two female employees held the youngest children. As if she knew what was going on around her, Lucy laughed and squealed with delight.

He hadn't thought they'd made a sound, but Caleb turned their way. He nudged Colleen who stopped filling plates for her children. Her mouth dropped open. She poked Sybil who nudged David. As the poking and prodding went around the room, it became silent. Everyone stared. Sybil grinned and winked. Caleb raised a glass in a toast. Using a corner of her apron, Cora wiped at the tears running down her cheeks.

As if he didn't understand the intensity of the situation, Charlie skipped over to Libby. "Hey, Mama. Whatcha doing with Mr. Bwad? Hi, Mr. Bwad. Why are you holding Mama's arm? Are we going to eat soon? I'm hungry. Are you hungry, Mr. Bwad? We're having fun, Mama. Even Wizzie is having fun. Is Santa coming tonight? Will I get presents? I'm sleeping with Davy in a big bed. The babies are sleeping in my room. That means I'm not a baby, doesn't it, Mama? Right, Mama?"

How did the child know who he was? He'd never taken his mask off in front of him.

Libby put a hand on her son's shoulders. "Hush, now, Charlie. Hush." She nudged the boy back to his friends. "Pretend like nothing is different and they won't make a big deal about you not wearing a mask."

Her voice was so quiet, he barely heard her, but he nodded. She was right. Not making a big deal would be the best. No explanations. Simply walk in as if nothing were unusual. As if everyone wasn't already staring, he clapped his hands to get their attention. "Thank you, everyone, for joining us on Christmas Eve. It's been a long time since I've hosted a gathering here."

Caleb snorted. "You got that right." Colleen elbowed him in the ribs.

"So, without further ado, let's bow our heads and give thanks for everyone's health and for the food your hands worked hard to prepare."

After a few moments of silence, which was all the children could take, Cora helped fill the children's plates and got them settled at their table.

Brad swept his hand at the food. "Guests first." Once his plate was filled, he went to the table, eyed the seating arrangement, raised an eyebrow at Sybil and Colleen, then took the only empty chair. The one next to Libby. "Sorry," he whispered.

"About what?" Libby sprinkled salt and pepper on her potatoes.

"They planned this."

Libby frowned. "Planned what?"

Brad shook his head. "Never mind." Evidently, she had no idea his family was trying to push them together.

Libby hadn't enjoyed a Christmas holiday like this in years. The laughter. The joy. The teasing. Gatherings with her family were quiet and tense. Even the addition of Charlie hadn't loosened her parents' disapproval of everything she did. Since she was an only child, their discontent was focused on her. Visits with Ben's family were better, but infrequent.

She'd often read where children were to be seen and not heard. How children in the past did not join their parents at their meals. They were fed in the kitchen and sent off to bed. Since being here, she knew it wasn't true. At least not at Whispering Pines. The children, even though at another table, were included in the adult conversations. Or rather, the adults kept their conversations to include the children.

When everyone was done eating, and with promises of a special story after their baths, Colleen and Sybil's nannies led the children from the room. Libby stood to help clean the table.

"Shoo, young lady." Cora flapped her apron at her. "There's enough helpers here tonight, I don't need you. You ladies go have a sherry in the parlor. The men have those stinky cigars and will join you soon."

Libby suppressed a burp. If she were in her own time, she'd let one rip and make Charlie laugh. She joined Colleen and Sybil in the drawing room. This was one tradition she didn't agree with. What did the men discuss that the women couldn't hear? Ridiculous.

Sybil poured them each a glass of sherry. "I'm amazed at how well the children are getting along. For a while there, I thought they'd come to blows trying to outdo each other to see who could talk first."

"And the loudest." Colleen took a glass from her sister-in-law.

"I'm amazed at how well you got the children under control." Sybil gave Libby her glass of sherry.

"It's the way Libby was when we were all here this summer."

"Too bad she wasn't able to knock some sense into your and Caleb's heads. I understand you two got into a little tiff. I don't know how you stay married to him. He drove me crazy when we were kids."

Colleen raised an eyebrow.

"I know. I know. You love him to death. I hear the same thing from David's sister. They thought I was crazy to marry him, but when you are crazy in love you want to be with them for the rest of your life."

Libby held back a sob. She was supposed to be with Ben until they died, which wasn't supposed to happen for decades. She held her twisted hanky to her lips.

Sybil jumped and knelt before her. "I'm so sorry, Libby. I wasn't thinking. Here we are going on and on about our husbands and you…"

"It's all right, Sybil. You didn't mean anything by it. Some days I'm fine and others it hits me like a semi."

Colleen and Sybil exchanged glances. "Semi?" they said in unison.

Damn. She needed to watch what she said. "It's… Um… It's what we call a large, uncovered wagon in Wisconsin."

Sybil frowned. "Really? I never heard of such a thing. In Massachusetts, we call them buckboards."

"Well, we do, too, but sometimes we say semi."

Colleen set her glass on a side table. "Tell us about your life in Wisconsin."

Libby's stomach dropped. What should she say? "I imagine it's a bit like here, except we have long winters with a lot of snow."

"That's not what I meant." Colleen clasped her hands in her lap. "I didn't want to ask questions this summer, but Charlie talked about the strangest things. I know children have active imaginations, but his is quite remarkable. Cars. Trucks. Televisions. Telephones. He even drew us pictures."

Charlie. What was she going to do about him and his big mouth? He was only three but seemed to remember everything. She giggled. "Well, that's Charlie for you."

"Then there are the strange shoes you wear."

Please, please would someone interrupt them? The pitter patter—or more like pounding of little feet—rattled the windows. A herd of elephants couldn't make as much noise. Libby jumped up from her chair. "I think the children are coming." Whew. Saved by the little monsters.

Caleb leaned an elbow on the fireplace mantle, took a sip of brandy, then glared at Brad. "So, when are you going to tell us what is going on?"

"What do you mean? I haven't heard anything more about the counterfeiters. Have you? I did get a telegram from Washington. They are sending more men to look into the situation."

David frowned. "What are you guys talking about? Counterfeiters?"

"It's not what I was going to talk about, but I guess we could discuss the situation. What about the telegram, Brad?"

Whew. Quick thinking on his part. He turned to David. "There's been counterfeit money and notes floating around. The printing is good enough to fool an untrained eye. People can turn the notes in for US money."

"How did you know they were phony?" David took a puff of his cigar and blew a perfect circle.

"Nice, David. Too many banks and businesses are getting the same type. When they won't accept the money or notes, the men trying to pass them off get violent. One bank clerk has been killed. One store owner had his cash stolen when he refused to take the money."

Caleb tried to emulate David's smoke ring. The men laughed when it resembled a wobbly square. "Because I had been in law enforcement before the war and before I married Colleen, the local constabulary contacted me. I, in turn, sent a message to my contact in Washington to inform them of what was happening. Even though Lincoln established the National Banking Act in 1863 to make currency standard, many places haven't abided by it. It was too easy for banks to print their own money."

"We, and I mean the government, is worried why all of a sudden these counterfeiters have started making so many types of notes to convert to gold and silver." Brad sat behind his desk and placed his glass on a blotter. "Since the dawn of time there have been people making fake money."

Caleb shook his head. "We are to keep our eyes open for anyone suddenly flush with money." He turned to Brad and smirked. "Nice try, Brad."

"What the hell do you mean? Nice try with what? I'm not making bad money."

"I know." Caleb chuckled. "I mean nice try in moving the subject off you and Libby."

Brad gritted his teeth. "There is no me and Libby. How many times do I have to say it?"

"Until you admit there is." David pointed his cigar at Brad. "I didn't hear her screaming and running from you when she saw you without your mask. In fact, I thought the two of you seemed quite cozy."

"And then there's all the strange things Charlie talks about. Colleen and I have discussed it. There's something unusual about her and her son. We want to know what it is."

Brad refrained from wiping his sweaty forehead. His heart raced. What should he say? He didn't want to break Libby's confidences. "You know what active imaginations children have. Remember when your oldest told you about the sea monster he found in the river? How he fought it with a saber and killed it? Remember?"

Caleb sighed. "Yes, I remember. But the things he says and draws are so vivid."

"Well, I can't tell you."

"Can't or won't?" Caleb glared at him. "She's not hiding something like—maybe she's part of the counterfeiting ring? If you are, not only will she be put in prison, but so will you."

Good heavens. Where did his brother get his ideas? Brad took a deep breath to calm the anger building in him. "She. Is. Not. Part. Of. The. Counterfeiters. Or. Anything illegal."

"Then what—"

Brad couldn't hide his relief when a knock came on the door. "Gentlemen, the children are ready for their story and need help hanging their stockings."

"We'll be right there, honey." Caleb crushed his cigar in an ashtray and stabbed a finger in Brad's chest. "This discussion isn't over, my boy. I'll find out what is going on if it takes me all weekend."

Which was what he was afraid of. Like his wife, once Caleb got his talons into something, he didn't give up until he had answers he was satisfied with. "Can this at least wait until tomorrow? I won't share Libby's secrets until I talk with her and get her permission."

"You have until tomorrow afternoon. Then..."

"Then what, Caleb? You have her arrested for no reason? Not likely. Besides, you can't take a mother away from her nursing child."

"Tomorrow afternoon, Bradley Kimble." As quick as a wink Caleb turned his frown into a smile. "Now, let's join the women and children so the little ones can go to bed." He swept from the room with David following.

With a houseful of guests, when was he going to find time to talk with Libby? The only thing he could think of was to take her aside tonight. Why had life become so complicated?

Chapter Eighteen

They tried to hide it, but something had happened while the men were gone. Even though they put on a good show and acted happy, there was an underlying current scaring her. Rather like in the parlor. The children's excitement about Santa's arrival overnight couldn't mask the tension in the air. With all the currents flowing around, they could float from here to the Gulf Coast.

As the eldest, Caleb read "The Night Before Christmas." With the help of the men, the stockings were hung accompanied by the children singing, *Hang the stockings with care. Hang the stockings with care,* so many times, Libby's ears rang and her head was about to explode.

"I should go with the children to put them to sleep." Maybe she could sneak into her room before any more questions were asked.

Before she could move, Colleen patted her arm. "That's all right. Bella will stay with the boys until they are asleep. June will take care of the girls."

"And Cora agreed to take care of the littlest ones."

Of course, she did. The woman wouldn't be happy unless there were babies in the house forever, but at some point, they all would grow up. Look how quickly Charlie was growing. Why, he would be four in February.

Colleen hid a yawn. "Well, then, I believe I'll retire for the night. Children, say good night to your parents and go with Bella and June. And go fast asleep so Santa can come."

Charlie stomped his foot. A tired tantrum was on its way. "But I want Bwad to put me to bed."

Brad knelt before him. "Do you know how special it is to have Bella put you to bed? Why, she put me to bed when I was a small boy like you."

She did? Libby peered beneath the woman's mobcap. If the woman had put Brad to bed, it had to have been when she was still safe in her mother's womb. The woman couldn't be more than eighteen.

Charlie's eyes widened. "She did?"

"Yes. And she did such a good job, I would fall asleep and not wake up until Santa had come." Brad kissed Charlie's cheek. "Now, go upstairs like a big boy and get some sleep. You'll need it for tomorrow. It's a special day."

"'Night, Mama."

Libby leaned over to receive a kiss on the cheek. "'Night, Charlie. Sweet dreams."

Once the children were gone, the noise level dropped dramatically. Colleen tugged on her earlobe. "I think my ears are still ringing."

Sybil stood next to her husband. "I know what you mean." She yawned behind her hand. "I believe it's time for us to retire, David. You know how I am at this stage."

Everyone halted in place. "What do you mean at this stage?" Colleen's eyes sparkled. "Do you mean what I think you mean?"

Sybil nodded. "Due in six months."

David beamed as if he didn't already have two children. Caleb slapped him on the back. Brad offered him a drink, which he refused. Colleen squealed and hugged her sister-in-law. Libby wasn't sure what to do. She only met Sybil this morning. While she liked the woman, she wasn't yet a friend and not family.

Simplest would be best. "Congratulations, Sybil. You, too, David. I can tell you are excited."

"We are." Sybil yawned again. "But tired. So, we'll say our good nights."

When they left the room Brad folded his arms over his chest and stared at his brother. "Well?"

What was that all about? Was Brad expecting news from Caleb and Colleen?

Caleb laughed. "Good heavens, Bradley. We have no news to share." He looked at his wife and raised both eyebrows. "Do we?"

"No, Caleb. We don't. I believe four is quite enough."

"Whew." He wiped a hand across his forehead. "I agree." He helped Colleen from her seat. "I believe it's time we go to our room, too. Those kids are going to be up before the roosters crow. You know how they are on Christmas morning." He bowed at the waist. "Good night, brother. Libby. Have a nice evening."

Libby stood. "I suppose it's time I retire, too. Charlie will be up before the crack of dawn."

"Wait." Brad put a hand on her arm. "We need to talk."

Had she done something wrong? She racked her brain over the events of the day. She'd assisted in getting the rooms situated. Helped with the children. Even though she'd been a nervous wreck, laughed when appropriate. Thought she'd used the correct utensils at dinner. Placed her napkin on her lap. Carried on a conversation. And most of all—didn't pick her nose.

Her stomach clenched. "What's wrong?"

Brad gestured to a red brocade chair before the fire. When she was seated, he pulled the other chair closer. "We have a problem."

He ran his fingers through his hair. She hadn't been lying when she told him he was handsome. Ben had been good-looking, but Brad carried it to another level. He closely resembled James Garner from the Rockford Files. To her, and obviously not to others, his scar only enhanced his looks.

"Is it one of the children? Your brother? Sybil? Is someone sick? Everyone seemed perfectly

healthy tonight." She gasped. "It's Cora, isn't it?"

He shook his head. "No. No one is ill." He ran his hands down his pant legs. "Caleb and David are asking too many questions."

Libby huffed breath and rested her elbows on the arms of the chair. "Must run in the family. So are Colleen and Sybil."

"Because of Charlie?"

She nodded. "Of course, Charlie."

"Is there any way to stop him?"

"Short of following him around all day, no. Besides, I don't want him to forget. What if we can go back to our time?"

"Do you want to?" Brad ran a hand over his mouth. "I don't understand all this time traveling."

"Neither do I. I can honestly say this is a first for me. And I have no idea why or how it happened."

"What if you went back to your time? Do you believe it will bring Ben back to you? He died in this time."

Heavens. Over the past months, she assumed if she went back, Ben would be there. What if he wasn't? What if she went back and people started questioning where he was? What if they thought she killed him and disposed of the body? This was getting more convoluted all the time. She closed her eyes and rested her head on the back of the chair. "I'm so confused." She opened her eyes. Brad held out a glass of sherry, one of the weakest drinks she'd ever had. "May I have some brandy?"

Brad raised an eyebrow. "Really?"

She nodded. "I need something stronger. An old-fashioned would be amazing."

The brandy decanter clinked against a glass. "What's an old-fashioned?"

"A wonderful Wisconsin drink."

"Do you know how to make one?"

Libby chuckled. "I do, but you probably don't have the ingredients for it. So, I'll settle for a plain brandy with a bit of water added." He handed her the glass with three fingers of liquor in it. If she drank all of it, she'd have to be carried to bed. A vision of Brad carrying her in his arms, laying her on her bed, or maybe his bed, flashed through her head.

She stared into the glass. He'd slowly remove her clothes, taking time to learn her body. His body was probably sculpted like a man who works outdoors. She'd seen him work horses, cut wood, clean a horse stall. He believed he should be able to do whatever he asked of his workers.

Her breath hitched, and heat rose to her face. One good thing about poor lighting, blushes were hard to see. Waving her hand in front of her face would be a poor choice, but she sure wanted to. Women used fans, probably to relieve heat from dreaming about men. She didn't have a fan. Couldn't snap one open like they did in movies. She'd probably poke herself in the eye. "Um. Let's get back to your family's questions."

Brad cleared his throat. There was no way he could read her mind. Had she said anything out loud? Could she bury herself in the backyard like Charlie thought his father was?

"Yes. We need to make a decision."

"About what?" The brandy was going down too easily. She set the glass on a side table.

"There are people who are counterfeiting money and bank notes."

"What does that have to do with me?"

"Caleb and David know there is something different about you and Charlie. They think you're harboring a deep secret. Caleb even intimated you're part of the counterfeiting ring and will have you arrested if we don't confess who you are."

Libby leapt from her chair. "What? Why would he think such a thing? He wouldn't really have me arrested, would he?"

"Please, sit down. Not unless we tell him the truth."

"But what if he thinks I'm crazy and sends me to a nut house?" She dropped onto her chair and held back flooding tears.

"Nut house?"

She shook her head. "An asylum. A place where they put crazy people."

"Trust me, I won't let it happen."

"So, you think I should tell them I'm from the future?"

"It certainly would help them understand the things Charlie says and does."

"Your family seems like an intelligent bunch. They aren't going to give up asking questions, are they?"

"Probably not." He downed the remaining brandy in his glass and refilled it. "They were mostly questioning the things Charlie says."

If he continued downing drinks as he was, she'd be carrying him up to bed. Her bed. Stripping— Stop it.

"Hmph. I made the mistake tonight of saying something about a semi." Brad frowned.

"Never mind. I can explain it some other time. Ben and Charlie were so into sports of all kinds and anything on wheels is ingrained in him. There is no way he would forget it."

"Can I assume by *into* you mean they really, really like them?"

"You don't have to assume. Ben lived for the weekends when he could watch football and explain the nuances to Charlie. After the game, they'd go outside and pretend to be a team."

"And I'm going to pretend I know what the hell you're talking about." He returned to his chair. "I reminded Caleb and David about children's active imaginations."

Libby crossed her legs at the ankles like a proper woman when she wanted to hook an ankle over her knee. "I told them the same thing. Do you think they bought it?"

"I highly doubt it."

"What do Caleb's kids say?"

"They love Charlie's stories and ask him for more."

"That's all we need is having them egg him on."

"Egg him on?"

"Make him say more." She raised her glass for a refill. "Go on. What else has he done?"

"Then there's the games he has them play."

She could only imagine. "Like what?"

"The football thing you mentioned. He gets frustrated because he doesn't have the proper... What did he call it?"

"Pigskin?"

Brad snapped his fingers. "That's it." He shook his head. "Then he finds a stick and a small rock and hits it with the stick to something called a goal. He calls it hockey. He was doing it around the dining room the other day until Cora told him to stop."

"Why didn't anyone tell me? I'll talk to him."

"He was having so much fun. In fact, he had Cora doing it until she was laughing so hard she nearly fell over. At least tell him to play his games outside."

Brad picked up a poker, pushed at the logs in the fireplace, and added a few more.

Libby moved closer to the heat. Someday she'll tell Brad about furnaces and central heating. She paused. What did she mean some day? She wanted to go home, didn't she? If she were in Wisconsin in December and the temperatures rose into the fifties, she'd be wearing short sleeved shirts and shorts.

"So?"

What was he asking her? "So, what?"

"What should we do? Should we share your story? Should we tell them Charlie's stories are true?"

If they did, what would happen? If they didn't, what would happen? Would she end up in prison? "Why do we have to tell them anything?"

"Oh, c'mon. You've met my sister. Can you imagine her forgetting her questions? Colleen and Caleb are the same. I'd bet my favorite racehorse, right now the four of them are not in their rooms but talking with each other. Comparing notes. Coming up with ideas which would be downright crazy."

"Crazier than time travel?"

Brad put the poker back in the stand. "You have a point."

"Here's a novel idea. Why don't we tell them the truth?"

His gaze went right through her. "The truth? He can't handle the truth."

Libby snickered and couldn't hide her smile at the famous line he'd quoted.

"What? You think this is funny?"

She shook her head. "No. You just said a line from a movie."

"Movie?"

Libby sighed. "Never mind."

"You keep saying never mind. I'm keeping track of every time you say it." He glanced at her over his glass before taking a sip. "So, you believe we should tell them."

"It's better than Caleb believing I'm a counterfeiter."

"What about the children? Do we tell them?"

"No. They wouldn't understand. And what if they say something to the wrong people? Charlie doesn't know or understand."

"I agree. We find a time tomorrow to tell my siblings and their spouses." He paused, looked into his glass again, and glanced up at her.

"What's wrong now?"

He rolled his head and sighed. "I have more to tell you. It's serious."

"More serious than having to tell people from 1870 I'm from over a hundred and fifty years into the future? I mean we're skipping nearly a century and a half."

"Well, it might be. Cora, Caleb and Colleen, and Sybil and Dave." He took drink. "Well, I'm not sure about Dave, but the rest of them are trying to get us together."

Libby chuckled. "Oh really? I hadn't noticed."

"All right. No need for sarcasm." He grinned. "I want you to know it's not my idea. I haven't said anything to them."

"You don't have to. It's pretty obvious."

"Well, they're not known for their subtlety."

"So, what do they think?"

He set his glass down on the side table. "There is something between us, and I should marry you. Evidently, there is talk out there about a widow living with a widower."

Libby snorted. "And don't they realize how chaperoned we are? And again. Why should we care what people think when they don't know the truth? I just lost my husband and had a baby. Like I'm going to jump into bed with the first man who comes along! People are too narrow-minded and nosy."

"Is it the same in the future? I mean, do people keep their noses out of other people's business?"

Once again, she snorted. "Not hardly. I guess some things never change."

Brad let out a breath and ran his fingers through his thick hair. "I believe we should tell them together so we each know what the other told them."

"Keep our stories straight?"

He took a seat beside her where his knee brushed against her leg. Even through her layers of petticoats and her dress, his heat sent a rush of unwanted feelings racing through her. What was wrong with her today when a simple, innocent brush of his leg sent her libido into overdrive? She moved away from him. No sense in inviting something she shouldn't.

"Let's think about this a minute and get it over with."

"You certainly know them better than I do. What do you think their reaction will be?

Brad shrugged. "Damned if I know."

Chapter Nineteen

Colleen brushed a non-existent wrinkle from her full skirt. Instead of heading to their respective rooms, they'd decided to talk in the dining room. "What do you think they're discussing?"

"Could be anything." Caleb took a sip of his whiskey. "Brad's been acting rather strange ever since he rescued Libby and her family. He's hiding something."

"Well, I think he's in love with her." Sybil smirked. "And her family. To think he delivered Lucy. He must have been scared to death."

Caleb snorted. "What make you think he's in love with her? She's only been here eight months."

Sybil tapped her fan against her palm. "I don't know. Even though, until tonight, he wore his stupid mask, there is something about the way he moves toward her. He always seems to be aware of where she is."

Her husband frowned. "How can you tell? I sure didn't notice anything."

"Me, neither," Caleb added.

"I think I know what you mean, Sybil. Maybe it's something only women can see."

Sybil turned to her sister-in-law. "And when she wasn't in the room, and he had his mask off..."

"Yes!" Colleen squealed. "Whenever her name was mentioned, his eyes lit up, even when he denied any feelings for her."

Sybil grabbed Colleen's hand. "Oh, my goodness. I nearly burst my stays trying not to laugh at his reaction."

"David," Caleb tipped his glass toward the women. "Do you have any idea what they are talking about?"

"No idea, my friend." He slapped his brother-in-law on the shoulder. "I think women have some sort of third eye noticing things us poor men can't."

"And don't want to."

Colleen pursed her lips. "Well, I can't imagine why they felt it was necessary to go off by themselves while we are here. Seems rather rude."

"Since we've ruled out marriage and we can't think of anything else they could be talking about, we should simply wait until they are done." Caleb went behind his wife and patted her shoulder.

Sybil stood and brushed out her skirt. "They've been in there quite a while. Since they aren't married, I believe we should check on them."

David chuckled. "You only want to eavesdrop."

"Well. Of course." She took her husband's arm. "Let's go."

Brad sighed. "Since they all went to bed, we'll have to do this in the morning." He held out his hand for Libby and helped her rise. Her hand trembled. "Nervous?"

"A little. What will they think I am? A witch? A liar? An occultist?"

"A what?"

"Never mind. They will probably have me committed somewhere."

"I won't let them. Besides, my family is more open-minded than most."

Brad placed her hand in the crook of his arm then put a finger to his lips. "Wait a minute. I hear something outside the door. Don't you?"

Libby cocked her ear to the door. "Sounds a bit like panting. Is your dog outside waiting for you?"

He yanked the door open. "What the hell is going on here?"

His sister toppled into the room, landing in a pile of petticoats. David tripped into her with Colleen and Caleb following. If Brad hadn't stepped to the side, he and Libby would be on the floor flailing among the arms, legs, boots, slippers, and cuss words filling the air.

He chuckled. "Should we leave them to their own devices, or help them up?"

Libby tapped a finger against her smile. "I wouldn't know where to begin." She chortled. "I mean, what if we pull up a hand thinking it was Sybil when it was actually Caleb?"

"I can't tell the difference. Why don't we let them sort it out?"

"Dammit, Bradley John Kemble." Sybil, at the bottom of the pile, screeched at him. "If you don't help us, I'll never speak to you again."

"Promises, promises."

Libby laughed. It was good to know siblings fought in 1870 like they did in her time. Some things never changed. She stood to the side as Brad gave Caleb, then David, a hand up. He let them help their wives.

Brad closed the door, leaned against it, and folded his arms over his chest. "What were you guys doing?"

"Um." Sybil patted her frazzled hair in place. "Why. Nothing. We were just..."

"Eavesdropping?" Brad shook a finger at his sister. "I know you, Billy. You were nosy as a child, and you're no different as an adult."

Sybil stomped her foot and glared at her husband. "Are you going to let him talk to me like that? We were only passing by."

"He's only speaking the truth, Sweetheart. You do tend to stick your nose in places where it doesn't belong."

"Well. I never." Sybil jabbed a finger in her husband's chest. "I didn't see you or Colleen or Caleb walking past the door. You were right behind me."

Colleen held up a hand. "It doesn't matter. We didn't hear anything, anyway. But we do want to ask you," she nodded at Libby, "a few questions."

Libby's heart sank. By Colleen's tone, she was going to be grilled. Maybe it was time to take the upper hand. "Why don't we all be seated again?" Brad stood by the fireplace, resting his arm on the mantle. At least she would be able to see him as she told a tale no one would ever believe. She took a deep breath, but before she could say one word, Brad spoke.

"We're going to tell you something. It can never leave this room." One by one, he glanced at his family. "You have to promise Libby and me." He raised an eyebrow at Sybil who sighed.

"I promise."

"We all do," Caleb added.

Brad stood next to her chair and patted her shoulder. What she wouldn't give to lean into him and let him absorb her fears. Let his strength flow through her veins. It was the same, yet different, from her husband. There'd been times when, without saying a word, Ben's presence calmed her, as if he'd taken on whatever was bothering her.

Caleb cleared his throat. "So, what is it you want to tell us?"

"You promise not to interrupt until we're done?"

Sybil shook her head. "Depends on what you're going to say."

"I guess it's all I can ask of you, but it would be better if you kept your questions to yourselves for now."

Dave poured a round of drinks. "Well, get on with it before we fall asleep waiting. I, for one, am exhausted."

Brad squeezed her shoulder. It didn't pass notice from the reaction by Brad's family. Their quick glances at each other. Sybil's smirk. Caleb's wink at his wife. They probably thought she and Brad were going to announce their engagement or something else crazy.

"I believe you all know the story of how I found Libby, her husband, and their son in their carriage the day of the strange storm."

Caleb chuckled. "You mean the one *you* encountered on the way from our place? The one which didn't drop a single leaf from the trees in my yard as well as from the driveway to the road?"

"That would be the one. And you know damn well there was a storm as you helped me cut up the fallen tree in the road."

Colleen tapped her husband on the hand. "Dear, we know your thoughts on the storm, let Bradley continue." She nodded to her brother-in-law. "And we know about delivering Lucy and taking care of Charlie."

"And burying Libby's husband," Sybil added.

"So, what we don't know," David sat on the arm of Sybil's chair, "is why all the secrecy? Why haven't Libby and her children returned to her home?"

"If you'd all be quiet, Libby can tell you."

Libby wiped her shaking hands on her dress. Here went nothing. Either they'd accept her story or have her locked up. Who would raise her children? She bit her bottom lip. "The reason I'm still here is I don't have a home to go to. I'm not from here."

"We know you aren't from around here, but how do you know you don't have a home anymore? And Cora says you haven't written to anyone nor have received any letters from your family. Surely, you have family where you're from."

"I knew it was too much to ask them just to listen," Brad muttered under his breath.

Libby stood and walked to the fireplace, said a short prayer, and faced the people whose expectant faces watched her. "When I say I am not from here, I mean I'm not from 1870. I'm from the year 2024."

The room was dead silent. Why wasn't anyone saying anything? Where was the denial? The laughter? The derision? A straight jacket?

David finally shook his head and wiggled a finger in his ear. "Could you repeat what you said? I think my ears quit working."

"If yours quit working, then so did mine." Caleb pointed a finger at Libby. "Did you say you're from two thousand and twenty-four?"

"I did."

"But... But..." Colleen put a hand to her lips. "That's..." She closed her eyes. "One hundred and fifty-four years from now. It's not possible."

Sybil jumped to her feet, ignoring the sherry splashing from her glass onto her dress. "Why, that's crazy. Bradley, you can't keep a crazy woman in your house."

Libby blinked back her tears. It was as she figured. They thought she was crazy. "I—"

Brad held up his hand. The desire to pull Libby into his arms and wipe the tears from her face was strong. If Sybil thought Libby shouldn't be in his house, what would she think if he hugged her? "Wait. Hear us out. I didn't believe it at first, either. Traveling through time was impossible. But there's been too much proof she is telling the truth."

"You've heard Brad's version of what happened, now let me tell you the story from my point of view."

Libby's instant composure solidified his idea of her strength. He couldn't think of any other woman who could have gone through what she had and not gone off the deep end. The longer she lived in his home, the more his admiration of her grew.

"My husband, Charlie, and I were driving from Wisconsin to West Virginia for a Civil War Reenactment."

"Why—"

Brad gave his brother a glare.

"Sorry." Caleb tipped his head at Libby. "Go on."

"Out of nowhere this strange storm came up. The radio went out. The car shook. The air turned freezing cold."

Caleb held up a hand. "Wait. What did you say you were driving? What's a radio?"

Colleen patted her husband's leg. "Caleb. What did Brad say? Let Libby finish her story. We can ask questions later."

Caleb huffed a breath and clamped his mouth shut. "Oh, all right. I'll try."

"Anyway, Ben lost control of the car and we started spinning. Luckily, Charlie was in his car seat and I had my seat belt on, so we weren't thrown out. I don't know how. I don't know why, but somehow when I woke, we were here. Because he wasn't wearing a seatbelt, Ben was thrown from the car and ended up beneath the buggy."

If he hadn't been worried about their reaction, Brad would have laughed at the four people simultaneously drinking from their glasses, eyeing each other in speculation. "It's the truth. While I don't understand how it happened, I was there to help them."

Caleb set his glass on a side table. "Can we ask questions now?"

"Sure." Libby took a sip of her wine. "Fire away."

"What about what you said about your husband flying out of the car? What hadn't he worn?"

"Seatbelts."

His brother ran a hand over his face. "You sound like Charlie when he starts talking strange."

"So, you believe me?"

Caleb shook his head. "It'll take more than your story for us to believe you."

"Traveling through time seems like something out of one of those books by Jules Verne you read. Something about traveling inside the Earth. Crazy talk." Sybil gave Libby a sideways glance. "It sounds... Well, it sounds..."

"Crazy?" Libby finished for her.

"Well, yes. Don't you think so?"

Libby slapped fists on her knees. "Of course, I do. Can you imagine how I feel? Why do you think Brad and I haven't said anything? When

Charlie talks about phones and television and cars, people can say he has a three-year-old's imagination, but when an adult says the same things, you say they are crazy. At least you haven't put me in a strait jacket yet or called the police."

For a few minutes no one said anything. What was his family thinking? Did they believe Libby? At least he had proof he could pull out if necessary. "Well?"

Sybil was first to break the silence. "Is this why you can't go home?"

"Nor why I haven't written to anyone. They haven't been born, yet."

Colleen raised a finger. "Wait, if your husband is dead in our time, does it mean you and Charlie are dead in your time?"

Brad hadn't thought about it. Had Libby?

"I don't know what to think. I've gone over this again and again." Libby twisted her hands in her lap. "I have no idea why or how I'm here, nor what to do about it."

David refilled glasses. "If you could, would you go back to your time?"

Brad held his breath. It was something he'd thought of at night when he couldn't get to sleep. Libby, Charlie, and Lucy had become an integral part of his life. What would he do if, somehow, she could go forward in time?

"I don't know. I miss my husband, but what if I go back and he's dead there, too?"

"At least you'd have family." Colleen accepted a glass of sherry from David. "Wouldn't you?"

Libby nodded making Brad's heart sink. She obviously would go back. And he'd return to his miserable, lonely life. Belinda Castlewood's face popped into his head. As much as she wanted him, he would never be desperate or lonely enough to fall for her fake charms.

Caleb put an arm around Colleen's shoulders. "I'm not sure I believe you. I mean, Charlie has some whopper stories, but like I said, kids have amazing imaginations."

Brad opened a desk drawer, took out a stack of papers, and handed them to Caleb, who glanced at them, and passed them on. "How do you explain these?"

"I would agree Charlie is creative, but it doesn't prove anything."

"Charlie is not just creative. These drawings show things from the future. Cars. Airplanes. Telephones." She pointed to each picture. "And here. Here is a picture of a spaceship."

Once again no one said anything.

Sybil rose and stood by her husband by the fireplace. "This doesn't make sense. It's so unreal."

"Tell me about it."

Sybil frowned. "Tell you about what?"

"Never mind. It's a saying from my time." Libby nodded at Brad. "You might as well show them the rest."

"Are you sure?"

"It's the only way they'll believe me. Obviously, they don't believe Charlie's pictures."

Brad pushed a button on the side of the fireplace. A wall to the right swung open to reveal a large safe in a hidden room. The first time he had shown her the hidden wall, she'd been thrilled. She'd read about hidden rooms but had never seen one. She'd insisted on his showing her all the ones in the house. Five small rooms cleverly hidden.

Not wanting Cora or anyone else to find her satchel in the attic, they'd decided to keep her belongings in the safe. Would they prove the truth of what she was to them?

After spinning the dial a few times, he tugged open the safe, removed her wallet, and handed it to her.

"This is my driver's license." At their blank looks she explained. "You have to have a special license in order to operate any vehicle." She stood and handed it to Caleb. "See. Here is my birthdate and the year it expires."

"Two thousand and two thousand ten?" He passed the card to David. "Impossible."

"Not to mention, her picture and the writing is in color." David held the card over a lamp. "And what is this strange mark here?"

"It's a special image called a hologram to keep people from making fake ones. Not that it helps any." She pulled some dollar bills from her wallet. "And here. This is our money. See the date? Nineteen ninety-two."

Colleen squinted at the dollar bill. "George Washington?"

"Yes. And Abraham Lincoln is on the five-dollar bill." Unfortunately, she didn't have any larger bills to show them. "And here is a credit card. Instead of using money, we use this card to charge things. Each month you get a bill to pay."

Caleb took the card from her. "So, you don't need money?"

"For some people, it's all they use, but some merchants only accept cash because they have to pay a fee to the bank for each customer transaction."

"Do people counterfeit them?" Caleb gave the card back to her.

Where did she start? There was no way she could explain computers, the internet, the dark web, identify theft. A simple answer was always the best. "Yes. It's awful."

Brad shook his head. "Some things never change."

Libby frowned. "What do you mean?"

"It's a story for another time."

Based on her knowledge of Civil War history and the period after, she assumed he meant all the money being counterfeited. Of course, it wasn't confined to this time period. Fake money had been made as far back as 400 BC by the Greeks covering less valuable coins with a layer of precious metal. But this was not the time to give them a history lesson.

Sybil pointed at the safe. "What else is in there?"

"Some of my clothing."

"Oooh. Can Colleen and I see?"

Brad shook his head. "Another time. It's getting late and the monsters will be up before we know it. We can talk more tomorrow."

David collected their glasses and put them on a tray. "C'mon, Sybil. Brad is right. It's going to be wild in the morning, and we need our wits about us."

"We have to put the presents under the tree first." Sybil stood and put her hand through the crook of his elbow. "Good night, everyone."

Caleb faced Libby. "We have a lot to think about, but whatever we decide, we'll keep what we talked about tonight to ourselves. Let's go, dear. Good night, Brad. Libby."

Libby sighed. "What do you think? Do they believe me?"

"They'll think about it and hash it over among themselves. I know my family. They are fair-minded and, based on what we showed them tonight, they'll have to believe us." Brad returned her things to the safe and Charlie's papers to his desk. "Do you have anything to put under the tree?"

"Yes. I have the doll for Lucy and wagon for Charlie you purchased for me." Huh. Since she had no money, he'd purchased them. "I don't know how I'll pay you back for them."

"Don't worry about it. Put Santa's name on it."

It went against her grain, but she had no choice. "Thank you."

"Let's get them so we can get some shut eye."

Libby followed him from the room to another hidden door in the dining room. A perfect place to hide things. Brad pushed against the edge of the door and stepped back when it swung open. She gasped. There were more than the wagon and doll in there. "Where did the doll cradle come from?"

Brad shrugged. "I made it for Lucy. She may be too little to play with it now, but it won't be long and she will be old enough."

"Oh. It's beautiful." She ran a finger over the scroll work similar to the cradle Lucy slept in. "And this?" She pointed to a wooden tricycle.

"I remade my old one."

"Amazing. Charlie is going to love it."

"I hope so."

"I know so." Libby picked up the doll and the blanket she'd made. "Let's get this done."

Presents were already under the eight-foot tree in the living room. It took them a bit to reorganize so they could fit their gifts beneath it.

"Oh, my. It's going to be crazy tomorrow morning."

"I have to admit, I'm going to enjoy it to the fullest. It's been a long time since there's been a Christmas celebration in this house."

Libby nudged the cradle with her toe. "Why?"

"As I told you, before I bought this house, it was the Carlisles.' Our families were good friends, so we spent a lot of holidays here. I bought it when Lucinda and I were married, but we always went to Caleb and Colleen's. It was easier for two people to go to a house filled with kids than for them to come here. After her death," he shrugged. "I didn't see the point in celebrating, so I would usually go over Christmas Eve, then come home."

"You spent Christmas alone?"

"I couldn't face all the celebrations."

Libby swept her hands down her dress. "Well, thank you for your help tonight."

"It was my pleasure." He followed her, then stopped beneath the door frame and glanced up.

"What?"

He pointed. She swallowed hard. Mistletoe. Was he going to do what she thought? Should she let him? She still missed Ben, but the missing wasn't as painful. Sometimes she had to think hard to picture him in her mind. She loved him, but what if she were stuck in 1870 for the rest of her life? And what if she hadn't been sent here and he'd died in their time? Would she have remained a widow focusing on raising her children by herself?

Brad lowered his hand and took hold of her fingers. "I know it hasn't been a year, but I've come to enjoy your being in my house. I've come to love your children. I admire you. I think about you all the time. When I'm working in the barn, the fields, or my office. You're the last thing I think about at night and the first thing in the morning. It's been a long time since I've looked forward to a new day."

Wow. She hadn't expected this. Looking deeply into his eyes, something shifted. Her heart raced. Shivers ran up and down her spine settling in her lower region, someplace she thought she'd have to forget about with Ben being gone. She smiled. "I have no idea who came up with the idea people needed to wait a year before they moved on after the death of a spouse."

"Probably some spinster or a minister set on ruining people's happiness."

"Well, since we are neither of those things," She put her hands on his shoulders. "Let's make use of the mistletoe."

The closer his head came to hers, the more her heart fluttered. When his lips met hers, her legs nearly gave out. His lips were soft. Warm. No. *Hot*. The heat spiraled clear down to her toes. Never had she thought another man would make her body react this way. Like she wanted to throw him down on the floor and have her wicked way with him. Luckily, before she did such an embarrassing thing, he stepped back.

Brad released a breath. "Wow."

"Wow is right." Would her heart ever stop racing like a hummingbird's wings?

"I'd best see you to your room."

"*What?*" Had he meant what it sounded like he did? She frowned up at him.

"Wait. That came out all wrong." He raked his fingers through his hair. "I didn't mean... I mean... I don't expect..."

Libby giggled. "Don't worry. I know you didn't mean anything by it. While your kiss nearly sent me to the moon..."

He lifted an eyebrow. "In one of Charlie's rocket ships?"

She giggled again. "Yes. I'm not ready for anything more. I need to figure out if I'll be sent back to my time."

"I understand." He bowed. "Well, m'lady. Let's go to our respective rooms."

Brad followed Libby up the stairs, trying to keep his eyes off her swaying hips. Their kiss was an act of heroism on his part. He'd kept it light, simple. Once his lips met hers, he wanted to deepen it. Taste her essence. Throw her on the floor and have his wicked way with her. It took everything he had not to. Thus—he was a hero. Right?

At her door she stopped and smiled at him. "'Night, Brad. See you in the morning."

He cupped her cheek. "'Night, Libby. Sweet dreams."

He entered his room and flung himself back on his bed. He thought he couldn't sleep before. Now, knowing what it was like to kiss her, it would be impossible.

Without warning, another emotion struck him. Guilt. How could he feel as if he'd been catapulted through the air when he still loved Lucinda? Was it possible to fall in love with this much passion twice in a man's life?

A flicker of light came from the corner of his room. The translucent body of a woman appeared.

"Lucinda?"

The woman nodded.

"I'm sorry I kissed Libby."

She shook head and patted her heart.

"Yes. I still love you, Lucinda, but I'm also falling in love with Libby. I'm sorry."

Lucinda shook her head again and mouthed *no*.

"No, I shouldn't fall in love with Libby?" This was frustrating. What was she trying to tell him?

She floated to his mirror. Words began to appear. *Don't be sorry. Fall in love again. No guilt. I'll always be in your heart, but there's room for more. Have children. Love you. Be happy. Goodbye.*

Before he could respond, the words disappeared as she floated from the room. He wiped at the tears flowing down his cheeks. His heart filled with something he at first couldn't identify. Then it came to him. Peace? Love? Happiness?

Now all he had to do was figure out how to keep his hands off Libby until she was ready. Or until she left. Would it be wrong of him to pray she stayed in his time?

Chapter Twenty

As Caleb came into the room, Brad tossed down his mail on the desk, leaving one particular, irritating note on the top. It was two days after Christmas, and except for an occasional giggle from Charlie and Lucy, the house was quiet and back to normal.

"Why the scowl?"

"What are you doing here? I thought you and your pack of rapscallions had gone home."

Caleb handed him a note. "Did you get one of these?"

Brad huffed a breath. "Yeah. What do you think?"

"I think Belinda is holding a New Year's Eve ball to try to get her clutches in you."

"Fat chance."

"You know she wants this property back. The only way she is going to get it is by either marrying you or getting rid of you."

"Yeah. The thought crossed my mind. I have to be careful when I ride into town. How she knows when I'll be there is beyond me. But I have a hunch."

"About what? Do you know something I don't?"

Brad shrugged. "Maybe. When I was in town last week, I saw her sitting in Smith's Restaurant with a man. If you ask me, they were a bit cozy."

"Did you recognize him?"

"Although he seemed familiar, I couldn't place him." He shook his head. "But there was something about him setting me on edge. Are you and Colleen going to attend the ball?"

"I think so. You and Libby need to go, too."

"Libby's name isn't on the invitation."

"Too bad. I have this gut feeling there is something going on I'm going to call in a few men to keep an eye on her."

Brad tapped the invitation. "Do you think it has anything to do with the counterfeiting?"

"I don't know. But for someone who has lost everything, she sure is living the high life. How can she afford to buy her house and hold a ball? Where is she getting her money?"

"The man you saw her with?"

"Possibly." Caleb put the invitation in his inside coat pocket. "Do you think Libby will mind going to a ball?"

"A ball? Did you say something about attending a ball?"

Libby stood in the doorway looking as fetching in her simple yellow blouse tucked into a blue skirt as a woman all decked on in her best finery. His heart skipped a beat. "I got an invitation from Belinda Carlisle for a New Year's Eve ball."

"Are you going?"

Brad couldn't help grinning at how she narrowed her eyes. Jealousy? "Not without you, I'm not."

"But I won't know anyone."

Caleb eyed them. "Colleen and I are going, so you can visit with us."

"I don't know how to do your dances."

Caleb folded his arms over his chest. "And what type of dances would those be? What dances do you do in your time?"

Was Caleb hinting he believed her, or was he simply being as ass?

"There are so many different ones, I couldn't begin to tell you them all. I can do the slow dance, polka, two step, but not much else."

"Polka I recognize." Would they have time to teach her other ones? What about the quadrille? The country dance? "I guess we'll have to practice every day. Would Colleen be able to come over and help us?" He'd need a buffer between him and Libby. Holding her close would be a problem. Not so much the quadrilles and other square dances, but the waltz.

"I believe she could get away. I'll ask her. When do you want to start?"

"If I'm to be believed that I know what I'm doing, as soon as possible."

Caleb sent a sly grin at Brad. "Maybe you two could start with the waltz. I'll send Colleen over tomorrow."

He knew darn well what he was up to. Could he stick his tongue out at his brother? "But who will be her partner? We need at least four dancers."

Caleb let out an exaggerated sigh. "I *suppose* I could dance with my wife if I *had* to."

"You'd better not let Colleen hear you say it like that."

"You're not going to tell her, are you, Bradley John?"

Brad chuckled. "Of course not."

"Don't you enjoy dancing, Caleb?"

"Of course I do. Especially with my lovely wife. We were referring to our mother forcing us to dance with girls at a time when we thought all girls were disgusting."

Libby giggled. "Guess things haven't changed."

Brad raised an eyebrow. "Boys still think girls are horrible until they realize they have better attributes? Girls think the same about boys?"

"Yep."

"I'd better let Colleen know what's going on." Caleb chuckled. "And I'll have my men keep an eye on things."

When his brother was gone, Libby crossed her arms and stared at Brad.

"What?"

"I want to know what's going on. I heard a bit of your discussion. Something about counterfeiting. Watching out for things."

"I don't want you involved."

"Since my children and I are living here, if there is any type of danger, I should know about it. Be able to take precautions."

Brad raked his fingers through his hair and huffed out a breath. "You're right. Caleb and I have been asked to help find some counterfeiters working in the area."

"By whom?"

"By the Secret Service. Since the end of the war, at least a third of money printed has been fake and is causing instability in the country's finances. We're concerned a lot of it is taking place in our area."

"What does that have to do with this Belinda's ball?"

"As you know, this farm used to belong to Belinda's family. After her father passed, she was more interested in dances and buying fancy doodads than running the farm. Eventually, she sold off her slaves, and I bought the land. She barely had enough to pay off her creditors."

Libby bit her bottom lip. "Let me guess. She's been trying to get you to marry her so she can have access to your money."

"I knew you were a smart woman. Every time I go into town or church, I have to keep a constant watch out for her. Once I even caught her heading upstairs."

"I'm sure she heard about the woman staying here and wanted to find out about me."

Brad nodded. "Or to warn you off."

"So, what does this have to do with the ball?"

"She's broke. I know she's broke." Brad rubbed the back of his neck. "So where did she get the money to put on a ball? I know it's another ploy to get me into her bed so I have to marry her."

"Do you want to marry her?"

"Hell, I mean, heck no!" Brad paced in front of the fireplace. "For one thing, she's not my type. For another, she'd bleed me dry within a year. Possibly less. And I don't only mean financially. She has a way of making a man feel inferior, while at the same time pretending to make him feel as if he were ten feet tall."

"So, you and Caleb believe she might be making fake money?"

Brad chuckled. "She doesn't have the brains to do it on her own. She has to have some accomplices. The other day I saw her with another man in a restaurant in town. They seemed pretty cozy. And how could she afford to buy the mansion in town?"

"I don't see the problem. At least she's not bothering you."

"True. I thought I recognized him, but I couldn't figure out from where. When I looked at him, I had flashes of the war, so it might have been from then."

"Was it something good?"

Brad shook his head. "No. I just wish I could recall."

"Maybe you're trying too hard."

"And maybe being at the ball will trigger something."

Libby tipped her head to the side. "So, I heard you say my name wasn't on the invitation. Do you think it's a good idea for me to show up?"

"You'll be arriving on my arm, so no one will dare question it. Besides Belinda, no one will know you weren't invited, and I need someone to protect me from the woman."

"And how do you expect me to do that?"

"Don't leave me alone or Belinda will latch onto me like a leech and won't let me go."

Libby giggled then huffed a deep sigh. "I guess I'll have to protect you at all costs. What an awful way to spend an evening."

"You're a smart aleck, aren't you?"

"So, I've been told." She stood, stopped before him, and ran a finger down his lapel. "So, when do we start the dancing lessons?"

Holding Libby in his arms and teaching her the steps? His arm around her waist? Maybe her breasts pressed against his chest? Not soon enough. "Tonight."

Chapter Twenty-One

The week between Christmas and New Year's Eve went by in a flash. Too fast. Every moment spent in Brad's arms as he taught her the various dances was special. Every moment made her return home less desirable. Charlie no longer asked about Ben, and, of course, Lucy had no idea who he was.

Butterflies filled her stomach. This would be the first time since ending up here when she'd be out in public. According to Cora, speculation about the woman with two children staying at Bradley's was rampant. Every time the housekeeper went into town, she came back with stories of people trying to get information from her. Well, tonight, they'd find out.

Libby tried to breathe. Even though she rarely wore a corset, the few times she had to, made sure she hated them. Bras had nothing on these torture contraptions. She turned sideways to view herself in the full-length, cheval mirror and patted her flat stomach. Even without a corset, her stomach had returned to its pre-pregnancy form.

Since she was going out in public, it was necessary to don widow's weeds. It was bad enough she was attending a ball, but if she wore any other color, it would create a scandal for Brad.

The bodice of the black dress wasn't deep and the lace attached to it covered a good portion of her chest. Whoever came up with the idea for women to wear black when a loved one died, wasn't a redhead with fair skin. Black was not her color. Even so, she wasn't used to having so much skin exposed. She turned sideways again and giggled. The bustle on the back of the dress made up for the lack of material in the bodice. Living in an era when women worried about their backsides being too big, it was funny to wear something to give the illusion of a large one.

She had to admit, even though it was black, the various layers of material were quite feminine and attractive. The long sleeves would help her stay warm. Too bad it had taken nearly thirty minutes for Cora to dress her in the multitude of undergarments and dress material. How many times would someone step on the short train attached to the bustle? No wonder Cora had put a small sewing kit in her small handbag. Hopefully, she wouldn't have to use it, for how in heaven's name would she be able to fix it without having to disrobe?

Cora came into the room carrying a black cape over her arm. "This was Miss Lucinda's and will be short on you, but I'm sure it'll be fine for tonight. Since it's not meant to go to the ground, it won't make a difference." She set the wrap, a pair of gloves, and a hat on the bed. "Now, all we have to do is take care of your hair. I used to do Miss Lucinda's all the time, but if you'd rather do it yourself..."

Libby bit back a laugh. Do her own hair? In the time she'd been here, she barely managed to put her hair in a bun so it wouldn't come loose after an hour. At least no one said anything about her daily French braids. "I would be grateful if you would do my hair, Cora." But how was she going to sit in her dress? Maybe if she lifted the bustle? She crossed the room to the stool before the dressing table. Actually, now would be a good time to practice as there was no way she'd stand all night.

Lifting the bustle, she lowered herself to the stool. The heaviness of the fabric flowing over the stool nearly sent her toppling backward. If Cora hadn't been standing behind her, she would have.

"Be careful, Miss Libby. I know you haven't worn a fancy dress since coming here, but you must remember not to flip the bustle so far back. At least there will be chairs to sit on tonight, so you shouldn't have a problem sitting down."

Thank goodness for small favors. Libby stood, eased the bustle over the back of the stool, and sat. Whew. She'd done it.

Watching Cora was like watching an artist at work. In no time at all, the housekeeper had her hair in a fancy updo, weaving a few springs of mistletoe through the tresses while leaving a couple of tendrils flowing down her cheeks.

"You did an amazing job, Cora."

"Thank you, my dear." Cora tucked a stray curl into her hair. "I love working with your hair. It's so thick and curly."

Libby laughed. "I always thought my curly hair was a curse. Never wants to do what I want it to."

Cora patted her black, curly hair. "It's why I keep mine short. Plus, it's cooler in the summer."

"I agree." Since Cora wasn't aware of who Libby was, she couldn't talk about air conditioning in homes and vehicles. After the summer, it was one of the things she missed the most. Besides Ben, of course.

Libby stared into the mirror. Besides fair skin which burned easily, another problem with red hair was light eyebrows and lashes. She was never one to wear much makeup, but mascara was always a must. Even though she knew where her mascara was, it was so old, it was probably goopy and gummy. She sighed. "I need something to put on my eyelashes. I hate how I can't see them."

Cora bit her lip then snapped her fingers. "I have an idea." She went to the fireplace, swiped a finger on the inside, and came back to Libby. "Face me. Now don't blink or I'll get ashes on your face."

Sitting as still as possible and holding her breath so she wouldn't blink, Cora touched her sooty finger against her lashes as gently as butterfly's wing. After ministering to each eye, she stepped back and wiped her finger on her apron.

"What do you think?"

Libby spun on the bench and stared into the mirror. Her eyes, once seeming tiny, now, with the black soot, looked large. "What a wonderful idea, Cora. I love it."

"So will Mr. Bradley."

She shouldn't worry about what he thought, but her comment made her heart skitter. He'd never seen her so dolled up. Would he like what he saw?

A light rap sounded on her bedroom door. "It's Brad. May I come in?"

Libby looked at Cora and raised an eyebrow. Even though he'd been in her room right after she'd arrived, he hadn't crossed the doorstep since. Men didn't usually go into a woman's bedroom alone unless they were married or living together. Before she could answer, Cora pulled the door open.

"Of course, you can come in, Mr. Bradley. I'm done fancying Miss Libby up." Without another word, she left the room and closed the door behind her.

Libby's breath caught. On a daily basis, she couldn't get over how handsome Brad was. Except during Christmas when he wore dress pants, shirt, and vest, she'd never seen him wear anything more than a work shirt, and heavy denim pants held up with suspenders.

Tonight, he wore dark dress pants, and a white shirt with a brocade vest nearly matching the color of her dress. The shirt had a wing-tip collar with the points tipping down over his black bowtie. If memory served her right, the striped, black waist-length coat with long, tapering tails in the back was called a tailcoat. The lapels were nearly as shiny as his boots. A pair of white gloves were tucked into a tailcoat pocket.

The overall effect had her heart palpitating so hard, she thought it would nearly split her corset in two. Her mouth went dry. Good heavens. Why didn't men dress like this anymore? If they knew how women nearly swooned if a man dressed in 1800s attire, they'd wear the outfit to bed.

Brad cleared his throat. His Adam's apple bobbed up and down several times. Was he as nervous as she?

"I know this isn't quite appropriate, but I wanted to give you something." He took a long box from an inside coat pocket. "It was my mother's." He opened the box and removed a gold necklace. "May I put it on you?"

"Of course." Her voice quivered, which was nothing compared to her body being ready to melt as he reached around her and placed the necklace around her neck. The light from dresser lamp reflected off the royal blue, oval stone dipping to the top of the dress' neckline. Four smaller, matching stones were strategically located on each side.

Brad's warm breath puffed against her bare neck. In the reflection in the mirror, his head disappeared behind her as he struggled to close the clasp.

Libby fingered the oval stone. When the necklace was closed, he placed his hands on her shoulders sending delicious shivers down her spine. "Oh, Brad. It's beautiful, but it's your mother's. I can't possibly wear it."

"Not as beautiful as you."

He leaned down. Was he going to kiss her shoulder? Her neck? Good thing he couldn't see her wobbly knees beneath the layers of her dress. Her skin was hot. Unfortunately, he took a step back.

"Please wear it. It's been sitting in my dresser for far too long." He pointed at the mirror. "And it goes perfectly with your dress."

Had Lucinda ever worn it?

As if he read her mind, he turned her to face him. "Besides my mother, no other woman has worn this." He lifted the stone, brushing his fingers against her heated skin. "I had many others more suited to Lucinda. I was saving this for when we had a daughter. If you're uncomfortable with it, wear it for tonight and give it back to me."

"Fair enough. Thank you, Brad. I'll be proud to wear it."

"Now, my dear. I believe it's time to leave. My carriage is waiting." He picked up her cape and gloves from the bed and waved a hand to the door. "After you."

Libby snatched up her handbag and a hat matching the cape. With his hand at her lower back, they went down the stairs. Cora waited at the bottom to fasten her hat before Brad helped her with her cape.

He winged out an arm. "Take my arm. It might be slippery."

Chapter Twenty-Two

The drive to pick up Caleb and Colleen was short, but long enough for Brad to regale her with stories of some of the people who would probably be in attendance, making her laugh and ease some of the nerves rampaging through her.

Since her name hadn't been on the invitation, would Belinda have her thrown out? Would she remember all the dance steps? What if someone else asked her to dance and she stepped on his toes? What if she spilled punch on herself or someone else? What if she couldn't lift her dress to use the bathroom?

Brad patted her hand. "Quit worrying. You'll be fine."

"How did you know I was worrying?"

He chuckled. "Those two little lines in the middle of your forehead are a dead giveaway."

Great, now she had to worry about worry lines in her forehead.

"Don't fret. No matter what, you are beautiful. The men are all going to want to dance with you, and the women will be jealous."

"Do you think Belinda will be jealous?"

"Oh. Most definitely."

"Do you think she'll do anything to me?"

Brad shrugged. "She'd better not. The only thing I can visualize is her trying to occupy my time. Maybe say some sarcastic remarks to you." He squeezed her fingers. "I am fully confident you will be able to handle her. The best thing is to not be alone with her."

Great. Add another thing she needed to agonize over. The list was getting longer and longer.

Joshua pulled behind a line of buggies waiting to discharge its passengers. As each buggy moved out of line and theirs came closer to the entrance of the massive two-story structure, her nerves grew. Finally, it was their turn. Brad exited first and held out his hand to her.

Getting into the carriage hadn't been too bad, but getting out was going to be a challenge. How did one hold onto a dress with a bustle, her small handbag, and Brad's hand without toppling head over heels to the ground? She took a peek out the door. Thankfully, it seemed no one was paying attention to her.

"You can do it, Libby."

"Easy for you to say. You don't have this stupid bustle to deal with."

"Drag it behind you. It shouldn't catch on anything."

"Shouldn't? That's reassuring." She was taking too long. If the carriages behind them were cars, the air would be filled with their horns telling her to get a move on. With a deep breath, she took Brad's hand, felt for the small step with her right foot, and stuck out her left one. In a matter of seconds, Brad had his hands around her waist and was setting her on the ground.

"Whew. Thank you. I thought for sure I was going to fall."

"I wouldn't have let you." He winged out his arm. "Madame, shall we?"

There were only three steps to maneuver up. She shivered.

"Cold?"

"No. Nervous."

"Nothing to be nervous about. All you have to do is follow my lead."

Colleen patted her arm. "You'll be fine. Remember, we'll be by your side."

The blast of warm air, loud voices, a string quartet, and perfumed bodies struck her like a semi hitting a wall. How was she going to survive this? In the past nine months, she'd become accustomed to the country's quiet.

A tall man in black tails took their wraps. "You may go right in. Refreshments are to your left." He sniffed, then turned away.

"Butler?"

Brad shrugged. "Probably. I never saw the need for one, but I guess Belinda is trying to impress everyone."

They walked down a long, dim hallway before entering the ballroom. "Do you see her?"

Brad guided her toward the refreshment table and tipped his head to the right. "She's greeting people over there."

Brad took two crystal glasses of champagne and handed one to Libby. Over her glass, she watched the swirl of dancers moving with precision across the dance floor. The various, bright colors of the women's dresses reminded her of a rainbow as opposed to her black as night dress. How was she ever going to be able to keep up?

"If you'll excuse us, we see some people we haven't see in a while." With their champagne glasses in hand, Caleb and Colleen crossed the room.

A petite, dark-haired woman stood at the door shaking hands and smiling at guests. Was this Belinda? Resembling Elizabeth Taylor, she was beautiful; one of the most gorgeous women Libby had ever seen. How could any man not fall for her? Were her eyes the same dark blue as Taylor's? She certainly had her figure. Narrow waist. Her low-cut dress showed breasts any woman would dream of having, and men of getting their hands on. Even her smile was radiant.

She didn't feel the need to, but how was someone like her going to compete with a woman like Belinda?

Brad leaned down and whispered in her ear. "Don't let her outward beauty fool you. She's like a barracuda. Sharp teeth ready to attack."

"Thanks for the warning."

"Good evening, Bradley." A man, slightly shorter than Brad, approached. If his bulging stomach was any indication, he enjoyed his food. "And who is this lovely woman? I don't believe I've met her before." Without her permission, he took her hand and kissed the back of it. "I heard you had a woman living with you." He eyed her from her head to her feet, stopping briefly at her chest before nudging Brad and giving him a wink. "I can understand why you've kept her hidden."

Thank goodness, she was wearing gloves. She repressed a shudder, but inside her stomach rolled. Yuck. The way he was looking at her, he must think she was good for a roll in the hay.

"Good evening, Frances. This is Mrs. Daniels. After her husband died in a buggy accident, she and her children are staying with us for a bit."

"Oh, I'm sure that's the story." He bowed to Libby. "Please save me a dance."

"By the way, Frances. Where is your wife tonight?"

Frances scowled at Brad. "She's here somewhere. I guess I must find her."

After he left, Libby shuddered. "What a disgusting little man."

"You don't know the half of it. Right after I married Lucinda, he had the audacity to try to seduce her."

"What did you do?"

Brad chuckled. "It wasn't what I did, but what Lucinda did. I have a strong feeling he wasn't able to walk for at least a week."

"Good for her."

"He stayed away after that." Brad had their glasses refilled and gave one back to Libby. "I'm not sure why he believes he's a ladies' man."

Libby tipped her glass toward the other side of the room. Belinda was bearing down on them like a heat-seeking missile. "Don't look now, but I believe Belinda is about to join us."

Brad groaned. "Great. I suppose it's too late to ask you to dance, isn't it?"

"Bradley, my dear." Pointedly ignoring his scarred side, she kissed him on his good cheek. "It's been so long since we've been together." She clutched his free arm and pressed it to the side of her breast making him spill a bit of his champagne on Libby's dress. "Oh, I'm so sorry."

As if Libby didn't know better, the woman had insinuated she and Brad had once shared a bed. She had also deliberately made Brad spill his drink. Ignoring the temptation to empty her glass down the front of the woman's overly exposed chest, Libby set down her glass, removed a hanky from her purse, and dabbed at the droplets. "No worries. I'm sure it won't stain."

How could a woman several inches shorter than her, manage to look down her nose at Libby? With her fan, Belinda tapped Brad on his chest. "You naughty boy, Bradley. Didn't you notice yours was the only name on your invitation, yet you brought a guest? I so wanted to spend some time alone. Maybe we can meet later in my library?"

Brad removed her hand from his elbow. "I don't think so, Belinda."

As Frances had done, Belinda eyed Libby from her head to her toes, then sniffed as if there was a foul odor in the air. "And who is this, Bradley?"

"As I'm sure you and everyone else here already knows, this is my houseguest, Mrs. Daniels. Mrs. Daniels, this is Belinda Carlisle."

"Oh, yes. I've heard about her." She sniffed again. "Didn't you show up at Bradley's house with a son and *with child* or some such thing? I would never press myself into a widower's home. That is so..." She flapped a hand in the air. "I don't know. So inappropriate." Her grin at Libby didn't reach her eyes. "Wouldn't you say, *Mrs. Daniels?*"

Brad coughed into his hand and nudged Libby's dress with his foot.

Having heard about Belinda's attempt at coming upstairs when Libby was recuperating from Lucy's birth, and how she showed up wherever Brad happened to be, the woman's comments were laughable. From where she stood and the few minutes she'd spent with Belinda, Libby already knew her to be cold, calculating, and a bitch.

"I don't know, Miss Carlisle. Mr. Kemble has been nothing but a gentleman, helping me after my husband died. I'm not one to chase after a man. You know, like showing up at his farm without an invitation or accosting him in stores or at church. With Cora and my children, we are never alone together."

Libby bit back a grin when Belinda's face turned an unbecoming shade of pink. Her words must have struck a chord—an off-key, minor one.

"Well, I for one, would never ever stay at an unmarried man's house for an extended period of time. It is simply beyond the pale." She gave Libby a stink eye. "I also would never attend a ball before my full year of mourning was over."

"Well, *Miss* Carlisle. When and if you ever have a husband and he passes away, you'll never know what you'd do. Until then, you shouldn't tell others what they should do."

Belinda opened her mouth to probably give her another scathing remark when Caleb and Colleen reappeared.

Colleen bussed Libby on the cheek. "Sorry we were gone so long, but it isn't often we get to see our friends."

"No prob—"

"Why, Caleb and Colleen. So, kind of you to make it to my party. I was telling Bradley and," she nodded at Libby, "this woman how I'd invited only Bradley. Evidently, Mrs. Daniels invited herself along simply to meet the competition."

Colleen raised an eyebrow. "Competition? Are we going to play games tonight? What are we playing?"

Belinda frowned. "Games? What are you talking about?"

Colleen was surely pulling Belinda's leg. Wasn't she? Libby bit her bottom lip while Brad coughed into his hand. At this rate people were going to think he had a cold.

Before anyone could answer, a tall, rather nice-looking man came up behind Belinda and whispered in her ear. "Excuse me, I need to take care of something." She kissed Brad on the cheek. "I'll see you later, Bradley."

"Not if I see you first," he muttered at her retreating back.

Colleen wiped a smudge of red from Brad's cheek. "Well, how interesting."

"I can't believe you pretended not to know what Belinda meant by competition." Libby couldn't hold back a laugh. "It was priceless. And to think I'm her competition."

"Quite ridiculous when you are far more beautiful than she'll ever be."

Libby frowned when Caleb and Colleen exchanged grins. "What?"

"Oh, nothing." Colleen took Caleb's arm. "Nothing at all. Let's dance, dear."

"I'll talk to you later." Caleb led his wife to the dance floor.

"Would you care to dance?"

The string group was playing a lovely waltz. Something she could handle with ease. "Of course."

Libby couldn't ignore the whispers from people staring at them as Caleb maneuvered her around the dance floor.

"I believe we are the talk of the evening."

His warm breath against her cheek sent her senses spiraling. "I think they're talking about me, not you. After all, I'm the hussy staying at a bachelor's home."

"Too bad, because without you, there is no me."

What did he mean? Was it a way of saying he was in love with her? Impossible. She was sure he still loved Lucinda. But then again, she still loved Ben, but was wildly attracted to Brad. "Umm."

"Maybe it's too soon, but I can't imagine you going back to your time. If there were a way to keep you here, I'd use it. You and Charlie and Lucy have brought me back to life."

Why did he have to say those words as they were dancing? How should she respond? She raised her head to stare into his eyes. The heat in them nearly melted her into a puddle on the floor. "You have to quit looking at me like that."

"Like what?"

"Like you want to devour me."

Brad tipped his head and grinned down at her. "Sounds like a plan to me."

Before she had a chance to respond, Caleb interrupted. "Hey, you two. If you want to be more obvious about your feelings for each other, keep dancing. But if you haven't noticed, the music has stopped."

Crap. Talk about being the center of attention, or in the center of an empty dance floor.

"There are no…"

Caleb didn't give her a chance to finish. He shook his head and chuckled. "Save it for someone who might believe you. Right now, I believe no one in this room would believe any denials you might profess."

Brad led her to the side of the room. If it were possible, every eye was on them. Whispers of the women were made behind fans. Men eyed her as if she were a piece of candy. Could they leave right now? She spotted Belinda standing by the refreshment table, downing a glass of champagne. If looks could kill, she'd have an arrow through her heart and lie prostrate on the floor.

The music started again. This time the song playing was for a quadrille.

"Do you think you remember the steps?" Brad took her elbow and followed Caleb and Colleen to the dance floor.

"I certainly hope so." Thankfully, it was a dance they'd practiced several times and managed to follow along as they switched partners, do-si-doed, and moved in circles. Relieved when the music stopped and she hadn't messed up, her stomach dropped when everyone remained on the floor.

"What's happening?" she whispered to Brad.

"I'm afraid to think." The group struck up several chords, then stopped. Brad groaned.

"What?"

"We have to dance with the two couples next to us."

Libby tried not to panic. "But we didn't practice anything with other people."

"I know. But the worst thing is who is part of the other couples."

She didn't want to look. She looked. "Tell me it isn't so."

"I wish I could." Brad nodded to the other group, which included Belinda. "I'll try to tell you what to do. Caleb and Colleen will, too."

After their side did their swirls and crossovers, it was time to include the other two couples. It wasn't an issue until the women had to take each other's hands and cross over. The first woman gently took Libby's and passed her. Then...

"You're a witch." Belinda's voice came out sounding like *she* was a witch as she dug her nails into the back of Libby's hand.

If Libby hadn't been wearing gloves, she'd have claw marks on her skin and would probably be bleeding. "Thank you." Probably a stupid thing to say, but it happened so quickly, nothing else came to mind.

Belinda stutter stepped as she passed her. Guess her response wasn't what Belinda expected. There was no way she could ignore her, but at least now she knew what to expect from the woman. Each time they touched hands, Belinda spouted another nasty term for her, until Libby's head was ready to explode by not responding to her digs. The less she said, the angrier Belinda became.

Finally, the tortuous dance was over. Brad guided her to the refreshment table and picked up two glasses of champagne. He handed one each to Caleb and Colleen and picked up two more.

Colleen took a sip of her drink. "What was going on between you and Belinda? I thought she was going to stab you or something."

"She was calling me names, some of which I didn't understand."

Brad frowned. "She called you names like a little kid at school? What did you say?"

"Thank you?"

Caleb spit out his champagne, dampening Brad's coat. "You what?"

"I was so surprised; it just came out of my mouth." Libby held out her hand. "Every time we had to take hands; she dug her nails into my glove."

Brad took her hand. "What on Earth? There are gouges in your gloves. If you hadn't been wearing them, she would have cut the back of your hand." He handed his glass to Libby. "I'm going to go talk to her."

"No, Brad." Libby handed the glass back to him. "Leave it be. I think she's simply looking for attention."

"If you say so." Brad stared at someone across the room. "Caleb. There's that man again. The one I saw Belinda with at the restaurant."

Caleb nodded. "I see him. I've been trying to figure out where I've seen him before, but I can't figure it out."

"Me, too. For some reason I believe it has to do with the war. I'm pretty sure he wasn't in our company, but I've encountered him somewhere." Brad shook his head and closed his eyes. "It's simply not coming to me."

Libby tried to picture Brad and Caleb fighting in the awful war. Reenacting battles was totally different from actually being in them. Cora had alluded to Brad's bad dreams. PTSD? Wouldn't be surprising. What those men saw had to have been horrific. Maybe someday, if she were to stay in the past, she could get him to open up about it. But only if he wanted to.

"Maybe if we both went over and joined in the conversation something would click."

Colleen patted her husband's arm. "Go ahead. Libby and I will be fine. We'll find a couple of chairs and wait for you."

Libby couldn't help admiring Brad's tall, slim form as he and Caleb wove their way around people to the other side of the room. In a matter of seconds, the men had insinuated themselves into the conversation. "Colleen, let's find somewhere to sit."

Brad nodded to the men he knew and struck out his hand to those he didn't. Although the only one he didn't know was the one he thought he should. "Good evening. I'm Bradley Kemble and this is my brother, Caleb. Are you new to the area?"

"Taylor Cobban. I grew up in what is now Virginia. I've known Belinda since she was a child and decided to pay a visit."

Strange. If he'd known Belinda since she was a child, why hadn't he ever met him? After all, their families had been friends forever. "And what it is you do, Mr. Cobban?"

"Please call me Taylor." He took a puff on his cigar. "A little bit of this. A little bit of that."

Which didn't explain much. He glanced at Caleb, who was studying his shoes. "Caleb and I each own farms in the area. In fact, I purchased the Castlewood place after Belinda's father passed."

Taylor raised an eyebrow and looked at his cigar. "Oh? I'm surprised she didn't say anything to me about it. But then, I'm not always easy to locate."

Something was fishy. If they'd been friends, he certainly would have known this house they were standing in wasn't Belinda's childhood home. "So, what are you planning to do while in our neck of the woods?"

"You ask an awful lot of questions, Mr. Kemble."

"Simply being neighborly." Brad gave the man a forced smile. "Thought maybe if you needed help with anything, I could offer my services."

"I doubt I would need the help of a *farm boy*."

"You'd be surprised what us *farmers* can do, Mr. Cobban." Where did he know this guy from? Even his voice was familiar. "I feel like I've met you before, but I can't think of where."

Cobban stared first at Brad the Caleb. "I don't think so." He tapped his chin. "Although, I tend to forget the lesser class of people. Too boorish."

Caleb put a hand on Brad's fist. "Not now," he whispered.

"Well, I'll figure out where I know you from." Brad bowed at the waist. "Have a good evening."

"Let's sit here, Libby." Colleen led the way to a set of chairs placed in front of a closed door.

Like trying to sit in the carriage, sitting on a chair was difficult. Sitting while holding a glass of champagne even more so.

"Sit on the edge of the chair and move your bustle aside with your foot." Colleen demonstrated. "Everyone does it."

After sitting precariously on the chair, Libby spotted Brad and Caleb speaking with a man. From Brad's clenched fists, it seemed it wasn't going well. "Who is the man Brad is talking to?"

"I don't know." Colleen took a sip of her drink. "I've never seen him before, but from the looks of it, the boys don't care for him."

Boys? There was no way Brad or Caleb could be construed as boys. They were both men through and through. "Yeah. It looks as if Brad would like to punch him."

"He wouldn't, though. Caleb would keep him in check."

"But who will keep Caleb in check?"

Colleen shrugged. "Brad?" She chuckled. "They're in trouble, aren't they?"

Brad bowed at the man, then he and Caleb wandered to another group of men. "The man is leaving."

"Good. The men Brad and Caleb are talking with are neighbors and friends of ours. They are safe."

They sat quietly, taking in the dancers and sipping their champagne. Thankfully, no one asked her to dance. A voice behind her took her attention away from *the boys*. "Shh. Do you hear that?"

"Hear what?"

"I thought I heard my name."

"It's coming from behind us."

Libby glanced over her shoulder. The door she had thought was closed, was open a crack. She put a finger to her lips. "Listen."

"I tell you we need to get rid of that woman."

"What woman?"

"The one staying at Bradley's. The hussy, Libby, whatever her last name is."

"Why do you want to get rid of her?"

"Taylor, use your head. While she's at his farm, there is no hope for me to insinuate myself into his life. I've seen the way he looks at her. As he was with Lucinda, he's in love with her. At least Lucinda had the sense to die."

"My, my, Belinda. You do have your claws out tonight, don't you?"

"Why can't Bradley fall in love with me? I'm beautiful. Have a great figure. We've known each other since we were children."

"Maybe that's the problem. He sees you as one would see an old friend."

"Are you calling me old?"

Taylor's sigh was loud and long. "Of course not. I meant it as you two have known each other for a long time. Maybe he can't see you as a desirable woman like I do."

The was a brief moment of silence. Were they kissing? How could she profess to want one man while at the same time kissing another?

"I need to get into his house. What I left there is worth a lot of money to both of us."

"We have plenty for our needs. What could be worth getting caught breaking into his house? We have the plates to make all the money we want."

"Oh, you don't understand at all. I have to figure out a way to get into his house."

"Well, you can't do anything tonight, so let's go back to your guests. You still have the evening to try your wiles on Mr. Kemble."

"You're right, Taylor. You're absolutely right. I'll show him who's the better woman. Me or the witch. I'll get her somehow."

Their voices drifted off.

"They must be coming back to the ballroom." Colleen took Libby's glass. "Let's move away from here in case they realize the door was open."

Getting up from the chair was as difficult as sitting. Especially since her shoe had caught on the hem at the front of her dress. "Damn." She reached down and released her shoe.

"Shh. Don't let anyone hear you cuss."

"Sorry. It tends to slip out when I'm not with the children. Besides, my being here before my year of mourning is up, is scandalous enough."

Colleen laughed. "Sometimes I have a hard time not cussing when the children act up."

"Ladies." Bradley held out his hand to help Libby stand. "Care to dance?"

"Of course."

Brad held her in a way society considered proper. There was something to be said about the way people did a slow dance in her time. The woman's arms around the man's neck. The man's arms around the woman's waist. Chest to chest. Hip to hip. Didn't leave much to the imagination, but so much more pleasant than being so far apart, you could stick another person between them.

"Did you learn anything about the man you were talking with?"

Brad shook his head. "No. But I still can't shake the feeling I know him. Plus, he was rather rude to Caleb and me as if we'd had some type of interaction with him." He spun her as they waltzed around the dance floor. "Did you enjoy talking with Colleen?"

Libby smiled. "I always enjoy spending time with her, but we heard an interesting conversation while we were sitting in our chairs."

"Really?"

"See the door behind the chairs we were sitting on?"

Brad glanced over her shoulder. "Yes."

"While we were waiting for you and Caleb, we overhead a conversation between Belinda and someone she called Taylor."

"He's the man we were speaking with. What did he say?"

"Besides wanting to get rid of me so Belinda can have you, she said there was something she'd left in your house. Something worth a lot of money."

Brad raised an eyebrow. "What did Taylor say?"

"He told her it wasn't worth getting caught breaking into your house, and they have plates to make lots of money. And we heard them kissing. Or at least it sounded as if they were kissing."

The music stopped and Brad led her to a corner of the ballroom. Caleb and Colleen joined them.

"Did Colleen tell you what they overheard?"

Caleb nodded. I think we know who the counterfeiters are."

"I agree, but what did Belinda leave in my house worth a lot of money?"

Libby tapped his arm. "I don't know but heads up. She's heading this way with the man you were talking with."

"Great. Is there somewhere I can hide?"

Caleb chuckled. "Afraid not. I know what Belinda wants, but why is Taylor heading this way?" He took his wife's arm. "C'mon, dear. Let's dance. If I have to listen to Belinda's simpering at Brad, I may... I'm not sure what I'd do, but it wouldn't be nice."

"Oh, Bradley, I finally found you. Would you do a woman a favor and dance with her?"

"I can't leave Libby by herself."

Belinda flapped a hand in the air. "Oh, pishaw. Taylor would love to dance with her, wouldn't you?" Without another word, she tugged Brad toward the dance floor.

Brad gave Libby a beseeching look over his shoulder. "I...uh..."

Taylor chuckled. "No one says no to Belinda Carlisle."

"I guess not."

"Do *you* want to dance? I'm not very good and don't really care for these country soirees."

Could the man get any more snobbish?

"I would rather have a glass of champagne." Where was he from to think a ball in their small town was something to look down on? There was only one way to find out. She followed him to the refreshment table. "So where are you from, Mr. Cobban?"

"How did you know my last name?"

"I saw you talking with Mr. Kemble earlier. He told me your name."

"I'm from New York."

He said it as if it were the most important place on Earth. Rather like people felt about the city in her time. Personally, she didn't care for the place. Too many people. Too much noise.

"So, what is it you like about New York?"

Taylor handed her a glass of champagne, stuck his nose in the air, and sniffed. "Oh, my dear. I guess you've never been out of this backwater town. You *must* visit it sometime. The music. The theatre. The food. All are simply the best."

If she hadn't heard him kissing Belinda earlier, she would have thought the man was gay. Or was it an act? "Well, Mr. Cobban. I've actually been to New York several times. I find it to be noisy, overcrowded, and dirty. And don't forget the crime. Why, when my husband and I were there for our honeymoon, we saw several cases of pickpockets, starving children, and, in one case, a shooting."

He sniffed again. "Well, I must say you must have been in the poorer parts of the city. *I* only stay at the best places. Like the Astor and the Grand Hotel on Broadway or the Fifth Avenue Hotel. Why," he leaned into her as if he were going to impart a secret. "I even got to ride on one of those elevators taking one up to the floor you want without having to use stairs. It was amazing."

Libby bit back a chuckle. If the man only knew about elevators whisking people within seconds up skyscrapers. How she wished to tell him about cars, planes, and movies. Being the ass he was, he probably wouldn't believe her. "I'm sure it was."

"Now. You must tell me all about your stay at Bradley's." He waggled his eyebrows. "I'm sure it must be most stimulating."

"I'm not sure what you mean by 'stimulating.' Mr. Kemble saved my son and myself from an accident. Unfortunately, my husband perished. My daughter was born shortly after. He and Cora have been wonderful to us."

"But when are you going home? I mean how long can you take advantage of Mr. Kemble before people start talking?"

Ooh. She'd love to dump her champagne over his pompous head. "It's no one's business how long I stay. But I must tell you, he's been gracious in letting me recover from my daughter's birth and keeping us during these cold, winter months. Traveling to Wisconsin in the winter months is not advised. Why, one could easily get stuck in a snowstorm and perish. I would never put my children through such a trip."

He raised an eyebrow. "Wisconsin, you say? So, when the weather gets better, you'll return to your family?"

Libby shrugged. "I'm not sure why it matters to you, Mr. Cobban. Now, if you don't mind, I'm going to find a place to sit." She nodded at him. "Thank you for the lovely visit." Asshole. Now, how was Brad faring with Belinda?

Chapter Twenty-Three

"It's so wonderful to see you again, Bradley." Belinda pressed herself against him. "I've missed you so much."

Brad eased her away from him. Trying to keep her at society's idea of what was proper for dancing was like trying to wrestle a pig wallowing in mud. Impossible. "I'm not sure why you've missed me. We haven't spent any time together." She tapped him on the nose. ON THE NOSE! What was she thinking? By acting coy, he'd succumb to her pretending to act like an innocent? Ridiculous.

"Silly boy. It's why I've been trying to find a way to see you." She nodded in the direction of Libby and Taylor. "It's all because of your house *guest*. I'm not sure why you're still letting her stay with you. Why, the way people are talking about you and her. Don't you care about your reputation?"

"My reputation isn't anyone's problem but mine. Nothing I can say or do will change those narrow-minded, gossipmongers' minds. I could say there is nothing between us until I'm blue in the face and no one would believe me. So, why bother?"

Belinda ran a finger down his lapel. "But what about the woman who'll be your next wife? Aren't you concerned about what she might think? I mean. I..."

He removed her hand from his chest. If there were anyone who should be worried about her reputation, it would be Belinda. People were staring at them. Was Libby? What was she thinking of Belinda's blatant attempt at public seduction? "Since I haven't met my future wife yet," Libby's face came immediately to mind, "she doesn't have anything to worry about."

Belinda bit her bottom lip and looked up at him through her eyelashes. "You haven't met your future wife? Why, I thought..."

It was extremely rude to leave a dance partner on the dance floor, but the temptation to do so was so strong, he had to grit his teeth to keep from walking away. "What did you think, Belinda?"

"Well, we've known each other almost all our lives. I was crushed when you married Lucinda. I know our parents were hoping for a match between us."

And there it was. Finally, out in the open. "Belinda, my parents never mentioned any hope of a relationship between us." In all truth, his father had warned him against scheming women like Belinda, and his mother had agreed.

"They didn't?"

Was that a tear? He nearly laughed. How hard did she have to work to squeeze out the one little tear rolling down her cheek? As an only child, her parents had doted on her. All she had to do was pout or force a tear or two and she got what she wanted. But it wasn't going to work on him.

"No, they didn't. Let me put it this way. I don't plan on ever remarrying." How easy it was to lie to Belinda. Now if she would only believe him. "Lucinda was my one and only true love. When she died along with our child, I was devastated and vowed to never marry again."

"Why, that's simply crazy. You're a young man. A young man with needs."

"And what do you know about a man's needs?" He had a good idea she was free with her favors. Another reason to stay away from the conniving witch." He stifled a groan. When would this song be over? He swore the musicians were playing the same song over and over. Wait. Had Belinda told them to do so?

"Well, I, uh. I've heard stories."

It was probably she who told stories. "What about Taylor?"

"Taylor? What about him?"

He swung Belinda toward the quartet. Could he give them some type of signal to make them quit playing? "How do you know him? Is he a friend or something more?" He was pretty sure Belinda's wide eyes and huffed breath were an act.

"Why, I only met the man a few months ago at a ball in Charleston." She tipped her head to the side and batted her eyes up at him. "We're...we're simply friends."

Another blatant lie. Should he call her on it? Probably not. She'd clam up. He needed to see how much information he could get out of her. "What does he do for a living?"

"I'm not really sure. Something about finance."

Bradley glanced over his shoulder at Libby, who was sitting along the wall carrying on a conversation with Mrs. Winthrop, an elderly woman who made it her business to know everyone else's business. What was she asking Libby? And why wasn't the woman doing her duty and making sure couples weren't dancing too close or for too many dances. Since Libby was safe, he returned his attention to Belinda. "Are you interested in him?"

Belinda tapped his chest and pouted. "Why, of course not, you silly man. If I were, would you be jealous?"

How should he answer? If he said yes, she'd probably consider it a sign she should up her game to get her clutches in him. If he said no, would she throw a fit? "I suppose I *could* be jealous, but if you care for Taylor, you should pursue him." Now if Taylor were to show an interest in Libby, he'd be livid. Stark-raving mad, ready to fight.

"Why, Bradley, how sweet of you, but it's only you I want. And as soon as you send your *guest* back to her home, we can be together. Of course, we'd have to be discreet."

Ah, hell. He moved Belinda to arm's length. Lucky he had long arms. "I'm not sure when she can go home. With it being winter and all, it would be dangerous for her to travel with two small children, one barely nine months old."

Belinda huffed a breath. "She seems sturdy enough, and children are adaptable. She could probably travel clear across the country to California with her children and never have a problem."

And more than likely hope they would all have died along the way. "Well, I wouldn't feel comfortable having her leave when it's so cold. It's only a few months until things warm up. I can't kick her out during winter."

"You must watch yourself, Bradley Kemble. Women like her know how to get their clutches into a man. I'm sure it's how she got her husband. She certainly isn't pretty enough to attract a man. Her husband must have been desperate to marry her."

Brad choked back a laugh. No, Libby wasn't pretty, she was beautiful. And, unlike Belinda, she was beautiful inside and out. "I'll be careful."

"You'd better. Who's to say she didn't do away with her husband so she could be with you."

Anger made his head spin. Kill her husband? "I'd be careful who you say something like that to. It would be rather hard for a woman close to delivering her child to tip over a horse and buggy on top of someone. Plus, she'd never seen me before then."

"Oh, Bradley. Don't be so naïve. Women will do anything to get the man they want."

Which would be the pot calling the kettle black. There would be no sense in convincing Belinda how wrong she was. Oh, not about a woman doing anything to get a man. *Look at her. Making up lies about a woman she's never met until tonight and trying desperately to get her claws into him.*

"Excuse me, Brad." Caleb tapped him on the shoulder.

"*Excuse me, Caleb Kemble.* You can't cut in. My dance with Bradley is not over."

"If you think I want to dance with you, you're crazy."

Brad held back a chuckle. His brother and Belinda had never gotten along. From the day their families had met each other, their mutual hatred was palpable.

"And I'd never dance with you. So, go away and leave us alone. Bradley and I have a lot to talk about."

Caleb ignored Belinda. "We have to leave. Colleen is not feeling well."

"Is she...?"

"Good heavens, I hope not."

"Another baby?" Belinda shuddered. "That's absolutely disgusting. Don't you have four already? No wonder your wife is getting plump."

Bradley held Caleb back. "You can't hit a woman."

"Watch me."

She glared at Caleb. "You wouldn't dare. And I would advise you to leave your poor wife alone."

"I never said she was with child. I only said she didn't feel well." Caleb smirked back at her. "Probably from something she ate or drank here."

"Ridiculous! I don't see anyone else getting sick."

"At the moment, I'm feeling a bit queasy myself." Caleb took Brad's arm. "C'mon. I want to get Colleen home before she eats any more tainted food."

"Bradley, you can't leave. We have so much more to discuss."

"I can't stay. Libby rode with us and it's only proper I see her home."

"Oh, for goodness' sake. Caleb can take her home. Can't you Caleb?"

"No, he can't." Brad peeled her fingers from his forearm. She was holding on so tight, even though his layers of clothes, he'd more than likely have scratches in the morning. "We took my buggy and picked up Caleb and Colleen on the way here. If I were to stay here, Libby would have to drive the buggy home by herself." He wasn't about to tell her Cora's husband, Joshua, had driven them.

"So, where is the problem?"

"I said no. It's dark and she wouldn't be able to find her way home. She's never been here before."

Belinda folded her arms over her chest, pouted, and stomped her foot. "Then you must come back after you drop them off. I need you so, Bradley."

Refraining from rolling his eyes, Brad shook his head. "I will not be coming back. Tonight, or any other time. Now, if you'll excuse us, we need to get Colleen home." He bowed. "Thank you for the dance and a lovely evening." As if the hounds of hell were behind him, he walked to Colleen and Libby. "Thank you for rescuing me, Caleb."

"I have to say I never thought the music would stop. They kept playing the same song over and over again."

"I believe Belinda told them to play forever so she could keep dancing. I've never seen a person so desperate." He stopped in front of the women. "How are you feeling, Colleen? Caleb says you're not feeling well."

Colleen waved her fan in front of her face. "I'm perfectly fine."

Brad raised eyebrow. "But..."

"We had to think of a way to get you away from Belinda." She yawned. "Besides, I am quite tired, aren't you, Libby?"

"Oh. Yes. Quite tired." She copied Colleen's yawn.

"All right, you two. Don't overdo it. Both those yawns looked quite contrived."

Libby rose. "Yes. Well. There are eyes watching us, so we'd better get going."

He didn't want to seem obvious and search for Belinda and Taylor, so he waited until Libby took his elbow and headed for the cloak room. Sure enough, with scowls on their faces, Belinda and Taylor followed their movements. Finally, Belinda stuck her nose in the air, snatched her skirts, and raced from the room, probably to shed more fake tears.

After the cigar and cigarette smoke, and over-perfumed bodies, the crisp outdoor air was refreshing. As one, they took deep breaths.

Libby held the sides of her cloak together. "I can't believe how stuffy it was in there. The cool air feels wonderful."

"Yes. It's why Caleb and I don't attend many balls, nor hold any in our home." Colleen took Caleb's hand as they waited for their buggy to arrive. "Can you imagine holding a ball with four children? Besides all the work, how would I ever be able to keep them in their rooms?"

Caleb chuckled. "I enjoy our peace and quiet too much to have a ball. People would come simply to see our home and what we have. And all the gossiping. No, Thank you."

"Plus, it would be an ideal time for Belinda to get into my house."

"You'd probably never be able to get her to leave." Colleen shook her head. "And she'd more than likely bring several trunks with her."

"I was happy to leave before midnight. I'm sure Belinda would have wanted me to give her a New Year's kiss." Brad shuddered. "Ugh."

Their carriage finally arrived, and after settling onto their seats and placing several heavy blankets over their laps, continued their conversation.

If only I could take Libby's hand like Caleb is holding Colleen's But he didn't have the right. She was wearing widow's weeds, for heaven's sake. At least for the ball she had. Only four more months and she could move on. But what if she disappeared before then? His heart was already engaged with her and her children. He couldn't survive losing them.

"Brad?" Someone kicked him in the shin. "Are you paying attention or are you too busy mooning?"

"I'm not mooning, just thinking about Belinda and Taylor." The carriage was small enough where each bump in the road made their knees come in contact with each other.

Caleb squinted his eyes at Brad. "It's exactly what we were talking about. If you were paying attention, you'd know that."

"Sorry. Please fill me in."

Caleb nodded at Libby. "Tell him your thoughts."

"I was thinking about the counterfeit notes and money you were talking about. Do you think Belinda mentioning plates means she and Taylor are the culprits?"

"Certainly sounds like it." Brad tucked the blankets under his legs. It was going to take a long time to warm up. When they get home, maybe he and Libby could spend some time in front of the fireplace in the parlor. Cora had probably made sure to keep the fire going while waiting for Joshua to come home. It was nice of her to volunteer to watch Libby's children, but he imagined Libby was anxious to get home to them.

"She has to be getting her money from somewhere." Caleb put his arm around Colleen's shoulders and pressed her to his side. "Maybe they'd been preparing to print it before she lost the farm."

Brad shrugged. "I'm not sure it makes sense. If they'd printed money then, she could have used it to pay off her debts."

"So, it means they must have more plates somewhere."

"I agree, Caleb. But why is she so determined to get the ones in the house? And how come I've never come across them before?"

This time Libby pulled the quilts tighter. "Probably because you weren't looking for them. We'll have to do a search in the next few days."

"My best bet would be in one of the secret rooms. Lucinda and I replaced all of the furniture with ours. Plus, Belinda took all of her families' belongings. If the plates were hidden in any of them, we wouldn't be worried about getting her hands on the plates."

Colleen clapped her hands. "Wait. What if the plates in their possession are small denominations? What if the ones she wants back are higher?"

Libby angled toward Brad. "She has a point. What bad bills are being used?"

"Huh. You have a clever wife, Caleb."

"Of course I do. She married me, didn't she?"

"She must have been blind."

"Blinded by my handsome face and wonderful physique."

"All right, you two." Colleen patted her husband's knee. "Stop acting like a couple of children and tell us what denominations are being used?"

Caleb grinned. "All right, but I believe I won this round." At Colleen's glare, he finally answered. "Mostly ones, twos, and fives."

"They would have had to print a lot of those for her to buy her house. So, what if her plates in the house are twenties and fifties? Or maybe higher notes?"

"Good idea. Libby. Not only had he fallen in love with a beautiful woman, but a smart one, too. "It's possible they are running low on the small bills. Or maybe she's over-extended herself again and needs the plates to make larger bills to pay off her creditors."

Caleb tapped his bottom lip. "But, besides more than likely helping print counterfeit money, where else would Taylor fit in the scheme of things?"

"After hearing them kissing, I believe I have a guess." Colleen giggled. "And I don't mean they're friends."

"And she tried to tell me she was innocent. She must think I'm a moron."

"Or blind to her beauty." Caleb shook his head. "She's been getting her way for so long, she can't fathom someone not falling for her so-called charms."

Brad tipped his head back and swore. "I know where I've seen Taylor before, but he didn't go by that name. It was... "He closed his eyes. "Gunther..."

"You're right. Gunther..." Caleb snapped his fingers. "Gunther Schmidt. Wasn't he in charge of supplies for our regiment?"

Brad nearly jumped from his seat. "Yes! Of course. Wasn't he given a dishonorable discharge for selling supplies on the black market?"

"No wonder I had a bad feeling about him."

"We're here," Joshua called from his perch. The carriage dipped as he got down and opened the door. "Here, Miss Colleen. Take my hand."

Caleb followed his wife then poked his head back inside. "Let me know if you find anything. The sooner we do, the sooner we can put them behind bars." He tapped his top hat. "Good night."

As soon as Caleb slammed the door shut, Joshua got the horses moving.

"It won't take us long to get home. Would you care for a sherry and warming up by the parlor fire?"

"Normally, I would. But I wasn't lying back at Belinda's when I said I was tired."

He lifted an eyebrow at her. "Sure looked like a fake yawn to me."

"It was, but I'm truly exhausted. It's been a long day. I need to check on the children, too."

"As disappointed as I am, I understand. Dealing with Belinda can make anyone fatigued. After I send Cora home, I'll head to bed, too."

As soon as they entered the house, Libby headed for the stairs.

"Wait a minute, Libby."

"What?" She really was tired, plus her ribs hurt from the corset and her feet were aching.

"May I please kiss you good night?"

With one foot on the bottom step, she paused. Why not? The whole having to wait a year was ridiculous. And, of course, it only applied to women. Men only had to wait six months. "I would like that."

As tall as he was, and even though she was tall, she stayed on the bottom step, making them eye to eye, mouth to mouth. He'd removed his gloves, so when he cupped her cheeks, her body zinged with the contact. And if her body zinged with the touch of his hands, his kiss electrified, banged on drums, played a trumpet solo, and awakened long denied parts of her body.

She moaned against his lips. He drew her closer to him, so her breasts were crushed against his chest. If she weren't wearing these cumbersome clothes, she'd jump into his arms and wrap her legs around his waist. Time stood still. Only their fast breathing filled the air.

"Now, that's what I like to see."

They broke apart, Libby nearly falling down the step.

"Cora. I didn't hear you come into the room."

"I heard the front door open and knew Joshua would be home." She tied a scarf around her head and buttoned up her coat. She smirked at them before going to the front door. "Good night, Mr. Brad, Miss Libby." Her wink probably meant she thought more would happen between them tonight. "Enjoy yourselves."

"How embarrassing." She picked up her skirts and raced up the stairs.

Halfway up, Brad called after her. "I don't regret it. Not one bit."

Libby paused and grinned down at him. "Me neither." She probably wouldn't sleep all night. It would take that long for her body to settle down.

Chapter Twenty-Four

Libby sighed and bit her lip from yelling at the noise Charlie was making playing a game of good guys and bad guys. Plus, every chance, he'd pick on his sister, who was learning to stand on her own. Every time he noticed she was on her feet, he raced past her, startling her and making her fall. Then Lucy would cry, Charlie would laugh his special evil laugh, and start all over again with his game.

Six weeks. Six weeks they'd been stuck in the house. Shortly after the ball, a series of snowstorms hit the area. Just when they'd cleaned paths to the barn and outhouse, another one would hit. By now they had received nearly three feet of snow. Charlie was going stir crazy. Cora was going stir crazy. And Libby believed she was simply going crazy. They needed to get out of the house. Somehow. Someway.

"Libby. Where are you?" Brad called from the kitchen. He must have come in from doing chores.

"In the parlor with the children."

Stocking-footed, hair slicked down from his stocking hat, he appeared in the doorway. "The sun is finally out. Cora says she needs to get some supplies in case we get another storm."

"Heavens, I hope not. How are you going to get to town?"

"I've hitched the horses to the sleigh. I thought maybe you and the children would want to go with us. The sun makes it feel warmer."

"I would love to, but I'm not sure it's a good idea."

"Why?"

"I guess I have cabin fever."

"Cabin fever?"

"It's when you're stuck in the house so long you're ready to go crazy."

"But wouldn't going to town help?

Charlie raced past, yelled at the top of his lungs, and pretended to shoot Brad. "Take that, you varmint."

Brad grabbed him and held him upside down, which only made Charlie scream louder. Lucy crawled over to him, pulled herself up by his pantleg, and started screaming, "Up. Up. Bird."

Libby closed her eyes. At least back home, no matter how much snow they'd get, it didn't take long for the road crews to clear the roads and they could get out of the house. The main ones, anyway. "Actually, what I need a break from is the little scoundrel. It would do him good to get out of here. Maybe make him run behind the sleigh and burn off some energy. What I really need is some peace and quiet."

"How about this." He set Charlie down and picked up Lucy, which at least made her stop crying. "We'll bundle up these little varmints. With Cora and Joshua along, we should be able to handle them. It should give you a few hours alone."

Libby kissed Brad on the cheek.

"Ooh." Charlie sang. "Mommy and Bradley sittin' in a tree, k-i-s-s-i-n-g." He made a kissing sound.

"Where did you learn that?"

"Cora. She said you and Brad would get married and he'd be my new daddy."

Brad's face burned. Probably as red as hers. "Cora?"

"Yep. She did."

"I'll talk to her on the way to town."

"But maybe not in front of big ears."

Charlie laughed. "Who has big ears? I know. Lucy has big ears."

"Charlie Benjamin Daniels. You will not say nasty things about your sister." If she weren't about to have some time alone, she'd make him stay in his room. "You say one more thing or pick on your sister, and you won't be going to town."

"I'm sorry, Mommy. I won't do it again."

Yeah, right. Maybe not for the next fifteen minutes. "All right. Let's get you and Lucy bundled up."

Half an hour later, Libby stood at the front door, waving to her family. Her family. Yes, it was what Brad, Cora, and Joshua had become. If she ever got back to her own time, she'd miss them terribly. Or would she remember them? Too bad there wasn't a book on time travel. Well, there were plenty out there, but not ones describing the ins and outs of actually traveling through time.

She closed the door behind her and soaked in the silence. The only noise was the ticking of a grandfather clock in Brad's office. She giggled. How much time did she have? What should she do? The options were open-ended. Take a bath. But there was no one to carry water. Have a glass of sherry? Not at ten in the morning. Clean the kids' rooms? No. No work. Search for the plates again? No. They'd already found them and Brad had given them to Caleb to pass on to the authorities. Make hot chocolate and read a book? Excellent idea.

Libby nearly skipped down the hallway to the kitchen. She poured milk into a pan and set it on the still-hot stove. Copying Cora, in a cup she added a teaspoon of chocolate powder, two of sugar, and a splash of vanilla. She mixed it together, and when the milk was nice and warm, poured it into the cup.

She picked up the book she'd been trying to read the past few days, and with the cup in her other hand, went into the library. Before sitting down before the fire, she eyed the wall where another room was hidden and where they'd found the plates. She set her book and hot chocolate on a side table by a green winged chair.

With the poker, she stabbed at the coals in the fireplace and tossed on more wood. She took a seat, propped her feet on a footstool and wrapped a blanket around her legs and feet. She'd taken to wearing a pair of her slacks under her skirts to help keep warm. Since they'd been her maternity pants, she'd taken in the elastic. She picked up one of her favorite books, *Little Women*. Not close to the romantic mysteries she enjoyed reading in her time, but better than some of the heavy tomes in the library. *War and Peace. Great Expectations. Crime and Punishment. Les Misérables*. All much too serious for her tastes.

She took a sip of her hot chocolate. Not bad, but not as good as Cora's. What had she done wrong? She stirred the mixture resting in the bottom of the cup. Better.

Now all she had to do was stay awake. Lucy was cutting teeth, or cracking teeth as Charlie said, and neither she nor her daughter were getting much sleep. The words on the page swam before her eyes. As much as loved the story, her eyes grew heavy. Her book fell onto her lap. Peace and quiet and a nap. Was anything better than this?

Chapter Twenty-Five

She dreamed of Ben. Her Ben. The one she'd loved since she was eighteen. The one she'd been married to for nearly six years. In her dream, they were dancing on a beach. He swung her around in circles. When he set her down, he took her hand, and they played tag with the waves.

The scene changed to a Civil War reenactment. Ben was by far and wide the most dapper man in his uniform. None of the other 'soldiers' came close. They were driving down a road. A storm. Her heart raced. Their car spun. Charlie. Where was Charlie? The baby kicked in her bulging stomach. Then everything went black.

Libby jerked awake, knocking her book to the floor with a thud.

"What was that noise? I thought you said no one was home."

"I saw them drive past. I swear it was the witch, Brad, her brats, and Joshua."

A man's voice rumbled a reply.

Someone was in the house. No one was supposed to be here but her. As quietly as she could, she unwrapped the blanket from her legs, and stood. The fire had died down, so the air was chilly.

"Where did you say they were?"

"In a hidden room in the library."

Crap. It was obviously Belinda and Taylor who were coming into the library. What should she do? If she opened the hidden door, they'd hear her. Their voices grew louder. They weren't far away. The closest place to hide was behind the couch. In the nick of time, she squatted behind the piece of furniture. The temptation to peak around the corner was strong. But those blasted skirts always swished when a woman moved. They'd for sure hear her.

"How do you open the damn door?"

"Oh, be patient, Taylor. I simply need to push this button." The door creaked open.

"Shhh."

"Oh. Be quiet yourself. I told you no one was here."

Their voices became muffled when they entered the room. Now was her chance. She stood, picked up her skirt in her arms and made a dash for the library door. Where to go? Once they realize the plates were gone, they'd not only be angry, but might tear the place apart. She ran for the dining room, opened the hidden door, stepped inside, and closed it. There were no lights, and with the door closed, no light came from the dining room.

She needed to find the lamp and matches Brad kept in here. With her arms outstretched she felt her way to where she recalled a table was. She struck a match and, in the dim light, located the lamp. She removed the glass chimney, raised the wick, and touched the almost burned-out match to it. Voices rose from outside the room.

"I told you I don't know where they went."

"You're lying. If I find out you're working on your own, I'll kill you."

"I swear, Taylor. You have the paper and press, so there is no way I can make money on my own. The last time I saw those plates they were in the room off the library."

"You'd better not be lying to me. Hey, do you smell something?"

"Smell what?"

"Smells like a burning lamp. Someone *is* here. If you lied about that, you're lying about the plates."

"I'm not lying. You were with me when their sleigh went past. You saw them."

A crack and cry came into the room.

"You didn't need to hit me, Taylor."

"Well, there's more where that came from if you don't find those plates. I think the smell of burning lamp is coming from behind the wall. Is there another room behind the wall?"

"Yes."

" Open it."

Damn. This was as good a time as any to swear. There was a stairway leading to the upstairs. She blew out the lamp and, as the door swung open, ran to the bottom of the stairs, and took them two at a time.

"See, I told you no one was here."

"Feel it. It's hot."

Breaking glass filled the room and up the stairs. Thank goodness she'd put the lamp out or he'd set the house on fire.

"All right. So maybe there is someone here. I'm not sure who it could be."

"Are those stairs?"

"Yes. I forgot about them. Must be where the person disappeared."

"Light, we need a light."

"Well, if you hadn't been such an ass and broken the lamp, we'd have one, now wouldn't we?"

Again, a crack and yell. Taylor was not one to mess with. At the top of the stairs, she slid open the door enough to slip through. On the other side, she turned the lock. At least this would give her time to find a place to hide.

Pounding came up the stairs. "Whoever you are, you'd better show yourself." Taylor banged on the door.

Libby turned left and pushed a button for another door. It slid into the wall. She ran through then closed it. There was no lock, but hopefully, if he got through the stairway door, it would take him a bit to figure out where she'd gone. But Belinda knew the house, so she was sure to know about this secret door.

She tiptoed down a short hallway, pushed through Brad's clothes in his closet, and entered his room. She slipped off her skirt and tossed it on his bed. It would be easier to run without the material twisting around her legs.

Thankfully, his door didn't make a noise when she opened it. Glancing down the hallway, she eased across the hallway to the back staircase leading to the kitchen. If she got there, she could find something to use as a weapon. Like a skillet or large knife. She held her breath when the top step squeaked. Why hadn't Brad fixed it like he always said he would? The next three also creaked.

"I hear something." Belinda's voice came from the upstairs hallway. "Whoever is here is using the stairway to the kitchen."

"Well, get your ass moving."

Taking two steps at a time, Libby raced down the stairs. Thank goodness she wasn't wearing her skirt. In the kitchen, she spun in a circle. Where to go? She didn't have time to get to another secret room. Outside. She was still in her stocking feet, which meant her feet would get wet and cold, but it was better than being dead and cold. She opened the back door and closed it as quietly as possible. Now where? The summer kitchen? The smokehouse? Outhouse? All those buildings were too small to hide in but were the closest to the house. The barn would offer more hiding places.

Taylor's voice roared from the kitchen. She dropped down below the back porch. If there weren't so much snow, she'd crawl underneath it. The back door opened.

"I don't see anyone out here."

"Stupid bitch. He could be anywhere out here. But there are too many footprints in the snow to tell if the person had come out here."

"They more than likely hid in another secret room. Plus, there are so many rooms in this house, it would be like a cat and mouse game."

"Since we are the cats and this person is the mouse, we'd better get on with the hunt. If he doesn't have the plates, he certainly knows where they are."

"Why do you keep saying 'he?'"

"I can't imagine a woman being smart enough to elude me."

"Idiot," Belinda muttered as she closed the door.

Libby had to agree with Belinda. While things had changed a lot for women since 1870, living back in a man's world was frustrating. But she could use it to her advantage. She crawled to the side of the house and peered into a kitchen window. No one was in the room. She took a minute to organize her route to the barn.

First a mad dash to behind the summer kitchen. Another to the smokehouse, and then the outhouse. From there, she'd have to sprint to the barn and hope neither Belinda nor Taylor looked out a window. There was no cover and a much longer route to the barn.

Taking several deep breaths, she made it to the first building, then the second. Behind the outhouse, which because it was winter didn't smell as bad as in the summer, she took a moment to slow her racing heart.

"One. Two. Three." She wasn't in as good a shape since she'd had Lucy and it didn't take long to become winded and her legs to tire. Back in Wisconsin, running was a part of her routine. Since being here, her life had become more sedentary. Something would have to change if she remained.

Instead of opening the large barn door, she stopped at a side door and yanked it wide. The scent of horses, cows, hay, corn, and manure brought back memories of her grandparents' farm. Even though Brad and Joshua kept the barn clean, it wasn't easy to get rid of the odors. Especially in the winter when they couldn't open up the barn.

She took a minute to catch her breath before heading to the steps to the hayloft. It was probably an obvious place to hide, but if they'd seen her, it would take them time to check all the places good for hiding. It would be warmer if she hid among the horses. Right now, she was freezing. Her wet, stockinged feet were like blocks of ice.

After climbing the stairs, she crawled to the farthest corner and piled hay around her. Now all she had to do, if they came into the barn, was to keep from sneezing. Time dragged. The hay was surprisingly warm. Heat rises, so it was fairly warm in the hayloft from the body heat of the animals. After what seemed like hours, the barn door was thrown open. Libby held her breath. It wouldn't take much movement for pieces of hay to fall between the uneven boards and float to the first floor of the barn.

"Get in there and look for him."

"You don't have to push me. You don't even know if the person we saw running actually came to the barn."

"Where else would he have gone? The other buildings were empty. Splitting up in the house only proved he wasn't there. Start checking the stalls."

"But I don't like animals. They stink and horses and cows are so big."

Taylor groaned. "Good Lord, woman. Will you please stop whining. No wonder no man wants to marry you."

"Bradley does."

"Like hell, he does. And if you were the last woman on Earth, I wouldn't."

"You're mean."

"And you're a witch. Now start searching."

"Where are you going to look?"

"The hayloft."

Libby sucked in her breath. Taylor couldn't find her. He'd more than likely kill her.

"Wait. I think I heard something at the other end of the barn."

"Well, go look."

"I can't. I'm scared."

"Or for crying out loud, Belinda. It's probably pigs or something."

"Or it could be rats."

If there were rats, maybe they'd scare Belinda and Taylor away from the barn.

"See, you dumb witch. It was pigs. Now I'm going into the hayloft."

Her reprieve was over. Don't move. Don't breathe. And for heaven's sake, don't sneeze.

The floor shook as Taylor climbed the stairs. Of course, her nose began to itch. She ran a finger beneath her nostrils. Closed her eyes. Thought about her children and Brad. Wondered how she was going to get out of this situation. And . . . sneezed. Damn it.

"Belinda, he's hiding up here. Come on out. You'll be sorry if I have to crawl through this damn hay to get you."

Libby didn't move. Maybe he'd think he'd heard a cow or cat. Okay, so the man was an idiot and arrogant, but probably not enough to believe a cow could sneeze. No one was so dumb, were they?

"Damn it. I said get out here."

Did he have a gun? A knife? Why hadn't she brought one of the pitchforks up here with her? After all, they were hanging right beside the steps. Which means, Taylor could have one.

"I'm going to count to three. If you don't come out by then, I'll take this pitchfork and start stabbing at the hay. Too bad if I manage to hit you."

"Taylor, you moron. If you kill him, he won't be able to tell us where the plates are."

Thank you, Belinda.

"Don't worry. I'll make sure not to stab too hard. Just enough to injure him."

She couldn't stay here forever, and she had to go to the bathroom. "All right. Hold your horses. I'm coming out." She pushed away the pile of hay and stood.

"Mrs. Daniels?"

"In the flesh."

"Who is it, Taylor?"

"You'll never believe it. It's Mrs. Daniels."

"Libby? That hussy? Maybe you should poke her with the pitchfork. Several times. But wait until she tells us where the plates are."

"Get over here, Mrs. Daniels."

Libby pushed her way through the hay. Loose hay was harder to get through than hay bales, but just as prickly. Not only did the bottoms of her feet hurt from running through the snow, but pieces of hay poked through her socks.

Taylor was standing on the top step glaring at her. "If you want me to come down, you'll need to move."

"No funny business." He disappeared.

What did he think she was going to do? Throw handfuls of hay at him? At least if these were bales, she could drop a few down on him and maybe knock him out. Instead of going down the stairs backward, she turned around so she could watch him as she descended. Maybe she could kick out her legs and bash him with her feet.

Luck didn't seem to be with her today. Both Belinda and Taylor stood several feet away from the steps. Taylor held a pitchfork in his hands. Belinda giggled.

"Looks like we got the almighty Libby in our hands. After we get the information we need, we can kill her and Bradley will be mine."

Libby chuckled. It may have been wobbly, but hopefully they wouldn't notice. "Do you think he'll want you? If he did, why did he marry Lucinda? Why has he been kissing me?"

"He's been kissing you? What else have you been doing?" Belinda stabbed a finger at Libby. "You hussy. He's mine."

"What were his words the other night?" Libby tapped a finger to her lips. "Yes. I remember. "If she were the last woman on Earth he wouldn't marry her.""

Belinda's face went red. She narrowed her eyes. "You're a liar. He'd never say such a thing about me. He loves me. And when he finds out how much money we can make, he'll definitely want me."

"I have a feeling all the money in the world wouldn't make him love you."

Belinda took a step toward her. "You're a liar. I'm not sure where you came from, but you need to leave. Leave Brad and me alone so we can make a life together. Besides, he'd never marry a scrawny thing like you."

Libby shook her head. "How long have you known Brad?"

"Nearly all my life."

"Has he ever kissed you? Said he loved you? Said he wanted to marry you?"

"Well, no. But I know he does."

"Enough, you two. I'm tired of listening to you fight over the man." Taylor waved the pitchfork at Libby. "We're going back to the house where it's warmer and you can show us where the plates went."

They followed her out of the barn, ignoring Belinda's taunts about Brad. Truth be told, she couldn't wait to get into the house and warm up. Hopefully, none of the fires had gone out. "By the way, I have no idea what plates you are talking about."

Taylor poked the pitchfork into her back. "You're a liar."

She couldn't say anything because he was right. They reached the back steps. How was she going to string them along? It shouldn't be long before her family returned. But how to warn them? The heat of the house wrapped around her like a heavy quilt. Her feet tingled as they began to warm up.

"Now show us where the plates are."

It would more than likely make them angry, but she couldn't resist. "Kitchen or dining room?"

Taylor frowned. "What are you talking about?"

"Plates. You asked where they are. We have plates in both the kitchen and dining room. There are the everyday plates, and the fancy Sunday and company plates. Which do you want?"

"Stupid woman." His jaws flexed.

Maybe he'd clench his teeth so tightly they'd fall out or he'd fracture his jaw. "Well, you asked."

Belinda smirked at her. "I have to agree she's stupid. We're not talking about plates for eating, but plates for making money."

"You mean counterfeit money?" Hopefully, they'd believe her act. "I had no idea people made fake money." She sat in a chair and aimed her feet at the stove. "How is it done? Can you really fool people with it?"

"We don't have time to explain it to you." Taylor grabbed her arm and yanked her to her feet. "If the plates aren't here, where are they?"

"I still have no clue what you're talking about, so, I have no idea." She certainly wasn't going to put Caleb's family in danger.

Taylor squeezed her arm. "Then Bradley must know."

Libby shrugged. "I wouldn't know."

"Taylor. Maybe we should wait until Bradley returns. We can threaten the children if he doesn't tell us. In fact, Libby, if you don't tell us, we'll kill your children."

Bile rose to her throat. "You wouldn't."

"Of course we would. I know how much he wants children. I'm sure Bradley loves your brats and would do anything to keep them safe."

Oh, Lord. What should she do? There was no way she'd endanger Caleb and his family, but the safety of her children was important, too. She yanked her arm from Taylor's grip. "Fine, I'll show you."

Taylor chuckled. "I knew she was aware of where the plates were."

"They must have re-hid them." Belinda frowned. "But how did you know about the plates?"

How much should she tell them? Enough to keep her children safe. "Caleb, Brad, and the authorities know there are counterfeiters in the area. They've been trying to find them. At the ball, Colleen and I were sitting outside a slightly open door. We heard you two talking about making money. We relayed the information to them. We spent weeks trying to find the plates. Since we've had so much snow, we couldn't get them to the authorities and put them someplace else."

Taylor growled. "Where?"

"I'm afraid I wasn't privy to the information."

"Then your children die."

"Libby? Where are you? We're home."

No! They couldn't be here already.

"Tell him where you are." Taylor shoved Belinda up the stairs. He grabbed a knife from the counter and followed her but remained on the first step. "Warn him and you're dead."

How did he think he was going to kill her? Unless he hoped to take Brad unaware and was going to stab him. But then he wouldn't get any information from him. Obviously, they hadn't thought out their plan very well.

"I'm in the kitchen. I'm making hot chocolate. Do you all want some?" Wait. Something was wrong. If Brad had the children with him, Charlie would be racing through the house yelling for her. Excited to tell her about their adventure in town. But other than Brad calling out to her, it was quiet. No stomping feet. No crying Lucy. No Cora scurrying into the kitchen with baskets full of food.

Brad pushed the swinging kitchen door open and mouthed *where?* With Taylor watching her every move, she couldn't let him know where they were hiding. And how did he know Taylor and Belinda were here? What should she do? Then it came to her.

"Brad, darling. I'm so glad you're home. I missed you so much. Come give me a kiss."

He raised an eyebrow but walked across the kitchen to her. "Of course."

Chapter Twenty-Six

What was Libby up to? If she'd only give some type of signal to let him know where Taylor and Belinda were. Without a doubt they were here. When they'd passed a carriage and a woman had peered out from a window, his body had gone into shock.

Belinda. What was she doing in a carriage on the road to his house? When Cora and Joshua agreed the woman was indeed Belinda, he snapped the reins to get the horses moving.

"What's wrong?" Cora held Lucy against her chest.

"I believe Belinda is going to try to find those plates I told you about. She probably thinks the house is empty."

Joshua grabbed Charlie and held him on his lap. "We goin' for the sheriff?"

"No. We're going to Caleb's. It's closer and we can leave Cora and the kids with Colleen. Joshua, you and I, along with Caleb, will come back to my place and see what's going on."

"Sounds like a good plan to me."

With the horses racing down the road, it didn't take long for them to get to his brother's. Caleb ran out of the barn.

"What's going on? I thought you were going to town."

"We were, but we passed Belinda's carriage. I believe she and Taylor are going to my place to search for the plates. Libby needed a break from her kids, so she stayed behind. If they find her, I don't know what they'll do to her. I want to leave Cora, Charlie, and Lucy here and go back.

"Do you have a gun with you?"

Brad reached beneath the seat. "Of course. Never go anywhere without it. To many wild critters around. Two- and four-legged."

"You get them settled with Colleen while I saddle up my horse and get my rifle."

It came as a surprise when Belinda's buggy wasn't in the driveway. But it could be behind the house or by the barn. He slowed the horses to keep the noise down and halted them short of the driveway in front of the house. "Caleb, you and Joshua go around back and keep an eye out. If either Belinda or Taylor come out of the house, stop them. I'll go in the front. All I have to do is figure out where they are."

As he approached the house, an idea came to him. He didn't bother to keep the noise down when he opened the door. "Libby. Where are you? We're home."

There was a long pause. His heart squeezed. Where was she? Had Taylor killed her?

"I'm in the kitchen. I'm making hot chocolate. Do you all want some?"

Making hot chocolate? Maybe he was wrong and she was alone. He stood in the doorway of the kitchen. She was alone. Shoeless. Socks wet. Wearing pants. Her hair in disarray with pieces of hay sticking out. Hay? What the heck was going on? Her lips trembled as she smiled.

"Brad, darling. I'm so glad you're home. I missed you so much. Come give me a kiss."

A kiss? She'd never asked him to kiss her before, but he wasn't one to deny himself something so amazing, but... He raised an eyebrow and walked across the kitchen. "Of course." He pulled her into his arms and tipped his head to her. "Is everything all right?" he whispered against her lips.

Her giggle sounded forced. "Is that a gun in your pocket or are you happy to see me?"

How did she know he had a gun? Then it hit him. Clever. They were being watched. "Yes."

"Good. Now about the kiss..."

Did Taylor have a gun pointed at them? If they were putting on a show, or if this would be his one last kiss in his lifetime, he'd make it a good one. He held her close and kissed her with everything he had in him. He licked her lips and when she opened her mouth, well...how could he resist? Lost in the world of passion, he almost didn't hear the screech filling the room. But he couldn't miss someone pulling Libby and him apart.

"Bradley, stop kissing the tart. You should be kissing me."

It took a moment for the haze filling his mind to clear. Belinda. Belinda standing between him and Libby with a fury he'd never seen before. Her face was red. Her eyes were squinted into mere slits. Her teeth were bared as if she were going to rip him to shreds. If she had a gun, Libby would be dead. But what about Taylor? What did he have?

"It's me you love, Bradley, not this witch."

Taylor stood at the doorway to the upstairs. "Belinda. Shut up. We're not here for you to fulfill some delusion you have about Bradley. We're here to get the plates. Remember?"

At least it didn't appear Taylor had a gun, but he was holding a long, wicked knife. The one used to butcher their animals. With the knife aimed at them he came toward them. Brad pushed Libby behind him. "Pocket," he whispered.

"What are you doing, Bradley? You don't want her. You want me." Belinda pointed a finger at Libby. "Why, look at her. She's wearing men's pants. No proper lady wears pants. Plus, she's a mess and smells like the barn."

Even so, she was beautiful, but right now, he couldn't take the time to stop what Taylor aptly called her delusions about him. Hopefully, Libby understood his whispered word.

"Where are the plates? Mrs. Daniels says they were given to the authorities, but I don't believe her."

"She's telling the truth, Taylor. Or should I call you Gunther?"

Taylor glared at him. "I thought I recognized you. You're the one who reported my thefts to the captain. Another reason to get rid of you. And now I don't believe you. Tell me where they are. Once we have them, we'll leave."

Now there was a lie if he ever heard one.

"He threatened to kill the children," Libby whispered behind him.

There was a tug on his coat. Good. She obviously understood what he'd meant before. But had she ever handled a gun? Most women were scared of them. Maybe she could give it to him. But then Taylor would see it. Where were Caleb and Joshua? They could storm into the room and in the ruckus, Libby could give Joshua the gun. Before he was able to think things through, Libby jumped around him. If he weren't so scared for her, he'd laugh. With her arms held straight out, she held the revolver with both hands. The hammer was pulled back. It wouldn't take much for the gun to go off.

"Put down your knife, sucker!" She screamed. "Now. Put down the knife." She nodded at Belinda. "Belinda, stand next to Taylor." Her voice held an authoritative voice he hadn't heard since the war.

"Give me the gun, Libby."

"No. I know what I'm doing. I've handled plenty of guns before."

Belinda skittered to Taylor. "Do something. She's crazy!"

"I'm going to count to three, and if you don't toss the knife to the floor and kick it to Brad, I will shoot you. It may be in the head. Maybe in the heart. What about between your legs?"

Taylor's face went white. Sweat beaded on his forehead. "All right. I'm putting it down. You just be careful, lady. The gun may go off on its own."

Libby chuckled. "Guns don't go off on their own. Someone has to pull the trigger. Which will be me."

Taylor put the knife on the floor and kicked it to Brad.

"Brad. There's a rope hanging in the pantry. Go get it and tie them up. No one—and I mean no one—threatens to kill my children. You're lucky I don't tell Brad to string you up from a tree."

Belinda took a step toward Brad then stopped when Libby told her not to move. "Bradley, you won't tie me up. You love me."

"And while you're at it, Brad, find a towel or something you can stuff into Belinda's mouth so we don't have to listen to her anymore."

Should he be scared or proud of Libby's actions? She was like a wild woman. Would she be like that in bed? He'd be a lucky man if he were ever to find out.

After retrieving the rope, he pulled out a chair, shoved Taylor into it, and tied his arms behind the back of the chair, then secured his ankles to the chair legs. All the while having to listen to Belinda screaming and crying. He took another chair and put it back-to-back with Taylor's, pushed her into it, and secured her arms and legs before wrapping a towel around her mouth. The silence was heavenly.

"Thank goodness we can't hear her."

"Let me take the gun."

After releasing the hammer and since there was no safety, she carefully gave it to him.

"Where did you learn to handle a gun? You were amazing."

Libby shrugged. "I grew up on a farm. We did a lot of hunting. Plus, I belong to a gun club. We shoot clay pigeons. I'm actually quite good."

Clay pigeons? Gun club? Before he could ask her what those were, the back door flew open and Caleb and Joshua strolled in as if nothing were wrong. "Where the hell were you?"

Caleb grinned. "Watching through the window. If anything had gone wrong, we would have helped. Now let's get these two to the sheriff."

Arms tied behind them, they loaded Belinda and Taylor into Belinda's buggy and hitched Caleb's horse to the back. "Joshua and I will take them into town." While Joshua got into the front to drive, Caleb held his gun on Belinda and Taylor. "By the way, nice show you put on, Libby. Very impressive. You have quite a woman there, Brad."

Woman? He thought Libby was his woman? She could be if she were able to stay in 1871. What would it take? More prayers? He glanced at her smiling face. Was she hoping for the same thing? Unless he asked her, he'd never know. He opened his mouth to ask, but she interrupted him.

"Let me change my clothes so we can get Cora and the children."

He held back a groan. He'd have to ask another time. If there was one.

Chapter Twenty-Seven

Three months later

March 1871

One year. It had been one year since their travel back in time. One year since Ben had died. Ben. At times she had trouble remembering his face. Or his voice. This would be the last day she'd don her widow's weeds. She'd even wear the black hat and veil she'd been wearing to church.

One year since Lucy was born. Her walking, laughing, giggly Lucy who wrapped everyone she met around her little finger. Ben would have loved her.

It was time to visit his grave. She hadn't been there since they'd taken Charlie to show him his daddy wasn't buried in the back yard. Her little boy was four. As rambunctious as ever. Followed Brad everywhere he went. Spoke less and less about his father. The memories must be fading.

She stood outside Brad's office. Bradley Kemble. A man she more than admired. One, if she had to admit it to herself, she had come to love. While they hadn't shared more than a few kisses, at night, in her lonely bed, she wondered what it would be like to share his bed. Then, after getting herself all hot and bothered, she couldn't get to sleep. Cora had mentioned a few times how tired she looked. She couldn't very well admit it was because she lusted after Cora's employer.

Taking a deep breath, she finally knocked on the door. When his deep voice called out to enter, she pushed the door open and held back a sigh at his amazing, good looks.

Like a gentleman, he stood when she walked into the room. "Is something wrong, Libby?"

"No. But I was wondering if we could visit the cemetery. It's been a year since Ben died. I'd like to pay my respects."

"Of course. I should have thought of it. How about if we do like we did last year? I'll have Cora pack us a picnic lunch. We can leave in about an hour."

"You're busy. I don't want to take you away from your work."

"Nonsense. I haven't visited Lucinda's grave in a long time, either. It's a beautiful, sunshiny day. Perfect for an excursion. Also, it would also be good to help Charlie remember Ben. I've noticed he talks less and less about him."

"I've noticed the same thing."

"Then I'll ask Cora to make us lunch."

"Thank you, Brad. I'll get the children ready."

Trilliums lined the one-lane road to the cemetery. She didn't recall them from last year. But then she'd recently had a baby and was in deep mourning.

"Mommy, I kinda remember this place. Have we been here before?"

Brad lifted Lucy and carried her on his hip while Charlie took a flying leap to the ground. Someday he was going to break a leg.

Libby took a quilt and lunch basket from the back of the wagon. "We came here a year ago. This is where your daddy is buried."

"I kinda remember him." Charlie took Brad's free hand. "He loved me, didn't he?"

A lump grew in her throat. Tears burned her eyes. "Yes, he did. He loved you very much."

"Why did he have to die?"

"I don't know, Charlie. Sometimes it simply happens, and we have to learn how to live without those who died."

"Like Brad's wife, Lucinda?"

Brad stopped and frowned. "How do you know about Lucinda?"

Charlie tugged on Brad's hand. "Oh. I see her in my room. She's pretty. Sometimes she stands and watches Lucy sleep. Then she comes and talks with me."

Libby glanced at Brad. His face was pale. A tear ran down his cheek. She hadn't seen Lucinda's ghost since Lucy was born. "What does she say to you?"

Charlie let go of Brad's hand and walked backward. "Oh. Things like my daddy loves me and Lucy. How I'm a good boy. How Brad should marry you."

Before she could respond, he skipped down the lane to the cemetery gate.

Brad set Lucy down to let her toddle after her brother. "I'm not sure I got all that. Did he say Lucinda talks to him?"

Libby sped up to catch her children. "Yes."

"And I should marry you?"

Oh, heavens. This was embarrassing. "I think so."

"Huh. Something I've thought about a lot."

"You have?"

He took the basket then her hand but didn't look at her. "Yes. I've fallen in love with you, Libby. But I'm afraid you'll disappear."

Libby's heart thumped against her rib cage. He loved her? Since he said it first, she was free to acknowledge her feelings for him. But he was right. What if she suddenly went back to her time? They reached the gate before she had a chance to respond.

They went to Lucinda's grave first.

Charlie placed a trillium blossom on her headstone. "Isn't this where Brad's wife is buried?"

Charlie could read a few words, but not a name on a headstone. "How do you know?"

"She's standing next to us. And she looks like the lady who comes to our room."

A tear rolled down Brad's cheek. "I see her, too."

"So, do I. She's smiling at us." Libby grabbed Lucy's hand before she climbed on Lucinda's headstone.

"Lady. Lady."

"I guess she can see her, too."

"Lucinda. I miss you."

Lucinda smiled.

"But it's time to move on. To fall in love again."

Lucinda nodded, pointed to Libby, and mouthed *family*.

Libby picked up her squirming daughter. "I think she wants us to be a family. I do, too. But how do we know I'll still be here next year, next month, or even tomorrow."

Brad shook his head and heaved a sigh. "I don't know."

Lucinda blew him a kiss and disappeared.

If she had been alone, she wouldn't have been sure what she'd seen was real. But with three others experiencing the same thing, it had to be. "Let's go visit Ben's grave, then find a place for lunch before these two have a fit about eating."

Ben's grave wasn't far from Lucinda's. Over the past year, the ground had flattened. A headstone had his name, age, and date of death. "Did you have this put up?"

"Yes."

"Thank you. I guess putting his year of birth would have raised a few eyebrows." She pushed away the black veil the wind had blown into her face.

"That's what I thought."

Libby knelt beside the headstone. "Hi, Ben. I miss you so much. You'd love Lucy and be amazed at how much Charlie has grown. They're happy. Even though we somehow were transported back in time, I'm happy. In fact, I've fallen in love."

"Is this where my daddy is?"

"Yes."

Like he had for Lucinda, he placed a trillium bloom on the headstone. "Do you think he misses us?"

She put her arm around Charlie's narrow shoulders. "I'm sure he does."

Brad picked up Lucy who, once again, was trying to climb a headstone. "Should we leave you alone?"

"No. But maybe step back a bit so Lucy doesn't become a headstone monkey."

"All right, Miss Monkey."

Libby rested her hand and head on Ben's headstone. "I'm not sure what's going to happen." No sooner were the words out of her mouth, than Ben, dressed in his Civil War uniform appeared. He held his hands over his face. Was he crying?

"I'm so sorry, Libby. We should never have taken the trip."

"You don't have to be sorry. We both loved those reenactments."

"But if we hadn't, we wouldn't have had the accident and you wouldn't be stuck in 1871 and me in 2025."

"Wait. What?" What he said couldn't be possible. "Did you say you were in 2025?

His image wavered. "Yes. I'm not sure why I stayed here and you went back."

"But we buried your body."

"And I buried yours."

"You mean I'm dead in 2025?"

"Yes. We did have a car accident. The impact brought on early labor. You were able to deliver our daughter before you died. I thought I'd died with you."

An image of a boy and little girl appeared beside him. This couldn't be happening. "Are Charlie and Lucy with you?"

"Yes. They are safe and growing like weeds."

"But they are here with me."

Ben shook his head. "I don't understand."

"I don't either."

Brad came up beside her. "I've tried to take care of them the best I could."

"Thank you, Brad. I know you have."

A young woman appeared at Ben's side. A young woman who resembled Lucinda. She had to be hallucinating. "Who is this?"

"I'm so sorry, Libby. I met Cindy at a grief meeting. Her husband died in a farming accident. She's been a great help to me with the children and in helping me overcome my grief."

"Do you love her?"

Ben nodded. "I will never stop loving you, Libby, but I do love Cindy and want to marry her."

A weight lifted from her shoulders. "I've fallen in love, too, Ben. I don't understand or know why time has messed with our lives but has given us reasons to move on."

"I don't understand, either, but I'm glad you're happy." His image began to fade. "I'll never forget you." He turned around, picked up Lucy, and took

Cindy's hand. With Charlie at his side, the foursome walked until they faded away.

Libby shook her head. "Oh. My. God. I can't believe this. How can he be in the future with the kids and me here with them?"

Brad knelt beside her. "I have no idea. But I believe you are destined to stay here. With me. With the children. If you went back, what would happen to them? There can't be two of them in the same place at the same time."

A jolt of happiness went through her. "So, does this mean I'm not going back?"

"I think so?" Brad removed her mourning hat and veil and tossed them to the ground. "Did I hear you tell Ben you'd fallen in love? Can I hope you meant me?"

With another lump in her throat, all she could do was nod. "Yes," squeaked from her mouth.

Brad took her hands and helped her to her feet. "I love you, Libby. I would like you to be my wife. I want to help raise Charlie and Lucy and any other children we may be blessed with. What do you say?"

Charlie tugged on her skirt. "You gotta say yes, Mommy. I want Brad for my new daddy." He jumped up and down. "Say yes. Say yes."

As she always attempted to copy her brother, Lucy tried to jump. "Yeth. Yeth."

Brad wrapped his arms around her waist. "Say, yeth, Libby. Say yeth."

Libby couldn't control the happiness spiraling through her. "Yes, yes. A thousand times yes."

Brad planted a kiss on Libby's lips. It was quick but packed a punch. He picked Lucy up and placed her on his hip, took Libby's hand, and with Charlie by their side, walked from the cemetery, and into their future.

About The Author

Tina Susedik is a multi-award-winning, multi-published author in both fiction and non-fiction. She is published in history, military, romantic mystery, erotic romance, and children's books, with forty-four books to her credit. Her books are in both print and eBook format.
She lives in northern Wisconsin with her husband of fifty-one years. She also writes spicier romances as Anita Kidesu.

Where to find Tina

Website: www.tina-susedik.com[1]
Facebook: https://www.facebook.com/TinaSusedikAuthor/
Pinterest: http://www.pinterest.com/tinasusedik/
Goodreads: https://www.goodreads.com/author/show/
1754353.Tina_Susedik
Newsletter: https://www.tina-susedik.com/contact

---

1. http://www.tina-susedik.com

Other Titles by Tina

<u>Romantic Mysteries</u>
Riding for Love
Never With A Rich Man
A Photograph of Love
Crazy With a Side of Love
Operation Santa – a Novella
<u>Historical</u>
The Trail to Love, An Oregon Trail Story
<u>The Darlings of Deadwood Series</u>
The Balcony Girl
The School Marm
The Proprietress
The Banker's Wife
Saving Ellis – A Novella
The Unconventional Blacksmith
<u>Fury Creek Series</u>
Missing My Heart
Missing Innocence
<u>Anthologies</u>
All I Want for Christmas is a Soul Mate
My Sexy Valentine
Sizzle in the Snow
The School Marm — Wild Deadwood Tales
Saving Ellis — Getting Wild in Deadwood
Rescuing Eliza — My Heart Belongs in Deadwood
The Pirates Ring - Hope Harbor Book 1
The Magic of the Whalehouse Tavern — Hope Harbor Book II

Finding Henrietta — Naughty and Nice – A Galena Holiday
Picturing Annabella — Lost and Found in Deadwood
Gruagh Gallagher – Hope Harbor Book III
The General – Galena Book II
Batty for Love – Taking A Chance in Deadwood
The Love Spoon – Galena Book III

<u>Children's Books</u>

Uncle Bill's Farm
The Hat Peddler
Peanut and Casey on Uncle Bill's Farm

Writing as Anita Kidesu

South Seas Seduction
Surprise Me
Surprise Me Again
Double the Surprise